S0-AJF-026

FEB   - 2023

HAUNTED BY THE PAST

BAEN BOOKS
by SIMON R. GREEN

ISHMAEL JONES MYSTERIES
The Dark Side of the Road
Haunted by the Past
Dead Man Walking (forthcoming)

Jekyll & Hyde Inc.

For Love of Magic (forthcoming)

To purchase any of these titles in e-book form, please go to www.baen.com.

HAUNTED BY THE PAST

❖

SIMON R. GREEN

HAUNTED BY THE PAST

This is a work of fiction. All the characters and events portrayed
in this book are fictional, and any resemblance to real people or incidents
is purely coincidental.

Copyright © 2022 by Simon R. Green

All rights reserved, including the right to reproduce this book or portions
thereof in any form.

A Baen Books Original

Baen Publishing Enterprises
P.O. Box 1403
Riverdale, NY 10471
www.baen.com

ISBN: 978-1-9821-9228-0

Cover art by Kurt Miller

First printing, December 2022

Distributed by Simon & Schuster
1230 Avenue of the Americas
New York, NY 10020

Library of Congress Cataloging-in-Publication Data

Names: Green, Simon R., 1955- author.
Title: Haunted by the past / Simon R. Green.
Description: Riverdale, NY : Baen Books, [2022] | Series: An Ishmael Jones
    mystery
Identifiers: LCCN 2022035881 | ISBN 9781982192280 (hardcover) | ISBN
    9781625798848 (ebook)
Subjects: LCGFT: Detective and mystery fiction. | Novels.
Classification: LCC PR6107.R44 H38 2022 | DDC 823/.92--
dc23/eng/20220728
LC record available at https://lccn.loc.gov/2022035881

Printed in the United States of America

10 9 8 7 6 5 4 3 2 1

HAUNTED BY THE PAST

CALL ME ISHMAEL. Ishmael Jones.

In nineteen sixty-three, a star fell from the heavens and landed in an English field. Or, to be more precise, an alien starship came howling down from the outer dark with its superstructure on fire, and crashed outside a small country town. The ship hit hard, and all of its crew but one died. This sole survivor was rewritten by the ship's transformation machines, changing its shape right down to the DNA so it could pass as human until help came. But the transformation machines were damaged in the crash, and they wiped away all memories of who and what I used to be, before I was human.

I might have thought it was all just a dream or a delusion, if it wasn't for the fact that I haven't aged a day since nineteen sixty-three.

The night sky is an ocean full of ships, sailing forever unseen and unsuspected by all the people down below, walking the Earth with their heads bent, intent only on the world before them. They don't know they share their world with monsters and angels, the unfamiliar and the uncanny, and all the dark wonders that lurk in the background of everybody's lives. They have no idea of how large this world really is, and how many weird menaces watch hungrily from the shadows of the hidden world.

That's why the world needs someone like me, the monster who hunts monsters. The alien who learnt to be human and found he loved it. I stand between Humanity and all who would prey on them, and if I do my job right, no one knows I was ever there.

I have spent most of my life working for secret underground groups, because only they possess the necessary resources to hide me from an increasingly suspicious and surveillance-heavy world. These days I work for the Organisation, a group so mysterious that even I'm not entirely sure who they are. But they respect my secrets and allow me to do good work, so we get along. Together with my partner in crimes, my true love Penny Belcourt, I investigate mysteries and check out the stranger corners of the world.

Because sometimes it takes a real outsider, to see what's really going on.

The problem with history is that it's not always content to stay in the past. The sins of yesterday have a way of sneaking up on people and ambushing them in the present. Murder, in particular, always has its roots in the past.

✦ CHAPTER ONE ✦
NO ONE GOES THERE

ALL OLD COUNTRY TAVERNS have one thing in common: they don't give a damn what outsiders think about them. Inns that have served generations of local people happily embrace traditions that go back centuries, even if some of them are frowned upon in these more civilised times. They still cling to the old ways, that have sustained them through any number of modern fads and fancies.

All old country taverns have their roots in the past, and so do the people who drink in them.

Penny Belcourt's latest acquisition, a vintage car possessed of more style than comfort, carried us deep into the ancient green dream of the English countryside. Trees and fields flew past in a pleasant blur, as we followed the long winding roads and the polite but firm instructions from the sat nav. Eventually we arrived at a quiet little drinking hole, The Smugglers Retreat, on the outskirts of a town called, for reasons best known to itself, Under Farthing.

The tavern actually stood some distance outside the town,

perhaps so its patrons could relax and be themselves, and not who their families and relations thought they should be. The small sturdy building was half hidden in a copse of tall leafy trees, and I only spotted the stone-walled car park at the last moment. I stabbed a finger at the narrow opening, and Penny spun the steering wheel with hearty bravado, sending the car flying through the gateway with barely an inch to spare on either side. We screeched to a halt in a spray of gravel, and Penny shut down the engine with a flourish. It was suddenly very quiet, and very peaceful, and I unclenched my hands from the seatbelt as though I hadn't been worried at all.

The Smugglers Retreat was a slumping stone-walled structure with tiny windows and a grey-slate roof, the kind of tavern that has been around for centuries and has no intention of going anywhere. No obvious frills or fancies, just a home away from home where local people could go to get some serious drinking done, and complain about the kind of things local people have always complained about. The hanging sign over the front door showed a stylised skeleton with glowing eyes, astride a rearing black horse.

"Not exactly a welcoming image," said Penny. "Nothing to say *Here is rest and comfort* to the passing traveller."

I considered the image carefully. "A skeleton on a black horse could represent all kinds of perfectly innocent rustic interests."

Penny looked at me. "Name three."

"Could be a famous local haunting," I said. "A well-loved folk song . . . Or a call to all those interested in a little quiet devil worship."

"You've been reading Dennis Wheatley again," said Penny.

"You can learn a lot from the classics," I said.

"Even so," said Penny. "All the images they could have chosen, and they went with that one?"

"It must mean something to the locals," I said.

"That's what I'm afraid of," said Penny.

We looked around the car park, taking our time. A dozen assorted vehicles stood scattered across the open space, sprayed with mud and other suspiciously organic country substances. They all looked shabby, well used, and very much the poor relation compared to the gleaming vintage car that had arrived among them like a cuckoo in the nest. I have spent most of my life carefully not standing out or doing anything to make an impression, but I knew better than to say anything. Penny was a deeply practical person, except when it came to her beloved cars. I gave the tavern my full attention, and the tiny windows stared back at me like so many suspicious eyes.

"Smugglers Retreat," I said thoughtfully. "Shouldn't that have an apostrophe?"

"You ask them," said Penny. "I wouldn't dare."

"Maybe they couldn't afford one," I said.

"I could use a drink," Penny said firmly. "In fact, I could use several drinks and a large drink chaser. Every time we get called in to investigate a mystery in the countryside, I just know things are going to take a turn for the worst. Because the evils in this part of the world have had so much more time to sink in and marinate."

I had to smile. "I thought I was the paranoid one."

Penny sniffed loudly. "If I see anything that even looks like a wicker man, I am throwing you to the locals and accelerating for the horizon."

"Let's check out the inn," I said. "And see if we can work out what it is we're here for."

We weaved our way between the parked cars, our feet crunching loudly on the gravel. Birds sang cheerfully in the surrounding trees, and there was a low hum from insects too lazy to bother us. It all seemed very calm and peaceful. The sky was a deep and vivid blue, untroubled by clouds, and the sun smiled warmly on the late afternoon. Penny pushed back her broad-brimmed black hat so she could look up.

"How can men do evil under such a beautiful sky?"

Penny Belcourt had sharp striking features under a mass of piled-up night-dark hair, a trim figure, and enough nervous energy to run a small factory. She was wearing one of her favourite outfits: a dress of black and white squares, with knee-high white leather boots. Penny always liked to maintain a glamourous presence, because it helped to distract people from the fact that she had a first-class mind.

I have always preferred anonymous clothes that allow me to pass as just another face in the crowd. I can't afford to stand out and be noticed. I have walked the Earth long enough to know how people treat things that aren't people. I have no intention of ending up locked in a cage or strapped to a dissection table.

The moment Penny and I walked into the gloomy interior of The Smugglers Retreat all conversation broke off abruptly, as the regulars stopped what they were doing to turn and stare at us. And yet there was none of the usual distrust of strangers, no signs of anger at being disturbed. Instead, they looked more like actors in a play surprised to discover that unfamiliar faces have joined them on stage. It felt as though we had interrupted something that the locals had no intention of discussing in front of strangers.

Penny smiled around the room, and I nodded easily, just to make it clear we weren't in any way intimidated. I could feel the weight of the patrons' massed gaze as I led the way through the crowded tables to the long wooden bar at the rear of the inn, with its impressive choice of real ales. All of which I was determined not to try. There's usually a good reason why ales with names like *Lucifer's Old Peculiar* and *Rutting Weasel Delight* don't travel.

The barman was the size of a bear, in an outfit so determinedly rustic you could have hired it at a costume shop. He had a round red face, and deceptively sleepy eyes that I just knew didn't miss a thing. He put down the pint glass he'd been polishing, flipped the cloth over his shoulder with a practiced snap, and treated Penny and me to his best professional smile.

"Welcome to The Smugglers Retreat, sir and madam! Always good to see new faces."

"Are you sure about that?" I said, nodding at the regulars sitting stiff and silent in their chairs.

"Oh, you mustn't mind them, sir," said the barman. "It's just their way. Now, what can I get you?"

I ordered a brandy, and a g&t for Penny, and the barman quickly went to work. A low murmur of conversation started up again, as the regulars got used to the idea that we were staying. But they all made a point of keeping their heads down, and not looking in our direction. I was half expecting the barman to point out some garlic hanging next to a wall of crucifixes and warn us not to go anywhere near Count Dracula's castle. He set our drinks down before us, and I handed him the exact change.

I never use plastic. It leaves a trail.

"The sign outside made a bit of an impression," I said. "Why does a place called The Smugglers Retreat have a painting of Death riding a dark horse?"

"No great mystery there, sir," said the barman. "This used to be prime smuggling territory, back in the day, and the local gangs would dress up as spooks and skeletons to scare people away. So they wouldn't see things they weren't supposed to. Might I enquire what brings you all the way out here?"

"We're just passing through," said Penny.

The barman raised an eyebrow. "Not often we get to hear that. It's not like we're on the way to anywhere. Bit off the beaten track, in fact. And most people around here prefer it that way."

Penny hit him with her most charming smile, and the barman visibly relaxed as he basked in the glow. Penny has always been more of a people person than me, but then, it comes more naturally to her.

"Is there a reason why visitors aren't welcome here?" said Penny.

"These days, the only reason people stop off here is because they're on their way to visit the old manor house," said the barman. "Glenbury Hall. No one local ever goes there if they know what's good for them. That house is dangerous."

"Really?" said Penny, smiling determinedly. "What makes Glenbury Hall so dangerous?"

The barman glanced at his customers, and then leaned over the bar. His voice became carefully low and measured, as though everything he was telling us was confidential.

"People have been known to disappear, in and around the Hall. We're talking about stories that go back centuries, of men and women who went out there and were never seen again. And as if that wasn't enough, the dead walk Glenbury Hall, along with the living." He paused to check our reactions and must have been reassured at what he saw in our faces, because he continued in an even lower voice. "The old Hall is famous for its ghosts. Not the traditional headless monks or walled-up nuns, no Ladies In White or phantom pipers. Just . . . presences, in the night. Things that come and go, intent on business beyond our understanding. There are all kinds of stories about the ghosts of Glenbury Hall, but none of them the kind you'd tell for a pleasant scare on a winter's night. They're warnings, for those with the sense to heed them. Some say there's lost souls that dance with the statues in the Hall's grounds, doors that won't stay shut and rooms that aren't always there, and something that prowls the house in the early hours, endlessly searching—"

"What kind of something?" I said.

The barman looked at me steadily. "They say: *It crawls...*"

And for a few moments, the hairs stood up on my arms. Penny and I glanced at each other. Down the years, we had gone up against all manner of monsters and out-of-this-world weirdness, but I had always been very firm that there were no such things as ghosts. Until we had reason to visit the House on Widows Hill. After that, I wasn't so sure.

"And it's not just the spooks and the spirits," said the barman, warming to his task of putting the wind up us. "There's the family that's owned the Hall for generations. The Glenburys. Everyone around here knows better than to have anything to do with them."

I kept my face calm, and my voice carefully even. "What's so bad about the Glenburys?"

"Bad blood in that family," said the barman. "Always has been. The Glenburys have made evil their religion, and they worship it in their hearts."

The hairs on the back of my neck stirred, at the calm certainty in his voice.

"Hasn't there ever been a good Glenbury?" said Penny. "Someone who tried to reach out to the town?"

"We know better than to let any of them get close to us," said the barman. "You can't ever trust a Glenbury. They're raised to be what they are."

"And what is that?" I said politely.

"Devils," said the barman.

"So which is the most dangerous?" said Penny. "The Hall or the family?"

"They belong to each other," said the barman.

Penny and I waited, but he'd said all he had to say. He turned away, to polish a glass that didn't need polishing, apparently feeling he'd done all that was necessary in the way of polite conversation. I nodded to Penny and we took our drinks to an empty table at the rear of the inn. I chose a chair that allowed me to set my back against the wall, and Penny sighed quietly.

"Do you have to be so obviously on your guard, darling?"

"Relentless paranoia is your friend," I said calmly. "I have learned the hard way not to trust anyone. Except you, of course."

Penny smiled at me sweetly. "Nice save."

"Well," I said. "I think it's obvious why we've been called down here, and what our mission is going to be."

"To sort out a spooky old house that eats people?" said Penny.

I shrugged. "The Colonel will give us the real details. When he gets here."

I looked around the inn. Golden light streamed in through the diamond-paned windows but did little to disperse the general gloom. There was no music, no television, and the locals sat hunched over their cards and dominos, voices pitched carefully low to keep their conversations to themselves.

The general layout looked like it hadn't changed in centuries; just an open space with a working fireplace, chunky tables and chairs, sawdust on the floor and a low half-timbered ceiling. In old taverns like this, it's often said that the walls have ears, but in this place, they had eyes. Everywhere I looked, dozens of stuffed and mounted animal heads stared back at me. Everything from foxes with snarling mouths, to stags with spreading antlers. If you could pursue and shoot something in the name of sport, its head was there. And every single face showed the same slightly surprised expression.

I had to wonder: if I was ever finally brought to ground, would my head end up as a trophy on someone's wall? With the same surprised expression on my face . . .

"I don't know if you've noticed," Penny said quietly, "but apart from the amateur taxidermy, there's nothing else in the way of decoration. No old maps or photographs, no horse brasses or interesting antiques. None of the usual conversation pieces. Either the locals don't care about their past, or they don't care to be reminded of it. Did the Colonel have anything to say about why we're meeting him here?"

"The Colonel was his usual tight-lipped self on the phone," I said. "Apparently someone has gone missing around here, under less than usual circumstances, and the Colonel wants him found."

Penny considered her drink thoughtfully. "That's a bit lightweight, for us. I mean . . . no monsters, no murders, just a few local ghost stories and someone who's gone absent without leave?"

I shrugged. "At least we got to drive out into this lovely countryside in your latest toy."

Penny fixed me with a stern stare. "A nineteen twenty-six Bentley, in its original night-black livery, is not a toy! It is a collector's dream, and still one hell of a smooth ride!"

"Then why didn't I get a chance to drive?"

She looked down her nose at me. "You know very well you are not allowed behind the wheel of any of my vintage cars."

"I have excellent reflexes."

"The way you drive, you need them."

Perhaps fortunately, the Colonel chose that moment to make his entrance. He strode into the pub as though he owned the place and was thinking of knocking it down. Once again silence fell across the room as the regulars turned their collective attention on the latest intruder. The Colonel stared coldly back, and the locals averted their eyes rather than meet his gaze.

A tall, elegant presence in his early forties, the Colonel was dressed in the finest three-piece suit that Savile Row had to offer. Ex-military in his bearing, right down to the expertly trimmed moustache, the Colonel might be an incognito authority figure, but he still wanted everyone to know it. Not that he was in any way the boss of me. The Colonel was simply the middleman, the go-between, my only point of contact with the Organisation, and both of us preferred it that way.

He passed between the crowded tables without so much as glancing at anyone, and when he finally joined Penny and me the regulars went back to minding their own business with a certain amount of relief. The Colonel removed a handkerchief from his top pocket, flicked some invisible dust from the remaining chair, and sat down opposite us, his back as straight and unyielding as ever. He replaced the handkerchief, took a moment to adjust his Old School Tie, and then nodded approvingly at the stuffed and mounted animal heads.

"What excellent trophies."

Penny's elegant eyebrows descended into a frown that would have placed a chill in the heart of anyone else.

"You hunt animals for sport?"

"I used to ride with the local hunt, when I was a young buck," said the Colonel. "All part of a country upbringing. These days, I hunt other things. Just like you."

"Why are we here, Colonel?" I said quickly, before Penny could take the conversation down a path I just knew none of us would find helpful.

The Colonel settled himself comfortably and addressed us in his usual *I am now lowering myself to lecture the subordinates* tone. I let my eyelids droop, as though I was about to drowse off. So far, honours even. Penny looked like she wanted to slap both of us.

"One of the Organisation's people, a minor functionary called Lucas Carr, was supposed to be attending an historical conference at a manor house some distance outside the town," said the Colonel. "Glenbury Hall had been left empty and abandoned for ages, but it was recently reopened as a centre for business meetings, conferences, and the like.

"Today was supposed to be their grand opening, and Carr was the first member of the historical society to arrive, at around ten o'clock this morning. He booked in at reception, collected his key, and went upstairs to his room. But he never got there. Somewhere between the lobby and his room, Carr just vanished. And no one has seen or heard anything of him since."

"Are we blaming this on enemy action?" I said carefully. "Or general weirdness?"

"Carr was one of us," said the Colonel. "So we have an obligation to assume the worst."

"You think he might have been kidnapped?" said Penny.

"It's a possibility," said the Colonel. "Though I wouldn't have thought someone on Carr's level would have known anything important enough to make him worth taking."

I gave him my best hard look. "If Carr isn't anyone important, what makes this case so urgent that Penny and I had to come racing all the way out here?"

The Colonel stared calmly back at me. "We really don't

like it when one of our own goes missing. There's always the chance it could be the opening gambit in an attack on the entire Organisation."

"So you don't care about Lucas himself?" said Penny.

"I'm here, aren't I?" said the Colonel. "And so are you. The very fact that I chose my best field agents to look into the situation should tell you how seriously the Organisation is taking this."

"We're your best agents?" I said. "Can I get that in writing?"

"Can we get a raise?" said Penny.

I smiled at her. "You always were the practical one."

"One of us has to be," said Penny, her gaze still fixed on the Colonel. "So there's nothing special about this Lucas Carr?"

"As far as I know, he's never done anything to stand out," said the Colonel. "Disappearing was the first interesting thing he ever did."

"What's our cover story?" I said. "Who are we this time?"

"As far as the Glenbury family are concerned, you are security experts," said the Colonel. "Brought in by Carr's employers to find out what's happened, because there are confidential aspects to his work. Which you, of course, are not free to discuss. The family have agreed to cooperate because they want this mess sorted out as quickly as possible, so they can get their business up and running again."

I sat back in my chair and looked at him thoughtfully. "But why choose us, for a missing person case? We usually only get the strange ones."

The Colonel shifted unhappily on his chair. "Glenbury Hall does have a long-established reputation as a bad place. And not just for people going missing."

"You're talking about the ghosts, aren't you?" said Penny. "The barman said there were all kinds of stories . . ."

"Which may or may not turn out to be at all relevant," said the Colonel.

I nodded. "What can you tell us about Lucas Carr? What sort of man was he?"

"A hard-working office drone," said the Colonel.

"What about wife, family, friends?" said Penny.

"There doesn't appear to have been anyone else in Carr's life," said the Colonel. "His only interest outside his job was this historical society."

"He sounds rather a lonely sort," said Penny.

The Colonel nodded. "I think we can rule out affairs of the heart."

"Not necessarily," I said. "It's always the quietest waters that run deepest."

"You should know," said the Colonel.

"What can you tell us about the historical group?" said Penny.

"The Ravensbrook Historical Society," said the Colonel. "Some sixty or so members, who usually only meet online. Today's conference was supposed to be their first chance for a small number of them to meet in person."

"What were they planning to do, at this conference?" I said.

The Colonel shrugged. "Present scholarly papers on their favourite subject, and then argue over the details. Their involvement does add an extra level of complication, in that there is an unsolved mystery at the heart of their special interest..."

Penny looked at me. "Didn't you just know he was going to say that?"

"I knew there had to be something weird and uncanny about this case, to justify bringing us in," I said. "And given the sheer number of ghosts involved, maybe we should mention our special exorcist's rate."

Penny beamed at me. "You see? You can be practical when you put your mind to it."

The Colonel gave us a look that indicated he was going to rise above us, and pressed on.

"Back in sixteen eighty-five, Lord Ravensbrook turned up at Glenbury Hall, to discuss putting together an armed uprising against King James II. But though he was seen to go into the Hall, no one inside ever saw him, and he never came out again. He simply vanished; without Ravensbrook to lead it, the rebellion never happened. He was widely assumed to have been assassinated by agents of the king, but there was never any proof, and never any trace of the body."

"So the Hall has an extremely long history, when it comes to people going missing," I said.

"Which may or may not have anything to do with what has happened to Carr," said the Colonel.

"How long can you give us, before you have to bring in the local authorities?" I said.

"Twenty-four hours," said the Colonel.

"Why the rush?" said Penny. "If there's no family or friends to raise a fuss?"

"Because after that the trail will go cold," said the Colonel. "And if this should turn out to be nothing to do with the Organisation, we have a responsibility not to muddy the waters for a more traditional approach."

I nodded. "Where is this Glenbury Hall?"

"Not far from here," said the Colonel. "Just follow the road away from town and it will lead you to an old manor house standing on its own; that's the Hall."

I suddenly became aware that everyone else in the pub was staring at us. I drew the Colonel's attention to our silent audience, and he made a point of turning unhurriedly around in his chair. Penny and I looked interestedly round the room, but not one of the regulars lowered their gaze, even when the Colonel hit them with his best *This is none of your business* stare. The barman cleared his throat in a significant sort of way and raised his voice so it carried clearly across the silent room.

"You're not really thinking about going to Glenbury Hall, are you? After everything I warned you about?"

"We have business there," I said. "And it will take more than a bunch of scary stories to put us off."

"The Hall is a dangerous place," said the barman. "No one goes there."

"Why not?" said Penny.

The barman took his time before answering, weighing his words as he considered just how specific he was prepared to be.

"No one in the town will go anywhere near the Hall. Every family around here has lost someone to that awful place. Disappearance after disappearance, going back centuries. It was left empty for decades, and everyone was happy for it to stay that way. When we heard the Glenburys were coming back, we knew nothing good would come of it. And when we heard that someone had gone missing out there this morning, none of us were surprised. That house should never have been opened up to visitors."

"Why not?" I said.

"The Hall is only safe when it's sleeping," said the barman. "It has an appetite. It takes people, because it can. We respect the old stories, and the old warnings, and stay safe."

"What warnings?" said Penny, favouring him her best winning smile. "And what stories, exactly?"

"You must have heard about the most famous one," said the barman. "Back in the nineteen fifties, two women arrived at Glenbury Hall to visit the family. They were surprised to find the grounds packed full of people in old-fashioned clothes. The two women thought it must be some kind of historical reenactment. They moved among the strangely clothed people, and listened to them talking in antiquated ways. There were stalls selling strange produce, outbreaks of laughter with a disquieting edge, and displays of swordsmanship that ended in real bloodshed. Somewhat confused, the women made their way to the front door and went into the Hall, to meet their friends.

"And that's when they found out there was no gathering or reenactment in the grounds. Nobody should have been there. When they all went outside, there was no one to be seen. You really haven't heard that story? There's been several books written about it, and a television documentary. Though none of us got paid for being in it."

"What do you think was going on in the grounds?" said Penny.

"Time isn't as nailed down as it should be, at Glenbury Hall," said the barman. "The past can appear out of nowhere to haunt the present, because that house's history has teeth, patience, and an endless reach."

"So . . . it's not just the Hall that eats people?" I said.

"Best not to talk about it," said the barman.

"Why?" I said.

"Because talking only makes things worse."

"How?" said Penny.

"It encourages the Hall," said the barman. "It likes the attention."

I looked at him steadily. "You talk about the house as though it's alive."

"There's a reason why the old Hall was built so far outside of town," said the barman. "It was because no one wanted the Glenburys anywhere near them. They did things, back in the day. . . . Terrible things, that poisoned the wood and stone of Glenbury Hall forever. It all comes down to the well, you see."

"What well?" said Penny.

"You don't know anything, do you?" said the barman. "It's in the grounds, right in front of the Hall. Legend has it the well used to be a pagan shrine, long and long ago, when people were sacrificed to something so old we don't even have a name for it anymore. The earth around the well was soaked with blood, and packed full of bones. The Glenburys ordered their house built there because they liked that."

I looked around as one of the regular drinkers suddenly stood up. He was wide and stocky, craggy-faced and grey-haired, with the air of a man beaten down by life, and other things.

"That's enough, Thomas! This is our business, not something to be shared with outsiders. They'll never understand."

"They have to be told, Nathan," said the barman. "They have to know what they're getting into."

"It won't help," said Nathan. "If the house wants them, it'll take them. You know that." He made himself look at Penny and me, and the Colonel. "You don't want to go there. It's not a healthy place."

I didn't get any sense of threat from the man, or from any of the locals watching us. They all seemed genuinely concerned, desperate to warn us away from a very real threat.

"We do have some experience, when it comes to the weird stuff," I said carefully. "We know how to protect ourselves."

Nathan just shook his head and sat down again. He wouldn't look at us anymore, because in his mind we were already dead.

I turned back to the barman. "Before today, when was the

last time someone from around here actually vanished out at the Hall?"

"We haven't lost anyone in decades," said the barman. "Because we still make it a point to tell each new generation the old cautionary tales. The last time ... would be back in the seventies. Those Glenburys were great ones for parties. Wild affairs, by all accounts, attracting like-minded souls from all over the county. Some people from town went out to the Hall, to work in the kitchens, or act as staff. They should have known better, but the money was just too tempting ..."

"And *they* never came back?" said Penny.

"Oh, they came back all right." The barman smiled briefly. "From the stories they had to tell, about things they'd seen, I'd say they earned their pay. Most of them wouldn't go back, but a few did. For the money, or because what went on at those parties spoke to something in them. And *they* never did come back."

"Didn't anyone go to the police?" I said.

"They didn't want to know," said the barman. "They knew they wouldn't be able to prove anything. The Glenburys have always been a law to themselves."

"Couldn't you do something?" I said. "I mean, if all the townspeople got together ..."

"It's not just the Glenburys," said the barman. "It's the Hall. Bad places call to bad people. The Glenburys have been monsters for generations; it's steeped in the blood and the bone. Now that they're back, it's all started happening again."

"We have to go there," said Penny. "It's our job."

The barman shook his head and started to turn away, but there was still one more thing I wanted to know.

"If everyone around here is so scared of the Hall, and you're all convinced it's so dangerous ... why do you stay?

Why go on living here when you could move to somewhere safer?"

"Because this is our place," said the barman. "And we will not be driven out of it—by the Hall or the Glenburys. And because someone has to be here to warn fools like you."

He turned his back on us and moved to the other end of the bar. He'd said all he was going to say. I looked at the Colonel.

"How much of that did you already know?"

"Find Lucas Carr," said the Colonel. "And don't contact me until you know something."

He didn't need to tell us we were on our own. We always were. The Colonel rose to his feet with unruffled elegance and strode calmly out of the inn. None of the locals so much as turned their head to watch him go. Penny and I looked at each other.

"Well, that explains why we were chosen for this mission," said Penny. "A family tree with its roots in Hell, and a house that devours people."

"If that is what's happened, we'll just have to make it cough Lucas Carr back up again," I said.

"And the family?"

"They're just people," I said. "We can deal with people."

Penny and I took our time finishing our drinks, to make it clear we weren't going to be hurried. When we finally got up to leave, I slammed the empty glasses down on the bar with some force, so the barman couldn't ignore me.

"Why are there so many stuffed animal heads on the walls?"

He met my gaze unflinchingly. "This has always been good hunting country. Everyone around here knows how to use a gun."

"Is that allowed, these days?" said Penny.

"If anything should come out here from the Hall," said the barman, "it'll find us ready."

"You think guns will protect you against ghosts?" I said.

"It's not just the dead you have to worry about, at Glenbury Hall," said the barman. "The house is bad, but the family has always been worse."

Penny and I headed for the door, and the locals watched us leave like they didn't expect to be seeing us again.

❖ CHAPTER TWO ❖
AT HOME
WITH THE GLENBURYS

"WHAT A FRIENDLY LITTLE HOSTELRY," said Penny, as we emerged into the open air.

"Couldn't do enough for us," I said, as we stood outside the door and took a deep breath of the evening air. "But whenever people tell me I don't want to go somewhere, that's when I really want to go there."

"Sometimes I think your ship's machines transformed you from some kind of lemming," said Penny. "Do you think any of those stories the barman told us could have something to do with Lucas Carr's disappearance?"

I shrugged. "Old houses always come with old stories attached. Locals think it adds character. *Our old house is spookier than yours.* But there's really only one way to find out for sure. Go to Glenbury Hall, ask a whole bunch of questions, and make such a nuisance of ourselves that the people there will tell us everything we want to know just to get rid of us."

Penny smiled brightly. "In other words, standard operating procedure. Of course, it is entirely possible that all of this weird stuff is nothing more than misdirection, to keep us from noticing what's really going on."

"Wouldn't be the first time," I said. "But after hearing so much about the terrible Glenbury family, I have to wonder... Did bad things happen because of the family who lived in the house, or did living in such a bad place affect the family?"

"In my experience, it's the bad people who make places bad," Penny said wisely.

"But now the old family is back in the Hall, and people have started disappearing again," I said. "I don't believe in coincidences. That's just the universe nudging your elbow, to get your attention."

Penny nodded. "And this is the kind of nudging that leaves bruises."

I looked at her thoughtfully. "What's your first reaction to Lucas Carr's mysterious disappearance?"

Penny shrugged. "If you believe everything the locals have to say, it must be something to do with Glenbury Hall. But what if Lucas stumbled onto something way above his pay grade, some secret information he was never supposed to know about? What if he tried to sell it to the wrong person, and it all went horribly wrong? You have to admit, that sounds far more likely than a house that eats people."

"Exactly," I said. "I don't believe the Colonel would have brought us all the way out here, unless this missing man is a lot more important than we're being told about."

"The stories about the Hall were interesting, though. Not your usual spooky stuff." Penny shot me a sideways look. "How do you feel about investigating a haunted house after your experiences in the House on Widows Hill?"

"That was a unique situation," I said steadily. "It's going to take a hell of a lot to convince me that there's any supernatural element to Carr's vanishing."

"But what if it turns out the ghosts really did take Lucas?" said Penny.

"Then we'll just have to persuade them to give him back."

Penny raised a single elegant eyebrow. "And how are we going to do that? Offer to buy them some nice new sheets and chains?"

"That is so last century," I said. "I thought maybe leathers and chains . . ."

"Goth ghosts and punk poltergeists?" Penny shook her head. "The horror, the horror . . ."

We laughed quietly as we made our way through the parked vehicles, and then came to a sudden halt as we looked at our car and what had been done to it. While we were busy being lectured on the evils and iniquities of Glenbury Hall, someone had painted a large white cross on the roof of the Bentley. The rough shape stood out starkly against the black paint, though the artist had made a sloppy job of it, presumably because he was in a hurry and didn't want to get caught. Drops of white paint stood out against the sides of the car, like elongated bird crap. Penny stood frozen in place beside me, wide-eyed and shocked speechless.

"I didn't see anyone leave the inn," I said, after a moment. "One of them must have sneaked out quickly, through a hidden back door. I should have known there'd be one. Remember, the barman said this used to be smuggling country. The locals would have needed a quick exit, for when the Revenue Men came calling. The cross is probably intended to protect us, if we insist on visiting the infamous Glenbury Hall."

"But . . . My car!" said Penny.

"They're just trying to be helpful."

"But . . . *My car!*"

"I wonder why they painted the cross on the roof, rather

than the bonnet," I said thoughtfully. "I mean, the bonnet would have been a lot easier for them. Less of a stretch. Is something supposed to see the cross from above, and be scared off? Or maybe . . . remember how the barman talked about the old-time smuggling operations? Perhaps some modern-day smugglers are trying to scare us away from investigating the Hall. No. That's a bit too Scooby Doo, isn't it?"

I stopped talking, as I realised Penny had torn her gaze away from the violation of her car so she could glare at me.

"What's the matter?" I said. "Is there something I should be doing?"

"*Are you kidding me?* I want you to march straight back into that poxy little pub, drive every one of them out here, and stand over them with a whip in one hand and an electric cattle prod in the other, until they have scraped every last bit of this mess off my lovely vintage car!"

"I don't think we have time for that."

"Why?" said Penny, just a bit dangerously.

"Time could be a factor, when it comes to locating Lucas Carr," I said carefully. "And making sure that he's safe."

Penny tilted back her head and let out a primordial howl of rage and despair that drove all the birds out of the surrounding trees. No one emerged from the tavern to investigate, which as far as I was concerned demonstrated good self-preservation skills. Penny lowered her head, breathed deeply, and then strode over to the Bentley without looking at me. She unlocked the doors and got behind the steering wheel, while I slipped in beside her, carefully keeping my opinions to myself.

I thought providing such obvious protection was rather sweet, myself.

Penny fired up the engine and crashed through the gears,

double-declutching like a wild thing as she sent the car roaring out of the car park. Gravel shot from under our wheels with such violence it pebble-dashed the parked vehicles and left them rocking in place. We put The Smugglers Retreat at our back and followed the narrow winding road away from the inn.

A pleasant summer evening was falling on the open countryside as it laid itself out before us: calm and contented and apparently entirely at its ease. But as I looked past the dry-stone walls bordering the road, I couldn't help noticing that all the fields were completely empty. No cattle, no sheep, no people out working . . . and not a single piece of farm machinery. The fields and meadows stretched away to the horizon without so much as a single scarecrow to break up the view. The countryside was completely empty, as though no one wanted to be out in the open, so far away from the town, because it wasn't safe.

After a while, the road narrowed so much we had no choice but to drive down the middle, with the way ahead often concealed behind the curve of an approaching bend. Penny took this as a personal affront to her driving skills and put her foot down. I clung onto my seatbelt with both hands, quietly hoping we wouldn't meet another driver in a similar state of mind coming in the other direction.

But we didn't encounter any other traffic on the road, even though we had to travel some distance to get to the Hall. Narrow country lanes are often a minefield of Land Rovers, cyclists, and slow-moving farm vehicles, but the road remained open and empty. I had to wonder whether that was significant, that no one would come out this way unless they absolutely had to.

Eventually the road straightened out again, and we

spotted a large house up ahead, squatting on the horizon like a great stone ogre. Penny yelled, "Tally-ho!" and aimed the car at it. The entrance to the private road wasn't sign-posted, and I swear we took that curve on two wheels, before we plunged into the entrance road and the car dropped back again. The wheels dug in, and we roared along a narrow track engulfed by tall hedges that buried us in shadows, until the road suddenly opened out into a broad open area next to Glenbury Hall. There were no marked parking spaces, so Penny brought the car to a shuddering halt right next to the single gap in the topiary trees surrounding the Hall's grounds.

She turned off the Bentley's engine and shot me a triumphant smile. I shook my head, lost for words, and fortunately she took that as compliment. We looked around, while the cooling engine ticked noisily. There were no other vehicles, and no sign of life anywhere. The parking area was just bare mud, with the odd tuft of grass here and there. Nothing at all between us and the wide-open fields that stretched away to the horizon. The long row of topiary trees formed a great green wall protecting, or possibly hiding, Glenbury Hall from the rest of the world. Each tree had been trimmed into a basic geometric shape: squares, triangles, and spheres.

"Brutal and yet unrelenting," I said. "Overpowering and intimidating and not in any way welcoming."

Penny nodded and pulled a face. "Functional and ugly wouldn't have been my choice, to make a first impression on the paying customers. Why would they want to conceal the Hall behind something as off-putting as that?"

"Maybe the old family valued its privacy," I said. "Unless... the trees were put in place to keep something out."

"Or something in," said Penny.

I looked at her. "Like what?"

"I don't know," said Penny. "That's rather the point, isn't it?"

I studied the trees appraisingly. "Makes me wish I'd brought my chainsaw."

Penny looked at me. "You haven't got a chainsaw."

"It was going to be a surprise," I said.

We got out of the Bentley. Penny carefully didn't look at the cross painted on the roof, and I didn't say anything, just in case. I did study the sky carefully, but there was nothing flying above us that struck me as threatening. In fact, there were no birds at all for as far as I could see. Which was just a bit unusual, this far out in the countryside.

Penny locked the doors carefully, while glowering suspiciously around her. There was no one else in sight, but the setting didn't inspire trust. Our footsteps made soft ghostly noises on the hard mud as we approached the opening in the topiary wall. We had to walk in single file and turn sideways to edge through the narrow gap, and then we were inside the grounds of Glenbury Hall.

A majestic lawn stretched away before us, with scattered stone statues caught in awkward and unnatural poses. They stood in strange patterns, all of them facing the Hall, like chess pieces on an unseen board. Their grey stone bodies were savagely scarred and pitted from long exposure to the elements, and spotted here and there with moss and mould, like some disfiguring disease. What faces I could see had been scoured away by the wind and rain, with nothing left but blank monstrous voids.

I couldn't even tell whether the statues were meant to be male or female, but they all had a certain strength to them, a sense of having endured despite everything the elements could throw at them. As though they had to be there, to serve some purpose.

"Why are they all facing the Hall?" Penny said suddenly.

"Maybe they're keeping an eye on the Glenburys," I said. "To see what they're getting up to. Or maybe the family deliberately had them arranged that way, so they could be sure of an audience for their sinning."

"Oh, that's just creepy," said Penny.

"They're just statues," I said.

I looked around the grounds, took a deep breath and then smiled suddenly, surprised by a pleasant scent.

"What?" Penny said immediately.

"Can't you smell that?"

"No," she said, just a bit resignedly. "What have you picked up this time, with your amazing alien senses?"

"The scent of freshly cut grass, still hanging on the air," I said. "Someone's been out here recently with a petrol mower. I can smell the fumes."

Penny took a few quick sniffs at the cool evening air, just to show willing, and then shook her head. We moved slowly forward, weaving in and out of the slightly sinister statues, until we could get a clear view of the Hall.

Topiary walls surrounded the grounds on three sides, with Glenbury Hall at the far end, a huge manor house of the old school. Two stories of old grey stone, buried here and there under great mats of moss and ivy, with arched and gabled windows. Suitably ugly gargoyles peered down past the guttering. Although the house had a good many windows, only a few of them had lights showing, and they were all right next to the front door. Which meant either there was hardly anyone home, or whatever walked there didn't need the light. Glenbury Hall looked dark and dour and threatening, the kind of place any self-respecting visitor would disappear from, the first chance they got.

"I am ready to bet you," said Penny, "that this crumbling

old pile turns out to be riddled with hidden doors, sliding panels, and secret passageways. Because houses this old nearly always are."

"Of course," I said. "You grew up in one, didn't you?"

"Dear old Belcourt Manor," said Penny. "Home to freezing draughts, coal fires that were always going out, and secret doors that might as well have had a neon arrow pointing at them. But just as I was getting old enough to take an interest, Daddy had them all nailed up and sealed over. He said, to make sure I didn't get lost in the hidden passageways. I always thought it was to stop me having any fun."

"This house does look like it has a reputation to live down to," I said. "An ancestral home held together by generations of grudges, and family secrets too grim to be shared with the outside world."

"Of course there are secrets," said Penny. "Or we wouldn't be here."

We stood together for a while, taking our ease in the evening air and studying our surroundings. The Hall stared back at us from out of the gathering gloom, just waiting for us to come within reach. The topiary walls cut us off from the surrounding countryside, and I suddenly realised how quiet it was. I couldn't hear any birds singing, and there was no buzz of insects, as though nothing in the countryside wanted anything to do with this place. Looking at the Hall, I could believe it. A house heavy with sin, home to a family steeped in corruption. If you believed everything you were told, which I try very hard not to.

"I've seen worse," I said finally.

"Really?" said Penny. "Because I'm pretty sure I haven't."

"First impressions can be deceptive," I said.

"Trust me," said Penny, "I am not feeling even a little bit deceived. This is a bad place, Ishmael."

"Let's go in and introduce ourselves," I said. "It's getting late." I shot her a stern look. "And don't even think of saying 'later than you think.'"

"All right," said Penny. "But I'm thinking it really loudly."

I started forward, and Penny was quickly there beside me. We had to weave our way between the distorted statues, but even up close there was no way of telling whether they were supposed to be family ancestors, local dignitaries, or mythological figures. They just stood around, staring at nothing and ignoring each other, like unpopular guests at a party.

"Remember the timeslip?" I said. "All those historical people filling up the grounds, like the echo of a gathering long gone?"

"That was a bit odd, wasn't it?" said Penny. "I mean, it didn't seem to tie in with all the hauntings and disappearances."

"I think we have to consider the possibility that the timeslip might have been just a madey-uppy story, to attract visitors," I said.

"Like the wishing well?" said Penny.

She pointed to the in-no-way-special attraction: a well so generic as to be completely lacking in character. We wandered over to take a look. A stone circle barely three feet high, recently white-washed by the smell of it, with a sloping roof that had recently been painted a virulent red, to make sure no one could miss it. There was no bucket on a chain, so it clearly wasn't a working well. A prominent sign announced: YE OLDE WISHING WELL.

"There's nothing about this to suggest an ancient pagan shrine," I said. "Never mind a setting for human sacrifice."

"Looks a bit twee, to be honest," said Penny.

We leaned over the stone wall and peered down into the depths. There was nothing to see but an impenetrable darkness. I produced a small coin and dropped it in, but there was no sound of the coin hitting water, or the bottom of the well.

"Must go down a hell of a way," I said finally.

"Did you make a wish?" said Penny. "Be a shame to waste the opportunity."

"I might have," I said.

"What did you wish for?"

"I can't tell you that," I said, "or the wish won't come true."

"You believe that?" said Penny. "You soft, sentimental creature from another world."

"Of course I don't," I said.

"Then why won't you tell me what you wished for?"

"Because it's traditional," I said firmly.

"Blow me," Penny said sweetly.

She headed for the Hall's front door, and I strolled along after her. As we drew closer, the front of the Hall looked increasingly old and decrepit. The stonework was as marred and pitted as the statues, and I had to wonder if the moss and ivy was all that was holding it together. There was only the one door in the front of the house, with a long banner nailed above it. One end had already worked loose and was flapping plaintively in the breeze, saying *Glenbury Hall welcomes the Ravensbrook Historical Society!*

"The group Lucas Carr belonged to," I said.

"Yes, thank you," said Penny. "I did pay attention at the briefing."

She came to a sudden halt facing the door and shuddered briefly. I stopped with her.

"Cold?" I said.

Penny looked at me. "Are you really not getting the same bad feeling I am? Like someone is dancing on your grave?"

"I'm not feeling anything," I said.

"Even after all the stories we were told about this place?"

"They were just stories. You should know better than to believe that kind of thing."

Penny scowled at me, and then at the Hall. "Normally, yes. But there's something about this house . . ."

I studied the Hall carefully, since it was obvious she was being entirely serious.

"Penny . . . It's just an old house."

"And you're not feeling any kind of threat?"

"No," I said. "Are you?"

Penny shrugged unhappily. "I'm not sure."

She stood and stared at the Hall, and I stood there with her.

"Do you want me to go in first?" I said, after a while. "You could always hide behind me."

Penny's head came up, and her chin jutted defiantly. "That'll be the day."

"Remember," I said. "We don't get scared, because we're the scary ones."

"Always," said Penny.

We strode up to the front door, which turned out to be a massive slab of dark-stained oak, with a raised pattern of black iron studs. There was no obvious bell, ancient or modern, just a heavy steel knocker that had recently been polished to within an inch of its life. The knocker had been fashioned in the shape of a horned demon head, with a ring thrust into the fanged mouth.

"The Glenburys were supposed to be devil-worshippers," said Penny.

"Would they really advertise it this openly?"

Penny shrugged. "That's the aristocracy for you."

"I'm surprised the current owners decided to hang on to such an ugly thing," I said. "It doesn't exactly make a good first impression, does it?"

"No one takes that stuff seriously, these days," said Penny. "The guests would probably think it adds character."

I took a firm hold of the steel ring and banged heavily on the door. The open grounds soaked up a lot of the noise, but the echoes seemed to carry on a lot longer than I expected. After a while, I reached for the door handle. I had no intention of waiting around like a poor relation, until the owners felt like answering. I threw the heavy door open and barged in, with Penny right beside me. Both of us prepared for anything, and more than ready to punch it in the face whether it was a ghost or not.

Perhaps especially if it looked like a ghost.

The lobby was a big sprawling affair, with a high wood-beamed ceiling and a great curving staircase. Widely spaced electric lights did their best to push back a gloom that looked like it had been around for centuries and wasn't going to give up its territory without a fight. The walls were buried under heavy wood panelling that looked like it could have used a generous application of wax and a lot of elbow action. The bare wooden floor at least looked like someone had attacked it with a mop fairly recently.

Hanging tapestries and faded paintings did their best to adorn the walls, while bulky old-fashioned furniture with no pretentions to style or elegance stood carelessly around the lobby, as though waiting for someone to take pity and move them to a more sympathetic setting. The last of the evening light slammed up against the diamond-paned windows, as though discouraged from entering by the general ambience. The only truly modern touch was the standard hotelier's reception desk on the far side of the lobby, directly opposite the front door.

Behind the desk, a man and a woman looked as though they'd been interrupted in the middle of a fierce argument.

They were both in their late forties, and clearly husband and wife, though currently not very happy about it. I slammed the front door shut, and the sound of the impact reverberated so loudly in the lobby I half expected to see layers of dust jump off the furniture. The husband and wife glared suspiciously at Penny and me, getting ready to demand an explanation for our sudden entrance, so I deliberately wandered over to inspect an historical display that had been set up next to the reception desk. Penny stuck her nose in the air and slipped gracefully in beside me.

It's always best to keep potential suspects off balance, if you want to get anything out of them.

The pokey little exhibit consisted of various farm implements, a bunch of old maps...and a prominently displayed CD in a blank case, next to a sign proclaiming that it was a dramatic audio reconstruction of the ghostly gathering witnessed by two women in the nineteen fifties. And that copies of this special treat could be pre-ordered, for a very reasonable price.

"Why an audio play?" said Penny.

"Presumably because making a film would have been too expensive," I said.

A shop window dummy had been dressed in a long scarlet brocade coat with gold piping, baggy breeches and stockings, flat shoes, and a silk cravat at the throat, and topped off with a long curly wig. The dummy stared blankly across the lobby, as though quietly resentful of the indignity that had been forced upon it.

Standing next to it, on a small easel, was a carefully labelled reproduction of a portrait of Lord Ravensbrook. A harsh-faced man, with cold eyes and a mouth that looked like it had never smiled in its life.

On the other side of the dummy, a laminated sign

provided details on the Monmouth Rebellion of sixteen eighty-five. I skimmed through the information, but there was nothing in it about Lord Ravensbrook and his planned rebellion. I stepped back so I could study the costumed dummy carefully.

"Is that supposed to be Ravensbrook?" said Penny.

"It's wearing the same clothes as the man in the portrait."

"Fashion can be a harsh mistress."

"Can we help you?" the woman at the desk said loudly, in a tone that suggested she really doubted it.

Penny and I gave our full attention to the frowning couple, and then sauntered over to the reception desk, hitting them with our best *We're in charge, you just don't know it yet* look. The husband and wife moved a little closer together, to present a united front in the face of strangers, but before either of them could say *Who the hell are you and what are you doing here?* I got in first.

"I am Ishmael Jones, and this is my partner, Penny Belcourt. We are security experts, called in by Mr. Carr's company to establish what happened to him. I believe you were told to expect us. . . ."

The man actually relaxed a little, relieved that help had turned up, but his wife was made of sterner stuff.

"Do you have any identification?"

I smiled. "People in our line of business don't carry IDs."

The husband and wife glanced at each other, and then nodded pretty much in unison, reassured the company hadn't sent just anyone to investigate their problem.

The woman drew herself up and put on a professional smile for us. "I am Marion Glenbury, and this is my husband, Arthur. We run the Hall."

Marion was tall and dark-skinned, with a shaven head under a violet silk scarf. She was wearing a smart navy-blue business suit with the kind of padded shoulders I hadn't seen since the eighties. Her back was straight, and her gaze was steady, and she looked ready to launch herself into battle at a moment's notice. Something in the practiced smile and thoughtful look made me think she was someone who would always be looking for the next fight.

She didn't offer a hand to shake, so Arthur quickly made up for it by thrusting his hand across the desk. His grasp was firm but fleeting, and while he didn't have any trouble making eye contact, there was no real warmth in his gaze or his smile. Tall and thin, he wore a smart suit as though he'd been told to, and looked like was carrying all the troubles of the world on his narrow shoulders. His face was pinched, and his receding hair was thickly streaked with grey.

Not exactly the dangerous scion of the Glenbury line that I'd been led to expect.

"Welcome to Glenbury Hall, home of my ancestors," said Arthur, flashing us a determined smile. "Though I fear that just at the moment, you're not catching us at our best."

Marion sniffed loudly. She kept switching her cold stare from Penny to me and back again, and seemed a little peeved that it wasn't bothering either of us.

"It's about time you got here," she said. "It's vital this unfortunate business is sorted out as quickly as possible. And preferably without having to involve the local authorities. I wouldn't trust them further than I could throw a wet camel."

"It has to be said, Mr. Carr's disappearance couldn't have happened at a worse time," said Arthur. "Right at the start of our grand opening."

"Why don't you want the police involved?" said Penny.

"Because no one in this area has ever trusted my family, or the Hall," said Arthur. "Of course, you can't really blame them for that . . ."

"I think you'll find I can," Marion said sharply. "It's nothing but rank superstition, from a community so invested in its past they'll cling to any old nonsense to justify it."

"My family has been here for some time," said Arthur, nodding to Penny and me almost apologetically. "And there's no denying some of my ancestors took advantage of their position . . . Small towns do so love to hang onto their old grievances even though the people responsible have been dead and cold and in their graves for centuries."

"Not everything is about your family," said Marion, and Arthur stopped speaking as though she'd hit a switch. She fixed her cold stare on me, as the most likely source of opposition. "You have to find Lucas Carr, as quickly as possible. If we can get this mess sorted out, it's just possible that the meeting of the Historical Society can still go ahead as planned."

"Assuming Mr. Carr is still alive," said Penny.

"Well of course he's alive!" said Marion. "Why wouldn't he be alive? We just can't find him, that's all."

"You don't seem too upset about what might have happened to him," said Penny.

"Of course we're concerned," Arthur said quickly. "But you have to understand, this man's disappearance could destroy everything we've worked so hard to achieve!"

"I don't see any reason to assume that anything bad has happened to Mr. Carr," Marion said firmly.

"The Hall does have a reputation," I said politely.

"And Mr. Carr isn't the first person to disappear from this house under mysterious circumstances," said Penny.

"Stuff and nonsense!" Marion said loudly. "No one really believes those old stories these days."

Arthur nodded immediately, but in a way that suggested he didn't necessarily agree.

"Let's start with the basics," I said. "How did Lucas Carr go missing?"

Marion stared at me. "Has no one explained the situation to you?"

"We'd prefer to hear the details directly from you," Penny said smoothly.

Arthur started to say something, and then stopped to look at Marion for permission. She nodded impatiently, and he launched into his story. It didn't take me long to decide he'd spent some time rehearsing what he was going to say, probably under Marion's direction, so he could be sure of presenting himself and the Hall in the best possible light.

"I was here at the reception desk, sorting out the last of the paperwork before the Historical Society arrived."

"Our very first booking," said Marion, unable to keep from butting in.

"Yes, dear," said Arthur. "I was about to say that."

"Well, get on with it," said Marion.

Arthur didn't actually sigh, but looked like he wanted to. "When you open up your home to visitors, your reputation stands or falls on how you treat your first guests. Marion and I had gone to great pains to make sure everything was in order, but I was still caught off guard when Mr. Carr turned up just after ten o'clock this morning, hours before the rest of the Society were due to arrive. I hadn't even finished working out the schedule for the day's events. You have to keep these people busy, or they don't think they're getting their money's worth."

"I was at the back of the Hall," said Marion, butting in again. "Working on the floral displays."

"Mr. Carr booked in," Arthur said patiently. "He signed the register, and then said he was tired from travelling and wanted to go straight to his room. So he could have a bit of a lie down before the rest of the Society arrived. I gave him his key."

"A proper metal key," Marion said proudly. "None of those plastic key cards, that only work when they feel like it. An old-fashioned key is just part of maintaining the proper historical ambience. It's the little touches that make all the difference."

"Mr. Carr almost collapsed, carrying his suitcases in," said Arthur. "From the sound the big ones made when they hit the floor, it was obvious they were really heavy. I offered to help take them up to his room, but Mr. Carr refused. He insisted on carrying both suitcases up the stairs himself. He had a smaller third case he wanted to take as well, but that was just too much for him. So he said he would leave it here, and come back down for it later."

"Didn't you offer to carry the smaller case?" I said.

"Mr. Carr was very firm, that no one was to touch his luggage but him," said Arthur. "So I just smiled and nodded and gave him directions to his room. Because the customer is always right, even when he's wrong. Mr. Carr put the smaller case down on the floor by the desk, and then struggled up the stairs with his suitcases, to his room on the next floor. Number Four."

Arthur gestured at the massive curving staircase, with its bare wooden steps and heavy bannisters.

I looked at Marion. "And you didn't see any of this?"

"No," she said flatly. "I already told you. I was at the rear of the Hall, arranging flowers in vases. I always say there's nothing like a few fresh blooms to add a touch of colour to even the grimmest of settings."

She didn't look around the gloomy lobby. She didn't have to. Arthur allowed the smallest wince to cross his face, but said nothing. I looked thoughtfully at Marion.

"So you never actually saw Lucas Carr arrive?"

She seemed a little startled, as though the thought had never occurred to her.

"Well, no. Not as such. Not in person . . ."

"Marion didn't join me here until after some time had passed," said Arthur. "Three quarters of an hour, maybe more."

He looked to Marion for confirmation, and she nodded impatiently. Arthur took a moment to pick up the reins of his story, and then continued.

"My wife noticed Mr. Carr's case was still standing by the desk. And that was when I realised he hadn't come back down for it."

"Even though it had been three quarters of an hour?" said Penny.

Arthur shrugged. "I was busy. I had a lot to do. I just forgot about it."

"I said I'd take the case up to Mr. Carr's room," said Marion, butting in again now it had become her story. "I wanted to check that everything was all right, because we really didn't need any problems, on our first day. I carried the case up to the next floor and knocked on the door to Number Four. There was no answer. I knocked again, and called out to Mr. Carr, but there was still no response. I was worried something might be wrong, so I hurried back down here and grabbed the pass key."

"We keep it here, for when it's needed," said Arthur, indicating the wall behind him.

"Where anyone could get at it," said Penny.

Marion let that one pass, determined to continue with her account of what had happened.

"Arthur and I went back upstairs."

"Why both of you?" I said.

"I felt I should be with her," said Arthur. "I was starting to get a bad feeling . . ."

"I wanted him with me," Marion said sharply. "As a witness, in case Mr. Carr might have fallen, or injured himself. You have to be careful, these days. It's a litigious world."

"Marion unlocked the door, and we went in," said Arthur. "Mr. Carr was nowhere to be seen. Neither were his suitcases. There was nothing to indicate he'd ever been in the room."

"We weren't sure what to do," said Marion. She was frowning now, as she relived the moment. "I mean, Arthur had seen him go up the stairs, so he had to be there, somewhere. We checked all the other rooms just in case Arthur had given him the wrong key, and then we went back down and searched the ground floor."

"Even though he couldn't have been there," said Arthur. "Because I would have seen him come down the stairs. We even went outside and looked round the grounds. There was no trace of him anywhere."

"What about his car?" said Penny. "We didn't see any other vehicle parked outside, when we arrived."

"Mr. Carr arrived by taxi," said Arthur. "The nearest railway station is in Marshford, the next town over."

He stopped, to take a deep breath. His hands were shaking. Marion moved in a little closer and Arthur seemed to settle, reassured by her proximity.

"I called the police and reported Mr. Carr missing," Marion said flatly. "At first, they didn't want to take the matter seriously, and just made stupid jokes about the Hall's history. I had to be very firm with them before they would even agree to send someone out. An hour or more went by, and there was still no sign of them. Arthur was in a real state. Finally, we got a call from the police station, saying they had relinquished the case to a higher authority, so it was nothing to do with them anymore. They sounded quite relieved, that they wouldn't have to come out to the Hall."

"Even after all these years," said Arthur. "Everyone around here is still scared spitless of Glenbury Hall."

"Not long after, we got a call from Mr. Carr's employers," said Marion, cutting in quickly. "Assuring us that they would be sending us some special experts to investigate the situation and determine exactly what had happened to Mr. Carr."

She paused to look down her nose, first at me and then at Penny. Apparently we didn't impress her as experts.

"We have a lot of experience," I said. "When it comes to getting at the truth."

"Really," said Marion. It wasn't precisely a question, more an expression of polite disbelief.

"Oh, lots and lots of experience," Penny said airily. "You wouldn't believe some of the cases we've investigated."

I nodded solemnly. "And we are very good at finding things that have gone missing. Whether they want to be found or not."

Marion looked like she was about to say something sharp, but Arthur spotted the danger signs and got in first.

"We're very pleased that you're here," he said firmly. "We've both been very worried, about what could have happened to Mr. Carr. It's like something just reached out and took him, before he could get to his room."

He made the suggestion quite casually, as though there was nothing out of the ordinary about it. I felt a cold breeze caress the back of my neck, and Penny moved a little closer to me. Marion looked at Arthur, but for once didn't have anything to say. Arthur just carried on with his story.

"Those stairs are the only way to get to the next floor. Mr.

Carr couldn't have come back down again without me being aware of it."

"Are you sure you didn't leave reception, even for just a few moments?" Penny said tactfully. "To take a look outside, to check out a noise, or just to pop off to the toilet?"

"No," said Arthur. He sounded very firm, and very definite. "I had a lot of paperwork to do. I never left the desk once."

"And there was no way he could have sneaked past you?" I said.

"Absolutely not," said Arthur, his voice rising in spite of himself. Marion put a hand on his arm, but he shrugged it off without even glancing at her. "Look at the stairs! Those are solid wooden steps. No carpeting. I would have heard him coming down long before I saw him. And I didn't."

"And why would he want to sneak out anyway?" said Marion, unable to hold herself back any longer. "Where would he go? We're miles from anywhere, and he had no transport. And if he is out there, somewhere, why hasn't he contacted anyone?"

"Those are all good questions," I said. "What about the Hall's security? Do you have any surveillance cameras?"

Marion didn't look at Arthur, but I could see the effort that took. "We made a decision not to have any. They would have detracted from the old-time ambience. Which is, after all, what we're selling."

"Do you still have the small suitcase that Carr left at reception?" I said.

"Of course," said Arthur. "It's right here."

I waited a moment, and then smiled at him politely. "Could we see it, please?"

"Of course," said Arthur.

He reached down and produced a perfectly ordinary case.

He laid it down on top of the desk and pushed it toward me, in a way that suggested it was now my responsibility and nothing to do with him. The case opened easily, but all it contained was a number of oversized and well-thumbed history books.

"I already looked through them," said Marion. "They're nothing special. Just books about the Hall, and Lord Ravensbrook."

I ran my hands around the interior of the case, checking for hidden panels or a false bottom where something might have been concealed, but there was nothing. I leafed quickly through the books, but all I could see was a lot of dense text interspersed with illustrations from the past. I put the books back in the case and closed it.

"I'm surprised there aren't any papers," I said. "Carr was supposed to be making a speech to his fellow enthusiasts in the Historical Society."

"What you saw is all there was," Marion said firmly.

I pushed the case back to Arthur, and he put it behind the desk again.

"Maybe Carr kept all his important papers in the two big suitcases," I said. "And that's why he made such a point of hanging on to them."

"But would he really have taken them with him, when he went wherever he went?" said Penny. "Given how heavy they were?"

"He might have refused to be separated from them," I said. "Even if he was being taken somewhere against his will."

Marion stared at me. "You think he could have been kidnapped?"

Arthur seemed genuinely surprised by the idea. "Why would anybody want to do that?"

Marion looked at him pityingly. "Because his job has

security connections, remember? That is why these people are here."

"No one else arrived at the Hall this morning," said Arthur. "I would have noticed."

And then we all looked round sharply, as heavy footsteps descended the wooden stairs. Arthur had been right; each separate step sounded out loud and distinct, echoing through the lobby like gunshots. Arthur couldn't resist shooting me a quick *I told you so* look.

A teenage girl hurried down into the lobby, and then stomped over to join us. Tall and more than fashionably thin, she had café au lait skin, close-cropped hair, and dark serious eyes. She couldn't have been more than seventeen, and wore distressed jeans, a blank white T-shirt, and sneakers that looked like their owner had taken through an assault course. She wasn't wearing any makeup or jewellery, either because she couldn't be bothered, or because she didn't think there was anyone around worth putting on a show for. She slammed to a halt in front of Penny and me, and glowered at us suspiciously.

"I heard voices. What's going on?"

"This is my daughter, Ellen," Marion said quickly. "And there is nothing going on here that need concern you, dear. Go on back to your room, please. I'll tell you all about it later."

Ellen ignored her mother. She gave every appearance of being a typical teenager, convinced everything in the world only happened to annoy and inconvenience her.

"Is it true?" she said, not even glancing at her parents. "Has someone really vanished into thin air? That's amazing!"

"Really?" I said politely.

"It's the first interesting thing that's happened since my parents abducted me from London and dragged me out here to the back of beyond," said Ellen. "Just so we could move into this creepy old house, miles from civilisation and all my friends."

"Now, Ellen, we talked about this," said Marion. "We all had to give up things, to come here."

Ellen continued to ignore her. She looked Penny over and dismissed her as just another adult, before deciding she might get more out of me.

"Do you think he was murdered?"

"Ellen, really!" said Arthur. He tried to smile at me, to show how ridiculous such an idea was, but couldn't quite manage it. "The things you say, sweetie.... There's no evidence that Mr. Carr has come to any harm."

"Of course not," said Marion. She looked like she wanted to laugh lightly, but wasn't sure she could bring it off. "The very idea! I really don't think you should mention this to anyone else, dear. That kind of gossip could ruin our business before it's even got off the ground."

Ellen looked at her for the first time. "Who could I talk to? I don't know anybody here!"

I studied her thoughtfully. "Were you at the Hall when Mr. Carr arrived this morning?"

"I was upstairs in my room," said Ellen. "Listening to music on my headphones. Mother insists on the headphones. She thinks my taste in music would upset the guests."

"Did you hear Mr. Carr walk up the stairs?" said Penny.

She shrugged. "I like my music loud."

"You heard us talking down here," I said.

She scowled at me. "I'd taken the headphones off. I don't wear them all the time."

I turned back to Marion and Arthur. "Is there anyone else present in the Hall, that you haven't got around to telling us about?"

"I didn't mention my daughter because I didn't think her

being here was relevant," said Marion. "She didn't see or hear anything."

"There's just the three of us," said Arthur. "We don't have any staff."

"The locals won't work here at any price," said Marion. "And it's not for want of us reaching out to the community." She shot Arthur another hard look, as though it was all his fault. "We have advertised for outside people, but so far no one wants to make the long journey for what we can afford to pay. I'm sure things will improve once we've got the business on a stable footing."

"To be fair," said Arthur. "Glenbury Hall does have a reputation..."

"Ghost stories!" Marion said scornfully.

"We talked about this, dear," Arthur said carefully. "The stories are already out there, so we might as well make use of them. They add to the ambience...catch people's attention and make them want to come here."

"Do you believe in ghosts?" I said.

Arthur surprised me then, by answering quite offhandedly. "Oh yes. I grew up in this house, and as a child I saw and heard all sorts of things I've never been able to explain."

Marion's voice actually softened as she looked at her husband. "I put a lot of that down to your parents, dear. The way they treated you..." She broke off abruptly and turned back to me and Penny. "I haven't seen anything out of the ordinary, in all the time I've been here. But then I never believed in ghosts, or any of that supernatural nonsense. I'll go along with the stories as long as they're good for business, but that is as far as I go."

I looked at Ellen, and for the first time she wouldn't meet my gaze. Her eyes dropped to the floor, and her voice was just a murmur.

"I don't believe in ghosts," she said. "But I'm still scared of them."

Something in the way she said that made everyone look at her, but she had nothing more to say. Her shoulders had slumped, and she seemed to have shrunk in on herself. I turned back to Arthur and Marion and had to clear my throat loudly to get their attention again.

"How many doors are there, giving access to the Hall?"

"Just the two," said Arthur. "The front door you came in through, and the back door on the far side of the house."

"I know you were watching the front door from your desk," said Penny, "but is there any way Mr. Carr could have got past you, and sneaked out the back?"

"I don't see how," said Arthur.

"I was out the back," Marion said flatly. "Carr would have had to walk right past me to get to the rear door. And you need to bear in mind that every floor in this house is just bare wooden floorboards. It's impossible to walk anywhere in the Hall and not be heard. I wanted to put down some nice carpets or a few tasteful rugs, but apparently that would have been out of character."

She shot Arthur another of her accusing looks, which he accepted with his usual long-suffering air.

I gestured at the display next to the reception desk. "Was this intended for the Historical Society people?"

"Of course," said Arthur.

"It was my idea," said Marion. "Arthur and I put it together, using things we found in the house. There's all kinds of historical junk just lying around, so I thought we might as well do something useful with it."

Arthur winced at her choice of words, but made no comment. Marion didn't even notice as she pressed on.

"The Ravensbrook Historical Society are obsessed with a

rebellion that never actually happened, but almost got its start here at the Hall. Arthur, you know all about this stuff. Walk them through it and fill in the details."

Arthur brightened a little, as we moved into his area of expertise. He stood a little straighter and did his best to look knowledgeable.

"King Charles II was a popular king, but his successor really wasn't. When Charles died and was replaced by the extremely Catholic James II, it made a lot of people very unhappy. Political and religious schisms sprang up all over the country, along with all sorts of people ready to take advantage of the situation.

"James Scott, the Duke of Monmouth, was Charles II's illegitimate son. He thought he could take the throne for himself. When the Monmouth rebellion finally began, in June of sixteen eighty-five, it was known as the Pitchfork Rebellion, because his army was mainly made up of peasants, with no access to proper weapons.

"The Rebellion was brought to a swift end at the Battle of Sedgemoor, in July of sixteen eighty-five. Peasants armed with scythes and pitchforks proved no match for King James' professional soldiers. It was a massacre. The surviving peasants ran for their lives, and Monmouth was captured, tried, and executed.

"I'm telling you all of this because it explains why Lord Ravensbrook thought he could mount his own rebellion. He came to Glenbury Hall in the Autumn of sixteen eighty-five, looking for funding to acquire enough mercenaries to form a proper army. But instead, he just disappeared into thin air."

"Why did Ravensbrook believe he would find support here?" I said.

"The Glenburys were distant cousins to Lord Ravensbrook,"

said Arthur. "And the head of the family at that time was said by some to be the lord's illegitimate son."

"But what did Ravensbrook have, that the Glenburys didn't?" said Penny. "Why would they need him to lead the rebellion?"

"Ravensbrook had a legitimate, if distant, claim to the Throne," said Arthur, "while the Glenburys were a widely hated and reviled family. None of them would have been allowed anywhere near the Throne."

"What did they do, that was so bad?" said Penny.

"Name a crime, and you could find some member of the family who'd been accused of it," Arthur said steadily. "It was believed by pretty much everyone that the entire family were devil-worshippers, and had been for generations. That they had called up things from the Pit, and made terrible deals with them, in return for wealth and protection. They were also supposed to have some unnatural source of power, linked to the old well. Born of ritual sacrifice, and the murder of innocents. There were all kinds of reasons for people to go missing, around Glenbury Hall.

"Not that anything was ever proved.

"Now, Lord Ravensbrook was seen to enter Glenbury Hall, but he never came out again. The family swore none of them ever saw him, and of course, there have always been weird stories about the Hall."

"What kind of stories?" said Ellen, looking at her father with new interest. He smiled at her.

"The original Glenburys were supposed to have summoned up a demon from the Pit and imprisoned it underneath the Hall. Something that had to be fed regularly, to keep it quiet…"

"And that's what people thought had happened to Lord Ravensbrook?" I said.

"Only the local people," said Arthur. "Everyone else believed the king had got wind of the meeting and sent his agents in ahead of Ravensbrook."

"But why make it look like Ravensbrook had disappeared?" said Penny. "Why not just execute him as a traitor, like Monmouth?"

"Because Ravensbrook had friends at Court," Arthur said patiently. "By making it seem as though the infamous Glenbury Hall had taken another victim, there was no evidence to point at the king."

"You know an awful lot about this," Penny said admiringly.

Arthur shrugged. "If Lord Ravensbrook had won his rebellion, and acknowledged his illegitimate Glenbury son, my family would have had a claim to the Throne. My parents talked about that all the time, when I was growing up. By then they'd lost most of their money, and this story was all they had to make themselves feel special."

"They didn't leave Arthur anything," said Marion. "Apart from the Hall."

"I never wanted anything from my family," said Arthur. "Except to be free of them. When my parents died, I thought I could finally live my own life. But here I am, back in the old family home and still talking about them . . ."

"We were told Glenbury Hall was left standing empty and abandoned for years," I said. "What brought you back here, Arthur?"

"The City turned on him," said Marion. "He lost everything."

"What happened?" said Penny.

"I was doing so well," said Arthur. His voice was calm and flat, his eyes lost in yesterday. "But finance is a slippery thing. It's all just numbers: nothing you can cling to, or depend on. And the financial winds can change direction in a heartbeat.

"The company I was working for made a series of bad investments. Suddenly the vultures were gathering, and my bosses started throwing people overboard. And despite all the good work I'd done for them, all the money I'd made for the company . . . none of that meant anything.

"Suddenly I had no job, no income, and no prospects. No one wanted to know me, because failure can be contagious. What savings I had didn't last long, so I had no choice but to come back here. To the one thing they couldn't take away from me. My heritage: Glenbury Hall."

"I came up with the idea of turning the house into a conference centre," said Marion. "It was supposed to be the saving of us. But then Carr had to disappear, and ruin everything!"

"What about the other members of the Historical Society?" I said. "Are they still on their way?"

"No," said Arthur. "Once it became obvious Carr wasn't going to just turn up, I got on the phone and told all the other members that their conference had been cancelled, due to a double booking."

"Why would you do that?" said Penny. "If you needed their money so badly?"

Arthur met her gaze squarely. "Because I couldn't risk them spreading the news about Carr's disappearance. Not until we've worked out what happened."

"I still say you should have talked to me first," said Marion.

"There wasn't time!" said Arthur, cutting her off for once. "We have to stay in control of the message. If the Society had turned up, what sort of comments do you think they would have left on Tripadvisor, and all the other social sites? What would that have done to our reputation, and the Hall's? Who would want to come to a house where people just disappear, with no warning or explanation?"

"We needed the money they were bringing," said Marion. She deliberately turned away from her husband, to fix her attention on me and Penny. "Old houses like this need a lot of upkeep. Even the most basic repairs and improvements took everything we had. We have to make this business work, because we don't have anything else!"

Arthur and Marion suddenly seemed to realise that they were revealing rather too much of their personal situation in front of strangers. And their fascinated daughter.

"Of course, parts of the Hall are really comfortable now," said Arthur. "Quite delightful, in fact."

"And we've added all kinds of modern features," said Marion.

"Like the wishing well?" Penny said sweetly.

There was a pause, as Arthur and Marion glanced at each other.

"According to some of the older stories," Arthur said carefully, "the well started out as a spring with miraculous healing properties. It later became a pagan shrine, though who or what was worshipped here is long forgotten. Later on, the original Glenburys turned the spring into a well, though it hasn't actually functioned as one for ages."

"So I made it into a wishing well," Marion said brightly. "Tourists love that kind of foolishness. They get to make a wish and we get to keep their money."

"I've been reading all kinds of sites about the old shrine," said Ellen. "No one knows how many people were killed here! You should put that on our business site; people love all that blood and horror stuff."

"We are not mentioning that," said Arthur. "There's a limit to the kind of visitors we want to attract."

"Do you talk about the hauntings on your site?" I said. "Some of the ghost stories associated with Glenbury Hall sound a bit off-putting. What sort of things did you see, growing up here in the Hall?"

Arthur took his time, considering how much he was prepared to talk about.

"I don't know if ghost is always the right word, for the kind of things that haunt Glenbury Hall," he said finally. "My father used to have a separate room to watch television in. His own private place. But he stopped going in there after the television started showing him things."

"What sort of things?" said Penny.

"He wouldn't tell me," said Arthur. "But my father wasn't a man who scared easily."

"What did he do about it?" I said.

"He moved the set to another room, and after that everything was fine," said Arthur. "The whole family would sit and watch with him, and we never saw anything out of the ordinary. Of course, it's always possible my father made all of that up, just to scare me. He did that a lot. He thought it was funny."

"Arthur's parents used to terrorise him," said Marion. "Some of the things he's told me, you wouldn't believe . . ."

"They said I needed toughening up," said Arthur. "That I'd never survive in the world outside. And they were right."

"I would like to point out that we have never encountered any problems with television sets in the Hall," said Marion.

"There are ghosts on my laptop," said Ellen.

Her voice was very quiet, and she'd gone back to looking at the floor. Judging by the expression on Marion's and Arthur's faces, it was the first time they'd heard about this.

"What kind of ghosts, sweetie?" said Arthur.

Ellen wouldn't look at him. "Sometimes the laptop turns itself on when I'm nowhere near it. Or the site I'm looking at will fade away and be replaced by places and people I never wanted to see, and voices saying horrible things."

"Why didn't you tell us this before, dear?" said Marion.

Ellen shook her head. "Most of the time, it's fine. And I didn't want to worry you."

Arthur and Marion looked at each other, and she gestured urgently for him to say something.

"I don't think it's anything you need to worry about, sweetie," said Arthur. "You're probably just picking up stray signals. Because we're so far from anywhere."

Ellen still wouldn't look at him. I decided to change the subject.

"Arthur..." I said, and his gaze snapped back to me. "Why did your ancestors have their Hall built so far outside the town? We heard some strange suggestions, in The Smugglers Retreat..."

"I'm sure you did," said Arthur. He didn't actually pull a face, but looked like he wanted to. "The locals might hate the Hall, but they do love to talk about it. You can put a lot of my family's bad reputation down to the old-time Glenburys abusing their power and privilege. That's what it was for, back then. But really, a lot of it comes down to the shrine. The townspeople have always been scared of it. Which is probably why the original Glenburys had their new home built right next to the shrine."

He broke off, his eyes once again fixed on the past.

"The Hall is very isolated. When I was a child, I was so scared of the dark... There were no streetlamps outside, so when my bedroom light was turned off it got very dark. Hardly any traffic passed by, but I would lie awake in my bed, hoping a car would come along. So that for a moment at least there would be light and noise, and I could be sure the world was still out there.

"My parents wouldn't allow me a night light. They thought any kind of pampering made you soft."

Marion reached across to take Arthur's hand. He hung onto it, but couldn't bring himself to look at her. Ellen looked a little embarrassed, to see such open emotion from her parents.

"I couldn't wait to get away from this house," said Arthur. "I dreamed of going to London, where it was always full of light and noise. But I had to come back. For the family."

"Are you still afraid of the dark?" said Penny.

"No," said Arthur.

But from the way Marion was looking at Arthur, I wasn't so sure about that. He took a deep breath, and then smiled around at everyone as though he thought he could change the atmosphere simply by adopting a more positive attitude.

"Of course, not everything that appears to be a ghost necessarily is one. Sometimes, when I was working alone down here, I would hear footsteps moving around on the floor above. And this was when I knew it couldn't be Marion or Ellen. No one else could be up there, because they would have had to get past me and I would have seen them. And yet over and over again, I was sure I heard someone walking about on the top floor. On a few occasions, I was so convinced I actually went upstairs to check, but there was never anyone there."

He paused, to take in our reactions, and then smiled.

"I finally noticed that I only heard people walking around upstairs after I'd been moving about down here. And that's when I worked it out. The reverberations from my footsteps were travelling through the wooden floor, up the wooden staircase, and then re-emerging in the wooden floor above. What I'd been hearing was the delayed echo of my own movements!"

He shared his pleased smile with Marion, who solemnly nodded her approval. Ellen looked impressed, that her father had been able to solve the puzzle on his own. She also seemed a little relieved, that a supposedly supernatural event could turn out to have an everyday solution.

"Ghost stories are fine when it comes to luring in the visitors," said Marion. "But that's all they ever are. Just stories."

I looked thoughtfully at Arthur. "What will you do, if your new business doesn't work out?"

"We'll have to put the Hall up for sale," he said steadily.

"We should get a good price for it," said Marion.

They didn't look at each other, and there was something in their voices.

"Are you sure about that?" I said.

Arthur slumped a little. "All right . . . The first thing I did was try to sell the Hall, but no one wanted it. The house needs a lot of repairs, and the ground it stands on isn't particularly desirable, because of the way the locals feel about it. We couldn't even find an estate agent who could be bothered to lie to us about our chances. Our business has to work out. It's all we've got."

"That's why you have to find Lucas Carr!" said Marion, glaring accusingly at Penny and me. "Why are you still standing around here asking questions, instead of doing something?"

"Because asking questions is how you find out things," I said.

"Well, what more do you want to know?" said Marion.

"How many people from the Historical Society were you expecting today?" said Penny.

"Twelve, including Carr," said Marion. "And we might still get them back, if you can dig him out of his hiding place!"

I just nodded, keeping my gaze fixed on Arthur. "You said Carr signed in. Can I see the registration book?"

He pushed it across the desk toward me. A large leather-bound volume, designed to impress. Arthur opened it to the first page, where there was just the one signature. I took a photo on my phone and e-mailed it to the Colonel and got an answer immediately, confirming it was the real thing. At least now I could be sure Carr really had made it this far.

"What happened to Lucas' room key?" said Penny. "Did you find it inside his room?"

"No," said Arthur. "There was no sign of it."

I looked around the lobby. "You don't have any surveillance cameras...but what about burglar alarms? Given that this is an isolated house, with a lot of antiques just lying around..."

"We don't have anything worth the taking," Marion said flatly. "And God knows we've looked. All the good stuff was sold off long ago, by Arthur's parents."

He smiled briefly. "The local museums and pawn shops are packed full of what should have been my inheritance. Towards the end my parents were selling off anything that wasn't nailed down, just so they could hang on to the Hall. The only thing they ever really cared about. But we don't have to worry about burglars, because no one local would dare come out here."

"There are burglar alarms, at the front and rear doors," said Marion. "Because the insurance company insisted. But the damn things are so sensitive we were always setting them off accidentally, so now we only turn them on at night."

"So Carr could have left through either door, without setting off an alarm," I said.

"He couldn't have come down the stairs without me hearing or seeing him!" said Arthur.

Yes, I thought. *You keep saying that. But you're the only one who saw him go up to the next floor. So which is more likely: that he vanished between the lobby and his room, or that you're lying?*

I kept all of that out of my face, and nodded at the wall behind Arthur. "I'm going to need one of your pass keys."

"There is only one," said Arthur. "We had it made specially, to open the doors of the visitors' rooms."

"For emergencies," said Marion.

Arthur took the key down from the back wall, and handed it to me. I tucked it away in my pocket.

"All right," I said. "Penny and I will search the upper floor, then down here, and finally we'll take a good look round the grounds. There's always the chance we might spot something you missed."

"Before you do anything," Marion said quickly, "you should know that while we were waiting for you to show up, Arthur and I decided we needed to bring in our own investigator, to make sure our interests would be properly protected."

"You can bring in whoever you like," I said, "but Penny and I will still be in charge."

"Who did you choose?" said Penny.

"Catherine Voss is a respected local historian," said Marion. "She's written a book about the Hall, and the Glenburys."

"On top of that, she's an old family friend," said Arthur. "She was like an aunt to me, when I was a child."

"Is she a properly accredited historical scholar?" I said. "Does she know her stuff?"

"Glenbury Hall is a fifteenth-century manor house, with sixteenth-century additions," said a calm and cultured voice behind us. "The house has been officially designated a Grade 1-listed building. Isn't that right, Arthur dear?"

We all looked round, and standing in the doorway was a

grey-haired little old lady in a baggy jumper and a long pleated skirt, clutching a battered carpet bag. She smiled happily at Arthur, as he quickly emerged from behind the desk and hurried across the lobby to envelop her in a hug. She patted him fondly on the back.

"Careful, dear, I'm a bit more fragile than I used to be."

Arthur gave her one last squeeze and stepped back. "I'm so glad you're here, Catherine. It's been a nightmare."

"I set off the moment I got your message," said Catherine. "Are these the security people?" She smiled at Penny and me, her blue eyes twinkling. "Don't worry, he hasn't told anyone else. He knows when to keep quiet about things."

"He told you," I said.

"Ah yes," said Catherine. "But I'm special."

"This is Ishmael Jones and Penny Belcourt," said Marion. "They're in charge of finding Lucas Carr."

Catherine came forward and made a point of shaking hands with both of us. Her tiny hand disappeared inside mine, so I was careful to treat it respectfully.

"I'm just here to help," she said sweetly, "not get in your way. But I do possess a great deal of specialised information about the house, and the family, that may turn out to be useful."

"We're grateful for any help we can get," said Penny. "Isn't that right, Ishmael?"

"Of course," I said.

"Just find Carr, or prove his disappearance has nothing to do with the Hall," said Marion. "And then we can set about getting the visitors back."

"We're about to start a search of the upper floor," I said to Catherine. "Perhaps you'd like to come with us, and give us the benefit of your expertise."

"Oh, how wonderful!" said Catherine. "Only in the Hall for five minutes, and already I get a chance to show off!"

❖ CHAPTER THREE ❖
A WALK THROUGH HISTORY

"YOU'RE GOING TO NEED a native guide," said Catherine. "I can answer every question you have, including the ones you don't know you need to ask."

"That would be helpful," I said politely. "I'm sure there are a great many things no one has got around to mentioning yet."

"We are here to find out things!" Penny said brightly.

"Then I think we should start with the grounds," said Catherine. "Studying the house from the outside will give you all manner of valuable insights. Glenbury Hall is steeped in the past and haunted by history, especially all the really appalling things the family did here."

"I'm getting a little tired of the way people keep skirting around exactly what it was the Glenburys got up to," I said. "Why make such a mystery of it?"

Catherine smiled. "Much will become clear, as we proceed on our grand tour."

"Only much?" said Penny.

"I'm afraid so, dear. It's that kind of family, and that kind of history."

"Then let's start with the grounds," I said.

"Well," Marion said quickly, just to remind us she was still there. "You won't be needing any more help from us, so we'll just leave you to it. We have work to do."

"I don't," Ellen said immediately. "I want to hear all these awful stories, about what our ancestors did."

"No, you don't," Marion said firmly. "You have homework."

Ellen scowled. "Hate home schooling."

"You have to do the work, if you want to get into a good university," Marion said sternly.

"I'm still thinking about that," said Ellen.

"No, you're not," said Marion. "It's been decided."

Ellen looked to her father, but he was deliberately staring in another direction and keeping out of it. Marion bustled her daughter out of the lobby, and up the stairs. Arthur gave me a *What can you do?* look and went after them.

"Families," said Catherine. "Makes me glad I decided never to have one. Follow me, my dears, and let the enlightenment begin. No. Wait a minute..."

She swept over to take a stern look at the historical display next to the reception desk. Penny and I waited patiently while Catherine carefully studied every detail. In the end she dismissed the entire affair with a loud disparaging sniff, like a bank teller who'd just been handed a three-pound note.

"Can't say I think much of this.... The farm implements date from entirely the wrong period, and the maps are all to do with the Monmouth rebellion. No one knows what plans Lord Ravensbrook had in mind for his campaign against King James' army. Something a bit more professional than Monmouth, one would hope." She paused, to run a grudging eye over the dummy. "At least the outfit is an accurate representation of what Ravensbrook was wearing, on the day he disappeared."

"How can you be sure?" said Penny.

"Oh, there are detailed contemporary accounts of what Ravensbrook was wearing when he left London," said Catherine. "He was quite the famous dandy, in his day."

"I thought he was supposed to be travelling incognito," I said. "So he wouldn't be recognised by the king's agents?"

Catherine shook her head sadly. "He was a lord. There was probably a limit to how far he could allow himself to hide his light under a bushel."

"What kind of man was Ravensbrook?" said Penny.

"Ambitious," said Catherine. "Admired, more than liked. And a man who fancied himself more of a soldier than a politician. He deserved a better end than he got . . . but of course, that's true for a lot of the people who disappeared at Glenbury Hall."

She squared her shoulders, turned her back on the display, and headed for the front door. Penny and I exchanged a look and went after her.

Outside, the sun was sinking down in the sky and the light was going out of the day. The Hall and its towering topiary walls shed lengthening shadows across the grounds. The dimming light gave the scattered statues an even more sinister aspect, their inclining heads suggesting they weren't just watching and listening, but taking an active interest. Catherine ignored them, striding briskly across the grounds until she'd gone far enough that she could turn around and take in the entire Hall with one look. Penny and I took up positions on either side of the old lady, and we all studied the house with critical eyes.

Glenbury Hall appeared even more grim and foreboding in the lowering gloom, a lurking presence with nothing of home or hearth about it. More like somewhere you would only visit for a specific purpose, and then hurry away from. While nursing a suspicion that you'd got out just in time. But even allowing for the impression it made, I still couldn't see anything obviously dangerous or threatening about the Hall.

Penny stirred uncomfortably. "We have been to some spooky places in our time, Ishmael ... but there's something disturbing about Glenbury Hall. It feels like just by being here we've walked into a trap, and something hiding in the shadows is grinning all over its face and rubbing its hands together ..."

I looked at her, over Catherine's head. "I'm not feeling anything like that. It's just an ugly house with an ugly reputation."

"The Hall was built to very specific instructions, by the original Glenburys," said Catherine. "They wanted a house no one but them would want to live in, and no one else would dare approach."

I nodded solemnly. "I would have to say they succeeded."

"I have very fond memories of my time here, when I was younger," Catherine said wistfully. "Paul and Mary, Arthur's parents, used to throw parties you wouldn't believe. Such good times ..."

"Just looking at the place gives me the shivers," said Penny. "It's like the architect had a nightmare, and then inflicted it on the world. I can't believe Arthur and Marion really thought a place like this would attract visitors."

"That's probably why they started with a group of historians already obsessed with the Hall," I said. "If they gave the place good reviews, others might follow."

"History isn't supposed to be comfortable," said Catherine.

I looked at her thoughtfully. "Why did you decide to write a book about the Hall, and the Glenburys?"

"Because there was so much fascinating material," Catherine said immediately.

"What was your book called?" said Penny.

Catherine had the grace to look a little embarrassed. "*The House with Its Roots in Hell.* My publishers insisted."

"Do you believe all the ghost stories that have accumulated around Glenbury Hall?" I said.

Catherine shot me a surprisingly serious look. "If enough people tell you something is true, you'd have to be a damned fool to disbelieve them."

Penny turned her gaze away from the Hall and scowled balefully at the closest statues.

"There's something odd about these figures," she said. "It feels like they were put here for a purpose. And that if we did anything to oppose it, they'd come alive and rise up ..."

"If one of them even looks at you funny," I said, "I will punch its stone head right off."

"Oh, there's nothing interesting about these statues," said Catherine. "The original family bought them as a job lot, because if you lived in a mansion house you had to have statues in your grounds. It was expected of you."

"So you don't have any idea who they're supposed to be?" I said.

"They're not meant to be anybody," Catherine said patiently. "Though of course, there are stories ..."

"I had a feeling there might be," I said.

"What kind of stories?" said Penny.

Catherine smiled knowingly. "Some say that on certain nights, when the moon is full and the wind blows out of the east, the statues come creeping forward to peer in through the windows and see what the people are doing."

"Okay," said Penny. "That is spooky."

"But unlikely," I said.

"Forget the statues," said Catherine. "Concentrate on the Hall."

The sun was setting behind the house now, surrounding the entire building with a halo of curdled golden light. The dark windows stared back at us like so many unblinking eyes, and the Hall seemed to crouch like some great beast lying in wait. I decided very firmly that I was letting my imagination get the better of me.

"Isn't it marvellous?" Catherine said cheerfully, clutching her carpet bag to her. "Still standing firm after all these centuries, despite decades of being left empty and abandoned."

"How did that happen?" I said.

"Arthur's parents were killed in a car crash," said Catherine. "Very sad, but somewhat inevitable given the way his father drove. Paul always aimed his car like he expected everyone else to get out of his way, until finally he met someone who drove the same way he did."

"Why did you become a substitute aunt to Arthur?" Penny said artlessly.

"Because he needed one," said Catherine. "Sometimes it seemed like I was the only one in that house who had any time for him. And perhaps I felt a little guilty, that I was having such a good time partying when he was so alone. I never wanted children of my own, but the two of us seemed to suit each other. Until I had to go away."

"Why was that?" said Penny. "Did something happen?"

"It was just time for me to leave," said Catherine. She stuffed her carpet bag under one arm, in a firm and emphatic way that said she was about to change the subject and didn't want any arguments. "Arthur was working in London when his parents died. I contacted him, to ask what he wanted to do now he was master of Glenbury Hall. He said, *Let it rot.* And so the Hall was left to its own devices. Normally you'd expect that kind of neglect to result in broken windows, graffiti on the walls, and local teenagers breaking in to steal what they could and generally trash the place . . . But not Glenbury Hall. No one from the town, or even the adjoining towns, wanted anything to do with a house they'd spent their whole lives being warned against."

"People are that scared of the Hall?" said Penny.

"Oh yes," said Catherine. "And with good reason."

"Does the house really eat people?" I said.

Catherine surprised me then, with a quick bark of laughter. "I've never heard it put quite that way, but yes, you could say that. Certainly the Hall has a long history of taking people who don't take it seriously enough."

"Why?" I said.

Catherine shrugged easily. "Depends which story you believe. I'd say the Hall does what it does . . . because it can."

"It's creeping the hell out of me," said Penny.

"And you don't creep easily," I said.

"Damn right I don't," said Penny.

"So what is it about the Hall that's getting to you?" I said.

She took her time answering. "I'm not sure. Maybe just a feeling that if everyone else is so scared, there must be a good reason for it. And the way those gargoyles are looking at us really isn't helping."

"Those aren't gargoyles, dear," said Catherine.

I gave her a stern look. "If you are about to tell us they are actually members of the Glenbury family suffering under a curse, and that they come to life at night and wander around the roof . . . then you and I are about to have a serious falling out."

"What a marvellous imagination you have!" said Catherine. "Of course they don't come to life! If they did, I would have heard about it. And the statues don't move around either, so you can stop peeking at them out of the corners of your eyes, Ms. Belcourt. I simply meant that figures like those on the roof are only called gargoyles if their mouths form part of the guttering. Otherwise, they are more properly referred to as grotesques."

"Let's talk about Lord Ravensbrook," I said. "What happened, when he arrived here?"

"This much is history," said Catherine. "He came to the Hall alone, on horseback, with no guards or retainers. Which was unusual as well as brave, in those turbulent times."

"Why would he travel alone?" said Penny.

"The most common explanation is that he was hoping to pass unnoticed by the king's agents," said Catherine. "He didn't know he'd already been betrayed, the poor dear."

"Do we know who gave him up?" I said.

"No one ever admitted anything," said Catherine. "Most likely it was one of the Glenburys, who didn't want the family involved in a new rebellion. Or it could have been one of Ravensbrook's contacts at Court. A lot of the nobility distrusted James, but still didn't want to risk plunging the country into another civil war. The general feeling among the movers and shakers of that time was that Ravensbrook was too ambitious for everyone else's good."

"Does anyone know what happened after he entered Glenbury Hall?" I said.

"No," said Catherine. "Every member of the Glenbury family swore they never saw Ravensbrook inside their home. The only record we have comes from servants working in the grounds, who saw Ravensbrook arrive."

"What about servants inside the Hall?" I said.

"They all swore they were somewhere else at the time," said Catherine.

"If the Glenburys were so famously evil," I said, "and the Hall was such a scary place . . . how were they able to attract so many servants?"

"Like calls to like," said Catherine. "And evil calls to evil. Anyway, all we can be sure of is that on that fateful day, Lord Ravensbrook walked through the front door into Glenbury Hall . . . and was never seen again."

"All right," I said. "Tell us about the timeslip. The gathering of people from the past who were seen in the grounds, back in the fifties."

"Ah yes," Catherine said happily. "I've always been fascinated by that story. Even though there isn't a shred of evidence to back it up, just the testimony of two very ordinary women who had no reason to lie."

"Did you ever talk to them?" said Penny.

"No, dear," Catherine said patiently. "I was a child, back in the fifties. By the time I was old enough to think about tracking them down, it was too late. They'd had enough of being mocked by the media, so they just retired from public view and refused to talk to anybody."

"Do you believe them?" I said.

Catherine took her time, considering her response. "The details in their written account were surprisingly accurate. There were none of the usual discrepancies you'd expect from someone who hadn't studied the period. I suppose it's always possible they did their homework, before making it all up. But that brings us back to the question, why would they? Neither of them made any attempt to profit from what they'd seen. Other people did that."

"What would a crowd of people have been doing here?" I said. "At such an infamous location?"

Catherine grinned. "The Glenburys have always been famous for the parties they throw."

"But if the family was so notorious," I said, "why would anyone want to party with them?"

"The allure of evil?" said Catherine. "I'm sure some people

came just to find out whether the stories were true. Others, because there was money and patronage to be had, for those who made the right kind of impression. And of course, the Glenburys always had the finest tobaccos and brandies, and all the other luxuries that had been taxed out of the grasp of most people. It was said that the Glenburys set the best table and had the best cellar outside the Royal Court. But in the end . . . I'd say people came here because like calls to like, and they were captivated by the thought of sinning on the same scale as the Glenburys."

"But what was it the Glenburys did, that was so awful?" I said.

Catherine frowned, choosing her words carefully. "The Glenburys handed the torch of corruption down from generation to generation, each one encouraging the next to do more. But you have to understand: no specific charge was ever made against any of them. Either because people were too frightened to speak out, or because the family had them silenced. It wasn't just the Hall that made people disappear. All we have are pamphlets, broadsheets, and books condemning the Glenburys, always anonymous, and only ever hinting at the really juicy stuff. Officially, the Glenburys were above reproach, and rich and powerful enough to ensure they stayed that way."

"So what did they do, in the juicy version?" Penny said patiently.

"Diabolism, human sacrifice, and all manner of depravity," Catherine said calmly. "The Glenburys were so far above the law they could look down on it. But to be fair . . . if they'd done everything they were accused of doing, they wouldn't have had time for anything but sinning."

"Human sacrifice?" I said. "Like with the old pagan site?"

"You know about that?" said Catherine.

"Not as much as you, obviously," said Penny.

"Throughout the history of this area," Catherine said slowly, "people claim to have heard a voice, singing and calling. First from the shrine, and later from the well. A siren song, that would draw people here against their will, to throw themselves in."

She strode over to the well, and Penny and I went with her. Catherine tutted disapprovingly at the new sign.

"I told Marion this was a bad idea, but she always has to go her own way. Never a good idea, at Glenbury Hall. The Devil is not mocked..."

"The Devil?" I said.

Catherine shrugged quickly. "Or whatever might once have lurked at the bottom of the well. Stories about the original shrine go back so far they were written in Latin. The Christian Church finally appropriated the spring, so they could claim its miracle cures as their own. But still the stories about the siren song persisted..."

Penny leaned over the stone wall, bracing herself on her elbows so she could peer down into the darkness. "It doesn't look dangerous now."

"Perhaps not, dear," said Catherine, "but I wouldn't risk upsetting whatever might still be down there, with something as frivolous as a wish."

"Too late," I said.

"Oh dear," said Catherine. "Never mind. Perhaps it wasn't listening."

"Is there anything else you can tell us about the well?" I said.

Catherine looked at me. "Isn't that enough?"

"Why weren't the Glenburys scared of the monster?" said Penny.

"Because the *Glenburys* were monsters," said Catherine. "I suppose it's possible they thought they could use the well's reputation to keep the local people at bay, so no one would find out what they were getting up to out here." She smiled familiarly at the Hall. "If those walls could talk . . . they'd probably scream."

"Do you know anything about the demon that's supposed to be imprisoned underneath the Hall?" I said. "Could it be connected to whatever was at the bottom of the well?"

"We are leaving history behind now, and moving into legend," said Catherine. "No one has ever reported a direct sighting of this demon . . . though there was supposed to be a portrait hanging somewhere in the Hall, of a member of the family who wasn't entirely human. Many years later, when I heard Paul and Mary had started selling off their paintings, I did make a few discreet enquiries, but nothing of the kind ever turned up at the auction houses. Despite a lot of enquiries from certain interested parties."

Penny nodded thoughtfully. "Were the grounds here really soaked with blood, back in the days of sacrifice? We were told the earth around the well was full of old bones."

"I doubt it," said Catherine. "The old storytellers would add whatever juicy details they thought would attract an audience. But the past is full of mysteries. Particularly at Glenbury Hall."

"What's your opinion of the well?" I said.

"Some say the original Glenburys were called to this location by some unknown voice," Catherine said carefully. "And that the family built first the well, and then the Hall, to protect whatever it was that summoned them. In return for wealth and power, of course."

"Which apparently ran out some time back," I said.

"Nothing lasts forever," said Catherine.

I leaned over the side of the well and peered down into a darkness so complete it defied even my eyes.

"Why does it go down so deep?"

"There are lots of stories about that," said Catherine. "But really, nobody knows."

"Could Lord Ravensbrook be down there?" I said. "It would be the perfect place to dispose of a body."

"You're not the first to suggest that," said Catherine. "But how could anyone have dumped a body in there without being seen by the servants in the grounds?"

"Servants might deny seeing anything, if they were paid or frightened enough," said Penny.

"Did anyone ever try to reach the bottom of the well to search for the missing lord?" I said.

Catherine nodded quickly. "Various attempts were made to plumb its depths, particularly when someone started a rumour about hidden treasure, but they all failed. Tunnels and earthworks constantly collapsed, killing the workmen. Waters from the spring would rise up and flood the diggings. And after a while, that was the end of that."

"But surely, these days..." said Penny.

"The well is unbelievably deep," Catherine said flatly. "I'm not sure the bottom could be reached even now, with modern digging equipment."

"Someone could always climb down," I said. "Or if the walls are tricky, they could be dropped in on the end of a rope."

"It's been tried," said Catherine. "After Ravensbrook disappeared, one of the Hall's servants was lowered headfirst into the well by a rope tied around his ankles. The Glenburys knew it had to be done before the king sent agents to do it for them. If only to make sure Ravensbrook definitely was dead, and no longer a threat.

"According to contemporary reports, the people at the top of the well became disturbed by how much rope they were having to play out, as their reluctant explorer descended further and further into the darkness. Suddenly the man started screaming to be pulled up, and when he was finally brought back into the light his hair was white, and his eyes were wild and staring. He kept babbling about the dark and the water, and the dark in the water. . . . No promise of money or threats or violence could persuade him to go back down again. Or anyone else, after that."

"And of course once that story got around, the king's agents wouldn't be able to persuade anyone else to go down," I said.

"You think the Glenburys faked the story?" said Penny. "To scare off future investigations?"

"I do seem to be spotting a pattern," I said. "When you get right down to it, all of these stories serve the Glenburys by scaring off their enemies and preserving their privacy."

"Sometimes there really is something to be scared of in the dark," said Catherine. "Local legend has it the well goes down as far as it does, because it has its roots in Hell."

"And we're back to the Devil again," I said. "How much of this stuff do you really believe?"

She smiled suddenly. "I like to believe six impossible things before tea-time, every day. It makes the world so much more interesting."

"But you're an historian," I said. "Isn't that all about the facts?"

"I am large," Catherine said grandly. "I contain multitudes. Some of whom aren't speaking to each other."

"If this well is so deep," said Penny, "how is Marion planning to retrieve the money the visitors drop into it?"

"I don't think she's really thought it through, dear," said Catherine.

And then she paused and leaned in close, so she could

speak confidentially. Even though there was no one else around.

"I came here once, to pay the Hall a visit while it was empty. I live not far away these days, over in Marshford, and I thought someone should take a look. But one visit was enough to convince me this wasn't the Hall I remembered. It felt as though the house wasn't entirely empty, and that something was looking back at me. I couldn't get out of the grounds fast enough."

"Does Arthur know you were here?" I said.

Catherine shook her head. "I thought it best not to bother him. Afterwards, I paid a visit to The Smugglers Retreat. Because I really needed a drink. Everyone there was still scared of the Hall, even though it was empty. In fact, the general feeling seemed to be that the Hall might actually be more dangerous without a Glenbury in residence to keep it in check."

"Thank you for your assistance," I said. "You can go back inside now."

Catherine looked a little shocked, at being dismissed so abruptly. "But there's so much more I could tell you..."

"You've given us more than enough to be going on with," I said. "But now, Penny and I need to make a thorough search of the grounds."

Catherine gave me a searching look, to make sure I was serious, and then nodded briskly.

"Very well, dear. I'll go and wait by the front door. Just in case you need to ask me some more questions."

She turned her back on us with quiet dignity and headed for the front door. Penny and I started our search in front of the Hall, moving slowly along together and studying the ground carefully.

"I'm not seeing any signs of digging," I said. "Nothing to indicate a recent burial."

"Have you given up on finding Lucas Carr alive?" said Penny.

"Not necessarily," I said. "But it is something we should consider."

"Someone in the Hall would have noticed a grave being dug," said Penny. "Unless you think everyone here is lying to us."

"Wouldn't be the first time," I said.

"But what possible motive could any of them have, for wanting to kill Lucas?" said Penny. "They'd never met him before today."

"So they say."

"But that brings us back to: why would they lie?"

I grinned. "Does complicate things, doesn't it?"

And then I stopped, as something caught my eye. I knelt down and ran my hands across one particular piece of ground. I could just make out a shallow depression, as though something heavy had been set down there recently.

"The grass here is flattened, and the earth feels compacted," I said. "Like something hit the ground, hard. Possibly something that fell from a great height."

I got to my feet again, and we both looked up at the roof. The grotesque faces stared back at us, giving nothing away.

"I'm not seeing any obvious gaps in the guttering," said Penny. "Nothing to suggest a missing gargoyle. There's no sign of any crumbling masonry that might have fallen. And again, I think people would have noticed."

"We'll have to ask Arthur how best to gain access to the roof," I said. "See if anything up there is damaged or missing."

"And look for clues?" Penny said hopefully. "You know how I love clues."

"A few would be helpful."

"What exactly would we be looking for?"

"I think we'd know it when we saw it."

Penny and I resumed our search of the grounds. We moved steadily back and forth checking the lawn, the statues, and every shaped tree in the topiary walls. It took some time, and the last of the evening light was wearing out by the time we gave up.

"These statues are starting to look increasingly sinister," said Penny. "It's the way they don't have any eyes to follow you around. Are you getting the feeling that they're crowding in around us . . ."

"No," I said firmly. "None of these statues have moved an inch. I memorised all their positions when we first entered the grounds."

Penny looked at me. "You memorised them."

"Of course."

"Why?"

"Self defence."

Penny shook her head. "Alien."

We walked back through the statues. Lights from a few of the ground-floor windows spilled out into the grounds, pushing back the gloom. Catherine was still waiting patiently by the front door, even though the evening had acquired a definite chill. She'd taken some knitting out of her carpet bag and was working industriously at something long and shapeless. She put it away as we approached.

"Find anything interesting, dears?"

"How well do you know Arthur?" I said bluntly.

"I was a close friend of his parents," said Catherine, entirely unaffected by my tone. "Paul and Mary were always great fun to be with, but they should never have had a child. They weren't suited to be parents. But they saw it as their duty to continue the line, the house of Glenbury."

"Does Arthur have any brothers, or sisters?" I said.

"Oh no, dear," said Catherine. "Paul and Mary decided very quickly that one child was enough. They were away a lot when Arthur was growing up, leaving the poor lamb to be taken care of by the servants."

"If his parents didn't want to look after him, why didn't they send him off to boarding school?" said Penny.

Catherine looked at her. "Is that what your parents did with you, dear?"

"We're not talking about me," said Penny.

Catherine shrugged. "Money was getting short by then, so Arthur was home-schooled by a series of inexpensive tutors. None of whom stuck around long. Arthur told me he was so lonely he tried sneaking out of the Hall and into town, hoping to make friends, only to find no one wanted anything to do with a Glenbury."

I studied her carefully. "Marion said Arthur's parents mistreated him."

"Oh, they did, dear," said Catherine. "But more through neglect and indifference, than anything else."

"They sound awful," said Penny. "Why were you their friend?"

"They weren't awful, dear!" said Catherine. "Just so wrapped up in each other, they had no time for a child's needs. Paul and Mary were very good company, back when we were young. Oh, the parties they used to throw! People would turn up from all over the county. You have to remember, the seventies was a very liberated time. Leave your clothes and inhibitions at the door and let the good times roll! I remember bowls full of car keys and condoms . . ." She laughed softly at the look on our faces. "You young people think you invented debauchery."

"Did Arthur know what was going on, at these parties?" said Penny.

"Once he got to a certain age, there was no hiding it from him," said Catherine. "Paul and Mary had to start holding their little get-togethers in other people's houses, and there's no denying they resented that. That's why they spent so much of their time away from the Hall, leaving the boy to his own devices."

"But he had you for company," I said.

"When I was around."

"When you weren't at the parties," said Penny.

"Well, quite," Catherine said. "I was his aunt, not his nanny."

I didn't have anything to say to that, so I led the way back inside Glenbury Hall.

The lobby was brightly lit, but there was no sign of Arthur or his family. Catherine smiled wistfully around her.

"It is good to be back. I always felt at home here."

"Really?" I said. "Isn't that a bit odd, given how much the Hall freaks out everyone else?"

She shrugged amiably. "Perhaps it's because I always had such good times here."

"Can you show us around the ground floor?" I said.

"Of course, dear," said Catherine. "What would you like to see?"

"You're the expert," I said. "Show us things we need to know."

Catherine grinned. "Just follow your native guide and pin your ears back."

She led us down a long gloomy corridor, pointing out one room after another. Most of the doors had been left standing ajar, as though inviting us to see for ourselves that nothing out of the ordinary was going on. The rooms held nothing but pieces of bulky furniture lurking under heavy dust sheets. Walls and floors had been left bare, and the floorboards creaked loudly under our weight, as though complaining at our presence.

"Arthur and Marion could only afford to renovate a few of the rooms," said Catherine, "so they concentrated on sprucing up the ones they thought the Historical Society would appreciate most. The Hall has fallen such a long way . . . It used to be so bright and cheerful here! So full of life! I remember running naked down this corridor with my friends, screaming with laughter, off our heads on the best wines and the best dope . . . It felt like the party would never end.

"But of course it had to, eventually. A lot of the family treasures had already been sold off, to fund Paul and Mary's lifestyle."

"Why was that?" said Penny.

"The family fortunes were finally running out," said Catherine. "They had no talent or skill for making more, and of course no one would lend to Glenburys."

"There's always someone," I said.

"But Paul and Mary would never mortgage the Hall," said Catherine. "Or take on any debt that would threaten it. So bit by bit, all the pretty things vanished, and as the settings got shabbier, so did the parties."

She pushed the thought firmly to one side and brightened up as she filled us in on the history of the house, and its family. She also seemed to have an endless supply of strange sightings and weird happenings. Of rooms that were sometimes there and sometimes not, and windows that occasionally showed views from the past.

"Like the timeslip?" said Penny.

"Exactly, dear. Time comes and goes, around Glenbury Hall. I sometimes think the family did something to break it."

Like the barman in The Smugglers Retreat, Catherine's ghost stories didn't involve the usual see-through ancestors, or animated suits of armour. Instead, she told subtler tales of people who looked into mirrors and saw someone else looking back at them. Of corridors that seemed to stretch away farther than they should, and guests who got the feeling there were more people in a room than they could account for. Dim figures seen walking the corridors at night, with horrid faces or none at all, and never making the slightest sound on the bare wooden floorboards.

"Some are supposed to be past members of the Glenbury family," said Catherine. "Walking these corridors because the sins they committed were so terrible, they're condemned to haunt the scenes of their crimes forever."

"The barman at The Smugglers Retreat mentioned one apparition that couldn't even walk," I said. "He said: *It crawls . . .*"

"Ah yes!" said Catherine, nodding enthusiastically. "One of the Hall's most notorious legends. Lots of people claim to have seen a terrible figure crawling along on all fours . . ."

"Why does it do that?" said Penny.

"Shape-changing was just one of the charges laid against the family," said Catherine. "And according to some accounts, this particular Glenbury hasn't lost his taste for human flesh just because he's dead."

"A ghost with an appetite?" I said. "Does he bring his own ghostly knife and fork?"

Catherine looked at me reprovingly. "The dead aren't just visions, in Glenbury Hall. The past has a strength all its own, that will not be denied. The dead can be a danger to the living, in this house."

"Was everybody in the Glenbury family mad or weird or evil?" said Penny.

"Pretty much," said Catherine. "They were very competitive."

"Mad, bad, and dangerous to encounter in the early hours," I said. "Apart from your good friends Paul and Mary. And Arthur, of course."

Catherine peered into the shadows of the corridor before us, so she wouldn't have to meet my gaze.

"Even inherited evil can wear out, if it passes through enough generations."

"But not the ghosts," said Penny. "They're still here."

"And yet Marion insisted that she's never seen anything weird, in all the time she's been here," I said.

Catherine sniffed loudly. "I'm not surprised. Some people are just blind to the hidden world. A ghost could walk right up to Marion and stare her in the face, and she wouldn't even know it was there."

"I don't think I like the sound of that," said Penny. "If something ghostly was happening to me, up close and personal, I'm pretty sure I'd want to know about it."

"Don't be too sure," said Catherine. "There are horrors and atrocities in this house that no one would want to see."

"You're being vague again," I said. "We need details."

"I don't think you do, dear," said Catherine. "Not really."

"It would take a lot to throw me," I said. "I've seen more than my share of bad things."

"It's true!" said Penny. "He really has. I was there with him, for some of them."

Catherine looked into our faces and nodded slowly. "I did get the feeling this wasn't your first supernatural rodeo. Very well . . . There are supposed to be things in this house that started out as people, but weren't at all human by the time they died. Or were put an end to. Certain members of the Glenbury family were said to have mated with things called up from the Pit, and only the offspring that could pass for human were allowed to survive."

"Really?" said Penny.

"The Glenburys were accused of every sin under the sun, and some that could only be committed in the dark," said Catherine. "And the worse the stories were, the more the Glenburys seemed to glory in them. They took a perverse pride in never denying anything."

"But have you ever seen any evidence to support these stories?" I said.

Catherine shook her head regretfully. "I have been in every room in this house, at one time or another, and I've never seen anything out of the ordinary. But you can't disregard the sheer number of people who swear they've seen things in Glenbury Hall."

"There are many ways in which things can be made to appear and disappear," I said. "Old houses like this one are often lousy with secret doors and hidden rooms."

"I asked Paul and Mary about that, back in the day," said Catherine. "They both seemed very sure that there weren't any."

"And of course, they would never lie to you," I said.

"They were my friends," said Catherine. "And Arthur spent ages banging on the walls when he was a child and never found anything. Remember, the usual reason for a hidden room was to serve as a priest hole, to conceal Catholic worship. But the Glenburys were always fiercely Protestant."

I stared down the corridor ahead of us, at all the doors still waiting to be investigated.

"How many rooms are there, on the ground floor?"

"Twenty-seven," Catherine said immediately.

"And does every room come with its own individual ghost story?" said Penny.

Catherine smiled. "It does feel that way, sometimes. Do you believe in ghosts, dear?"

Penny looked at me. "You want to field that one?"

"I try to keep an open mind," I said.

"Oh no," Catherine said solemnly. "You don't want to do that, dear. You can never be sure what might walk in."

"They'd get a shock if they saw what's inside my head," I said.

"Why are you so fascinated by ghosts, Catherine?" Penny said quickly.

"I was a product of the seventies, that most haunted of decades," Catherine said proudly. "When there were all kinds of spooky shows on television, and supernatural events turned up regularly on the local news. I still remember watching reports about haunted stone heads, poltergeists in council houses, and the Beast of Brassknocker Hill . . ."

Penny and I looked at each other. We didn't say anything, but Catherine caught something in the look.

"You know about that?"

"We had an experience, on Brassknocker Hill," I said.

"Nothing to do with the Beast, though," said Penny.

Catherine waited for a moment, until it became clear we had nothing more to say on the subject. She presented us with another of her loud sniffs and continued her tour of the ground floor.

"It all comes down to what you believe ghosts are," she said over her shoulder, as we hurried after her. "The unquiet dead, condemned to walk the Earth, or simply past events, endlessly repeating. There's no doubt some Glenburys did things in the Hall that were so vile they stained the atmosphere forever."

"What do you think people see here?" said Penny.

"I've always said I'll make up my mind after I meet a

ghost," said Catherine. "If there is anything in this house, I am determined to come face to face with it before I leave."

"That's the spirit," I said. "But please remember, we are here to discover what happened to Lucas Carr. That takes precedence over everything else."

"Well of course, dear," said Catherine. "But I feel I should remind you, an awful lot of people have come to the Hall, looking for answers to all kinds of questions...only to be bitterly disappointed. No one has ever found any of the people who've been reported as missing. The Hall holds its secrets close to its chest, and its mysteries remain mysteries."

"The Hall never met anyone like me," I said.

We completed our little excursion without uncovering anything useful and returned to the lobby. It was still empty. I went over to the reception desk and banged on the old-fashioned brass bell with my fist, and then called out for Arthur or Marion, but there was no response.

"Where is everybody?" said Penny.

"Oh, I'm sure they have lots of work to be getting on with," said Catherine.

"More likely they're hiding from us," I said.

Catherine raised an eyebrow. "Why would they want to do that?"

I smiled briefly. "When we find them, I'll ask them."

"First rule of investigating a mystery," Penny said brightly. "Everyone has secrets."

"And everyone lies about them," I said.

"That's two rules," said Catherine.

"And that's just the start," said Penny. "If it was easy, everybody would be doing it."

I checked out the route from the reception desk to the foot of the staircase. There were no obvious signs of violence. I knelt down, put my face right next to the floorboards and had a good sniff. Traces of a dozen different scents filled my head, most of them to do with cleaning products. I studied the floorboards carefully, with my better than average eyes, but couldn't make out the faintest remnant of a blood spot. There was nothing to indicate that any kind of struggle had taken place. Whatever had happened, it hadn't happened here.

I realised Catherine was watching me closely and sighed quietly. You'd think that after all these years, I'd be better at hiding my true nature from innocent bystanders. But sometimes a weird situation can't help but bring out the weird in me.

The starship's transformation machines were only supposed to make me human, but given my superior strength and speed, and sharper senses, I couldn't help wondering whether the machines had taken advantage of the situation to try for a few improvements on the basic model. Not that I had any reason to complain. It isn't just my outsider's viewpoint that helps me solve mysteries.

I got to my feet again and looked back at Penny and Catherine.

"I'm not picking up any trace of blood, or death."

Catherine gave me a hard look, and then turned to Penny.

"He's part bloodhound," Penny said solemnly.

"Really, dear?" said Catherine. "Which part?"

They both got the giggles. I gave them a pained look and moved to the foot of the stairs. Penny and Catherine followed on behind, doing their best to smother their laughter.

"This is quite definitely the only way to get from the ground floor to the top," said Catherine. "Mr. Carr had to have gone this way, to get to his room."

I started up the bare wooden steps, with Penny and Catherine sticking close behind me. The sound of our footsteps on the uncovered floorboards was loud and carrying. Halfway up the stairs I came to a sudden halt, and the others almost bumped into me.

"Arthur was right," I said. "There's no way he could have missed hearing sounds like these. If he was where he said he was."

"You can trust Arthur!" said Catherine, sounding shocked that I could even think otherwise.

"Ishmael doesn't trust anyone," said Penny. "Except for me, of course."

I took off my shoes and continued up the stairs in my socks. The boards still creaked loudly under my weight.

"I should put those shoes back on, dear," said Catherine. "There are bound to be splinters..."

I slipped into my shoes and led the way to the top of the stairs. A long passageway stretched away before us, disappearing into an unrelieved gloom. Catherine went straight to the main light switch, but the bulbs were so few and far between they left more in shadows than they illuminated. It was so quiet I could almost hear the dust falling.

"I'll take the lead again, shall I?" said Catherine. "I know the territory."

"More ghost stories?" said Penny.

"Oh, loads and loads!" Catherine said cheerfully.

We followed her down the passageway as she chattered happily away. Paintings still covered most of the walls, and Catherine had a story for all of them. It made a change from the spook stuff, though strictly speaking she was still talking about the dead.

Most of the portraits were so stylised as to be basically anonymous. Only the differing outfits marked the passing of time. But Catherine could still put a name and a potted history to most of them. This one was a bad lad, and came to a bad end. That one should never have married into the Glenburys, should never have poisoned her husband, and certainly shouldn't have been caught so easily. This one went missing, and this one. And that one was sent abroad because he went too far, even for the Glenburys.

"Jacob was what they used to call a Remittance Man," said Catherine, pausing before a particularly saturnine face. "Paid regular sums by the family, as long as he promised never to return to England."

"What did he do that was so bad, even the Glenburys were ready to disown him?" said Penny.

"He got found out," said Catherine. "I gather there was some disquiet over what Jacob might say about the rest of the family if he was ever brought to Court. Sending him abroad seemed the safest option for everyone. Except for the people abroad, of course."

The portraits gave way to hunting scenes, mostly from the naïve school. Nothing too realistic, and given the sheer number of disembowelled deer involved, that was probably for the best. They made me think of all the stuffed animal heads at The Smugglers Retreat.

"Why was everyone around here so keen on killing things?" said Penny.

"Tradition," said Catherine. "Sport . . . And of course the Glenburys always took a special pride in savouring the kind of pleasures other people didn't or couldn't."

There were even a few paintings of glowing skeletons on horseback, riding hell for leather across a moonlit scene.

"I saw a similar image outside The Smugglers Retreat," I said.

"For a long time, this was serious smuggling country," said Catherine. "And the smugglers would go to great lengths to scare the locals away from their special routes. Because the Revenue Men would pay good money for that kind of information."

"Were the Glenburys involved in smuggling?" said Penny.

"I don't know about involved," said Catherine, "but you can bet they were regular customers. The Glenburys always had to have the best of everything."

We pressed on, our footsteps sounding out loud and clear, as though to warn any ghosts we were on our way. I made a point of at least glancing inside every room. Penny suddenly shuddered, as though troubled by a cold breeze. Catherine shot her a knowing look.

"You feel it too? Everyone does, who stays in the Hall long enough. That pressure of unseen eyes . . . Even back in my partying days, we all preferred to go back to our own homes once the fun started winding down. Paul and Mary had bedrooms to spare, but everyone always had an excuse."

"Weren't Paul and Mary bothered by the atmosphere?" I said.

"No. They laughed at us. But then, they grew up here."

"Where do you think the feeling comes from?" said Penny.

"The past is always with you, in Glenbury Hall," said Catherine. "Often right behind you and peering over your shoulder."

I suppressed an urge to look behind me, and we moved on. I still wasn't seeing anything strange, or out of the ordinary. Just a whole bunch of antique furniture, battered and scratched and in need of a good dusting. And the wall panelling wasn't much better. The whole of the top floor looked like someone's forgotten attic.

"Arthur and Marion haven't made make much of an effort here," said Penny. "They could have spruced the place up a bit, for their first visitors."

"Catch-22, I'm afraid," said Catherine. "Renovation costs money, but they can only get money from visitors. They cleaned and polished those areas near to where the Historical Society would be staying and left the rest for later. Besides, a lot of the time this is what people like that would want to see in old houses. The patina of the past."

We reached the end of the floor without finding anything useful, turned around and made our way back to the top of the stairs. I asked Catherine which room belonged to Arthur and Marion, and she pointed to the first of a row of doors near the top of the stairs. The door wasn't locked, so I pushed it open, and we looked in. An ordinary, modern, and perfectly comfortable room. Ellen's was next door, and seemed much the same, with the addition of a great many posters displaying scowling rap artists I didn't recognise.

"No wonder Marion insisted Ellen use her headphones," I said. "Not exactly suitable background music, when you're expecting a dozen historical scholars."

"The whole point of young people's music is that it doesn't appeal to anyone else," Catherine said wisely. "I was a huge Hawkwind fan, when I was her age."

I closed the door carefully.

"It's still hard to believe Ellen didn't hear anything when Lucas disappeared," said Penny.

"Maybe there wasn't anything to hear," I said.

"Or she wasn't where she said she was," said Penny. "In fact, why isn't Ellen in her room now? Her mother said she had homework."

"They're probably having a family meeting," I said. "So they can get their stories straight."

Catherine shook her head. "How can anyone be so cynical?"

"Years of experience," I said. "Where were the Historical Society supposed to be staying?"

Catherine pointed out half a dozen doors, next to the Glenburys' rooms.

"How do you know all this?" said Penny. "I thought you hadn't been inside the Hall in ages?"

"I consulted over the renovations, after Arthur brought his family back here," said Catherine. "I was quite touched when he reached out to me. We'd drifted apart. Just Christmas cards, and the like."

"Did you approve, when he said he was coming back?" I said. "You said you didn't like the look of the abandoned Hall."

"It's wasn't my place to approve or disapprove," said Catherine.

"But did you try to talk him out of it?" said Penny. "You were his aunt, in all but name. He must have valued your opinion."

Catherine took her time before she answered. "I told him I thought it would be wrong to let the Hall fall into ruin. It's an important historical building. And I did point out that by opening the Hall to visitors, he could probably make a good living from it. But in the end, I think he was more persuaded by his wife. Which is of course as it should be."

"Hold it," said Penny. "You only pointed out six rooms, but Marion said they had twelve members of the Society booked in."

Catherine had the grace to look a little embarrassed. "Arthur couldn't afford to modernise more than six rooms, so he told the visitors they'd have to double up. They didn't seem to mind. They were so keen to finally get inside Glenbury Hall, I think they would have slept in hammocks in the kitchen if that was what it took."

The door to the first guest room was locked, but I opened it with the pass key, and we looked in. The room seemed cheerful enough, though dominated by a large double bed.

"There you are," said Catherine. "Easily big enough to sleep two."

"I think this room will do for us," I said to Penny.

Catherine looked at me sharply. "You're staying overnight?"

"Penny and I aren't going anywhere until we find out what happened to Lucas Carr," I said.

Catherine smiled suddenly. "Me too!"

"You're staying the night as well?" said Penny.

"Of course," said Catherine. "You're going to need my expertise, if you're planning on searching this house from top to bottom."

"But you never wanted to stay overnight, back in your partying days," I said.

"That was then," said Catherine. "This is now."

"Do you still want to see a ghost?" said Penny.

"Oh yes!" said Catherine. "If only because there are so many questions I could ask it, about the history of the Hall."

I got the feeling any sensible ghost would run a mile, faced with Catherine's determined interrogation, but I didn't say anything. I locked the door again.

"Are all the rooms the same?" said Penny.

"As far as I know," said Catherine.

I was ready to start back down the stairs, when my attention was caught by an old-fashioned grandfather clock standing on its own.

"Catherine, why isn't that clock working?"

She stared at me. "How do you know it isn't?"

"Because it's not ticking."

"You must have really good hearing," said Catherine. "But

you're quite right. That clock hasn't worked since eighteen eighty-eight. Something bad happened, right here, and that clock was the only witness."

"Then how do you know something bad happened?" said Penny.

"Because Jacob wouldn't stop boasting about it, dear. Right up to the point when they sent him abroad."

"What happened to him?" I said.

"Oh, he died, dear. Very suddenly, right after he disembarked from the ship. No one in the family seemed at all surprised."

"So not every Glenbury got away with it?" I said.

"The family did find it necessary to throw a few particularly rotten apples to the wolves, now and again," said Catherine.

"Why did no one ever get this clock fixed?" I said.

"Oh, they did, dear. Many times," said Catherine. "There's nothing wrong with the mechanism. The clock just refuses to work. Some say it's still in shock."

"This house is seriously weird," said Penny.

Catherine beamed at her. "You have no idea . . ."

And then we all looked round sharply, as we heard raised voices down below. I hit the stairs running, leaving the others to catch up.

❖ CHAPTER FOUR ❖
NEW AND OLD SECRETS

THE ARGUING VOICES grew even louder as I raced down the stairs, with Penny in close pursuit. Somebody in reception was giving the Glenburys a really hard time. When we finally reached the bottom of the stairs, I could see Arthur and Marion standing behind the desk, and so close together they were practically on top of each other.

A short, middle-aged woman in a baggy tweed suit and a battered Panama hat was facing the Glenburys down at the top of her voice and hitting them with both barrels. Her vocal assault filled the lobby, pushing the shadows back into corners as she set out her complaint, and every time she made a point she hammered on the desk with her fist. Arthur winced every time she did that, but Marion held her ground and didn't bat an eye. The new arrival was a stocky, pugnacious bulldog of a woman, with a lined face and slate-grey hair, not unattractive, but clearly one of those women with no time for the usual feminine touches. A bulging suitcase squatted patiently at her feet, like an obedient dog.

Fascinated as I was by this new drama, I suddenly realised I hadn't been hearing something I should have. Penny and I had descended the stairs accompanied by the usual low thunder of feet on bare wooden steps, but there had been only silence behind us. I turned and looked back up the long stairway, but there was no sign of Catherine anywhere. For whatever reason, she had chosen to stay on the top floor and ignore what was happening downstairs. I made a mental note to find out why later on, and then gave my full attention to the primordial clash of forces taking place in the lobby. Everyone involved was so taken up with their war of words they hadn't even noticed Penny and me arriving. So we took up a position at the foot of the stairs and settled back to enjoy ourselves. I didn't even think of interrupting; it would have been like trying to hold off a tropical storm with a leaky umbrella. Some things you just have to let run their course.

The newcomer was Wendy Goldsmith, a member in good standing of the Ravensbrook Historical Society. She repeated this at regular intervals, in between establishing her complaint, just to make sure Arthur and Marion knew exactly who they were dealing with. She had turned up at Glenbury Hall despite being told not to; in fact, she'd probably done so precisely because she'd been told not to come. Apparently, she was damned if she was going to be messed about with like that. Or cheated out of a weekend she'd been looking forward to for months.

"I paid good money to be allowed access to Glenbury Hall, at long last!" she said loudly. And the fist came hammering down again. The room keys on the wall behind the reception desk jumped on their hooks, as though volunteering to press themselves into Wendy's hand if she'd only stop shouting. Wendy paused for breath, and Marion jumped right in.

"We did offer a full refund," she said quickly, in her best *I am being reasonable about this because one of us has to be and it clearly isn't going to be you* voice.

"I don't want my money back!" said Wendy.

"Then what do you want?" said Arthur.

Surprisingly, Wendy seemed to calm down a little when presented with a straightforward question.

"I couldn't believe you cancelled the Society's meeting at such short notice," she said. "I was so angry about that I came all the way here from London just so I could complain in person, and now you tell me there wasn't a double booking after all? That it was just something you made up, to disguise the fact that Lucas Carr vanished into thin air before he even got to his room? How is that even possible? No one's disappeared at Glenbury Hall for ages!"

"But what is it that you want?" said Arthur, sticking to the one question that seemed capable of derailing her.

Wendy drew herself up to what passed for her full height and folded her arms in the manner of someone prepared to stand where they were until infinity ran out, if that was what it took to get her way.

"I insist on being allowed to stay in the room I booked, in advance, until someone can tell me what the hell is going on here. Or else..."

"Or else what?" I said interestedly.

Wendy looked round sharply, as she finally realised she had an audience. Arthur and Marion looked too, and seemed a little relieved at the prospect of reinforcements. Wendy took a good look at me, and then at Penny, and deepened her frown into a scowl to make it clear she wasn't even a little bit impressed. When she addressed us, her voice was more a growl than anything else.

"What do you mean 'or else what?'"

"Well," I said, keeping my voice carefully reasonable, because I knew that would annoy her more than anything else, "when someone says *Or else*, it usually means *Give me what I want, or I will do something you really don't want me to do.* I was just wondering which particular threat you had in mind."

"Or else," Wendy said heavily, turning the full force of her glare back on the Glenburys, "I will be forced to go to the local police, and inform them of my suspicions!"

"And what might those be?" Penny said politely.

Wendy seemed thrown for a moment, but quickly rallied.

"I will tell them that since the Hall's management has made such an effort to put me off . . . something suspicious must be going on here!"

There was a pause as we all considered that, and even Wendy seemed to realise it wasn't as impressive an argument as she'd hoped. But she still stood her ground, arms tightly folded, refusing to give an inch.

"Did you know Lucas Carr?" I said.

"Only by name and reputation," Wendy said grudgingly, as though afraid she might be giving ground. "And of course I was very familiar with the excellent work he did for the Society. I read all the papers he submitted to our site. Including some remarkable pieces detailing Lord Ravensbrook's precarious position at the Court of James II, and his constantly shifting political alliances. Lucas also came up with some fascinating theories as to what shape Lord Ravensbrook's rebellion might have taken, if he'd been able to get it off the ground. I don't know what sources Lucas had access to, but he was able to quote all kinds of people who were directly involved."

She paused for a moment, her bulldog expression suggesting she might actually be a little jealous Lucas had been able to discover sources that had eluded her. She quickly recovered and stared at me challengingly, as though daring me to catch her in a contradiction.

"That was Lucas for you: tenacious as a terrier when it came to digging up rare and elusive facts. Though of course he had more time to spend on his investigations than the rest of us. I don't think Lucas had anything else in his life, just his fascination with this particular area of history."

"Do you think Lucas had discovered something important?" said Penny.

"Absolutely!" said Wendy. "If Lucas said he had something, then you could take that to the bank and get a receipt. I never once knew him to make a claim he couldn't back up, unlike some members of the Society I could mention but won't."

"Did Lucas have any close friends, inside the Society?" I said.

"Well, not friends, as such," said Wendy. "There were people he was always ready to chat with on the site, but he'd never met any of us in person. I got the feeling he didn't get out much. In fact, I think we were all a bit surprised when he announced he would be joining us at Glenbury Hall. From things he let slip in his posts, I'm pretty sure he found travelling, and meeting new people, a bit difficult. I think it was only his discovery of this important new information that gave him enough strength to make the effort."

And then she stopped, and fixed me with a suspicious stare. "Who are you? What right do you have to question me?"

"I am Ishmael Jones, and this is my partner Penny Belcourt," I said easily. "We were brought in by Lucas Carr's company, to find out exactly what happened to the man."

Wendy smiled knowingly. "Of course . . . His disappearance matters, because his job has security connections! That's it, isn't it?"

"You know about that?" said Penny.

"Oh, Lucas loved to boast about how important his work was," Wendy said airily. She'd unfolded her arms, and seemed a little calmer now she seemed to be getting somewhere. "He loved to drop the word *Security* into a conversation and then back off, without giving anything away that might pin him down. You don't need to worry, though. He never told us anything about what his work actually involved. He could have been just the tea boy, for all we knew."

"So this would have been Lucas' first trip away from home," said Penny. She nodded to me. "That would explain the over-packed suitcases. He had no experience when it came to what he might need, so he brought everything."

"I know he was very determined to make a good first impression," said Wendy. "His last few posts were brimming over with enthusiasm for what he had to tell us." She shrugged, just a little unhappily. "It is possible that we weren't all as supportive as we might have been. Lucas didn't cope well with teasing."

She broke off, suddenly realising that she was giving away more information than she was getting.

"Anyway! I was looking forward to meeting him at last, if only so I could buy him several drinks, back him into a corner, and finally get some straight answers out of the man. And I was really looking forward to hearing his presentation. He'd been talking it up for months, promising us exciting new material that would completely change the way we saw Lord Ravensbrook, and the Glenburys' role in what happened to him!"

She stopped for a moment as she ran out of breath, and then fixed me and Penny with an inquisitive stare.

"You think something bad has happened to Lucas, don't you?"

"Foul play can't be ruled out," I said carefully.

Wendy shook her head and seemed to shrink into herself a little. "Poor bastard. After all the effort he made to get here the Hall betrayed him, because that's what it does. I can't believe people are still going missing here, in this day and age..." She turned her glare back on Arthur and Marion. "I demand to know what efforts are being made to find him!"

"You'll have to ask Mr. Jones and Ms. Belcourt about that," Marion said immediately, pleased that she could turn the problem over to someone else. "They're in charge of the investigation."

Wendy planted her fists on her hips, to back up her glare, and sniffed loudly. "So his disappearance is connected to his job!"

"We haven't uncovered any evidence to support that, as yet," I said.

"But we are concerned about what might have happened to him," said Penny.

Wendy decided she'd got as much out of us as she was going to, and resumed her attack on Arthur and Marion.

"I want my room! The one I paid for. So hand over my key, because I am not leaving this house until Lucas has been found!"

"Then you could be here for some time," murmured Arthur.

"Let her stay," I said. "Her knowledge of the Hall's history, and of Lucas Carr, might come in handy."

Arthur looked to Marion, who shrugged quickly and gestured at the keys on the rear wall.

"Give her Room Five." She pushed the ledger across the desk to Wendy. "You'll have to register."

Wendy snatched a proffered pen from Marion's hand, while Arthur went to fetch the key. Wendy nodded at Lucas' signature, and added her own underneath. She finished with a flourish, and then underlined it for emphasis. Just to remind them who they were dealing with. She smiled triumphantly at Marion, and tossed the pen onto the desk.

"When will you be calling us for dinner?"

For the first time, Marion was caught off balance. "It's a bit late for a meal..."

"No, it isn't!" Wendy said immediately, with the air of someone not prepared to compromise even a little bit. "I have come a long way to be here! The least you can do for a paying guest is to provide them with an evening meal!"

"Oh, very well," said Marion, recognising a lost cause when it was glaring right into her face. "I'm sure we can rustle up something..." She looked at me and Penny, and we both nodded solemnly. "All right, something for all of you."

Arthur came back to offer Wendy her key, and she grabbed it out of his hand as though afraid he might change his mind. Penny leaned in close to me.

"Why do you want her to stay?" she said quietly.

"Because she might not be exactly who she says she is," I said, just as quietly. "In which case it's better to have her here, where we can keep an eye on her. And just maybe, she can tell us things about Lucas Carr. We really don't know much about the man, considering he's at the heart of this mystery. I'm also interested in this historical paper Lucas was going to present to the Society. The one that was going to change everything. Not everyone likes change."

"You think someone might have arranged his disappearance, over an academic paper?" said Penny.

"People have killed each other over less," I said. "And, I think it might be a good idea to compare Wendy's knowledge of the Hall with Catherine's. Just in case our sweet little local historian has been telling us things that aren't one hundred per cent accurate."

Penny looked a little shocked at the implied accusation. "You don't trust her?"

"Do you?"

"She has been very helpful," Penny said thoughtfully. "Perhaps a little too helpful? And she does seem very protective, when it comes to Arthur."

"She's been doing everything she could to steer us towards a supernatural explanation, and away from the historical," I said. "Wendy might be able to help us figure out which facts we can depend on."

"And whether any of it has anything to do with what really happened to Lucas," said Penny.

"Exactly," I said.

"If you two have quite finished muttering together!" Marion said loudly.

Penny and I looked round, to find Marion, Arthur, and Wendy all glaring at us. I stared calmly back at them.

"Just crunching a few theories," I said. "You know how it is."

"You must have turned up something useful by now," said Marion. "You've been all over the Hall."

"And yet, there's no sign of Lucas anywhere," I said.

"Didn't you find anything?" said Arthur.

"A few things," I said.

I think he would have liked to press me on that, but we all stopped and looked round as we heard footsteps coming down the staircase. Catherine Voss descended leisurely into view, showing us her usual sweet smile, and finally joined Penny and me at the foot of the stairs.

"I heard raised voices," she said. "I do hope everything's all right."

"Why didn't you come down with us?" I said, as casually as I could.

"I had to go to the bathroom," said Catherine. "It was right where I remembered it, but then, things don't change much in Glenbury Hall. That's rather the point."

Wendy stared at her, openly suspicious. "And who might you be?"

"Catherine Voss, local historian and expert on Glenbury Hall."

Wendy surprised us all then, with a broad smile that lit up her whole face.

"Of course, I've read your book! *Roots in Hell*, and all that. A bit sensational in places, but solid in the facts department. And never afraid to draw a daring conclusion! Our Society has adopted it as a standard text."

"Really?" said Catherine, beaming all over her face. "I'm afraid my little book didn't attract many positive reviews, so sales weren't what they might have been..."

"I thought you did first-class work!" said Wendy. "Lucas found a few things to argue with, but then he always did."

I made a mental note, to consider a possible argument between Lucas and Catherine. There's no one more touchy than a specialist scholar defending their territory.

Catherine smiled politely at Wendy. "I'm sorry, I'm afraid I didn't catch your name..."

"Wendy Goldsmith, from the Ravensbrook Historical Society. I'm staying here."

"Are the others on their way too?" said Catherine.

"I doubt it. Takes a lot, to get them off their backsides." Wendy fixed Catherine with a thoughtful look. "You know, while I was fascinated by your grasp of the Hall's history, I really couldn't be doing with all the spooky stuff. That kind of thing just gets in the way when it comes to uncovering the facts."

"Unfortunately, it's difficult to separate the supernatural

from the historical at Glenbury Hall," said Catherine. "The one does tend to reinforce the other."

Wendy shook her head firmly. "When you strip away all the weird shit, what you're left with is what matters."

Catherine smiled happily. "Oh, we are going to have such fun, arguing about this!"

Wendy smiled back. "That's what scholarship is all about."

I moved forward to face Arthur and Marion. "Penny and I will be needing a room as well."

"You're staying overnight?" said Arthur.

"We're staying until we find Lucas Carr," said Penny.

"Or what happened to him," I said. "We want the guest room at the top of the stairs."

"The one Lucas was supposed to have?" said Arthur.

I looked at Penny. "Didn't you just know he was going to say that?"

"Not really, no," said Penny. "Is it too late to change our minds?"

"Yes," I said. "If that was Lucas' room, we don't want anyone else having it."

"You're doing it again," said Marion, just a bit dangerously. "Muttering to each other, keeping secrets, and leaving the rest of us out of it."

"All part of the job," I said.

"Get them the key to Room Four," said Marion, not even glancing at Arthur. She looked at me steadily. "Do you have any luggage?"

"No," I said. "Travel light, travel fast."

"Oh. I didn't bring anything either!" said Catherine. "I was in such a hurry to get here, I didn't stop to think about that."

"You're staying as well?" said Arthur, halfway to the rear wall.

"Of course, dear," said Catherine. "You're not to worry

about anything, Arthur. I'll be here for as long as you need me."

"You can have Room Six," Marion said resignedly.

I wasn't sure how pleased Arthur was about that, but he didn't say anything. He collected two metal keys from their hooks, and presented them to me and Catherine.

"I'm sure we can provide you with whatever personal items you might require," he said.

"For a price," Marion said quickly.

"Just work out what we're going to need," I said to Arthur. "And then send the bill to Lucas Carr's company."

Marion shot Arthur a look, and I could almost hear them planning on how best to pad the bill. Which was fine by me. Technically, I'm supposed to get my expenses paid every time I work for the Organisation, but they make such a fuss about receipts I don't usually bother. Arthur came out from behind the reception desk, and gestured at Wendy's suitcase.

"Would you like me to carry that up to your room?"

Wendy lifted the heavy case easily, her bicep bulging the tweed sleeve. "I have important historical texts in this case. And some very interesting documents."

"But the Society meeting has been cancelled," said Marion.

Wendy smiled coldly. "There are still things I plan to check out for myself, while I'm here." She glowered fiercely at Arthur. "And I am perfectly capable of looking after myself!"

She did look like she could punch her weight. I pitied anyone who tried to abduct Wendy on the way to her room.

Arthur just nodded, and led the way up the stairs.

Once we'd all reached the top floor, Arthur indicated which room went to whom, and then stood back. It was obvious he had something on his mind and was working on how best to say it. I'd just got the key in the lock when he cleared his throat awkwardly, and kept on doing it until we'd all turned to look at him.

"Before any of you go into your rooms, I feel I should point out that due to circumstances completely beyond our control . . . none of the guest rooms are, technically, en suite."

There was a long and slightly ominous pause, as we all stared at him.

"Does that mean what I think it means?" I said.

Arthur didn't quite squirm, but looked like he wanted to. "There are no . . . individual bathrooms."

"You mean, no toilets?" said Penny.

"For what you're charging?" said Wendy.

"I'm afraid not," said Arthur. He drew himself up, and did his best to sound managerial. "There is a communal bathroom, further down the hall. The blue door, on your left. Bath, shower, and toilet."

"It's very comfortable," Catherine said brightly. "Though the flush chain was a bit stubborn. I had to be very firm with it."

Arthur winced. "Please. Treat the chain with respect. I don't want to have to reattach it again."

Wendy shook her head. "This was definitely not mentioned when the Society booked these rooms."

"We were planning to make all the guest rooms en suite," said Arthur, "but we couldn't get a plumber to come in from town. We've been trying to find someone from further afield . . ."

"So there's just the one toilet, between four of us?" said Penny.

"Actually, between seven people," said Arthur. "Including my family. But there are chamber-pots under the beds! For emergencies."

Wendy glared at Arthur with such venom that he actually fell back a step.

"Do I look like the kind of person who squats on chamber-pots?"

Arthur started to say something, and then quickly decided not to.

"Is there anything else you feel you should be telling us?" I said.

"No, no; that's it," said Arthur. "Just call down to reception if you need anything. There's a phone in every room."

He seemed to realise how sad it was that he had to point this out, and turned quickly away to hurry back down the stairs. Wendy shouldered her door open, stormed into the room, and slammed the door behind her. Catherine nodded cheerfully to Penny and me, went into her room, and closed the door quietly behind her. I led the way into our room, and once we were both inside, I locked the door behind us. Penny raised an elegant eyebrow.

"We don't want anyone barging in while we're busy discussing the case," I said.

"You think that's likely?" said Penny.

"In this place?" I said. "For all I know, someone is already kneeling outside our door and peering through the keyhole." I stopped, looked back at the door, and then shook my head. "No . . . I'd have heard something."

"You and your senses," said Penny.

We took our first good look around the room that should have been Lucas Carr's. It seemed modern enough, even comfortable, but completely lacking in character. The walls had been painted instead of wallpapered, and the furniture looked like it might have been self-assembled. There was an old-fashioned fireplace that clearly hadn't been used in ages, and a single wall radiator. The room smelled strongly of cleaning products, and when I ran a fingertip across a few surfaces, I was pleased to discover that at least someone had dusted recently.

Penny strode over to the large double bed in the middle of the room, knelt down, and thrust a hand underneath. She swept it back and forth, and finally pulled out an antique china chamber-pot. She studied it for a moment, and then showed it to me. A large open eye had been painted on the inside of the bowl, with the words *Eye see you!* inscribed above it. I nodded solemnly.

"Yes. That's definitely a chamber-pot."

Penny thrust the china bowl back under the bed, got to her feet, and gave me a hard look.

"Give me one good reason why we shouldn't just drive back into town, and spend the night at The Smugglers Retreat?"

"Because you can't solve a case like this from a distance," I said. "We need to be here, on the spot, so we can observe our suspects interacting. And, so we can go sneaking about at night and see things we're not supposed to."

Penny scowled around the room, looking for things to find fault with, and only gave up because there were too many of them.

"I can't believe Arthur and Marion really thought they could squeeze two people into a room this size. There is such a thing as too much togetherness."

"If you have to get up in the middle of the night, I promise I'll look the other way."

Penny smiled suddenly. "I might need you to hold my hand, to help me balance."

I smiled back at her. "You know I'm always there for you."

I picked up the landline phone on the bedside table, and listened carefully.

"What are you doing?" said Penny.

"Making sure it is connected," I said.

She shook her head admiringly. "You don't trust anything, do you?"

"The world has given me cause," I said. "I think we need to treat everything in the Hall as our enemy, until proven otherwise."

"Because the house is alive, and eats people?"

"Because it might have been booby-trapped, against anyone who came looking for Lucas," I said. "I don't believe we have any friends here."

"Situation entirely normal," said Penny.

I took another look around the room. "No television, or even a radio, and no sign of an Internet connection. It's all a bit spartan, isn't it?"

"Maybe the Glenburys thought modern toys would clash with their old-timey mood," said Penny. "Why were you so determined to stay in this particular room?"

"Because it's set between the Glenburys' rooms, and the other guest rooms," I said. "I thought that might be significant. Particularly when Marion chose not to give it to Wendy. Now we know Lucas was supposed to stay here, we need to search this whole room thoroughly for clues."

"But Lucas never got this far," said Penny. "He disappeared on his way here."

"Maybe there was something in this room, that Lucas was expecting to find," I said. "Something he couldn't be allowed to have. And that's why he had to disappear before he got here."

"I love the way you can think 'round corners," said Penny.

"Comes with the job," I said.

"And not being entirely human."

"Well, naturally."

"All right; let's see what there is to see," said Penny, looking around the room and metaphorically rolling up her sleeves.

I pulled out every drawer in the chest of drawers, checking each one in turn to make sure nothing had been taped underneath or on the back. Penny searched inside the wardrobe, and even pushed it away from the wall to make sure there was nothing hidden behind it. We carefully examined every piece of furniture, took a really good look under the bed, and peered into every nook and cranny... but didn't find anything. In the end, we stood together in the middle of the room, looking around us.

"If there was anything here, I think someone has beaten us to it," said Penny.

"It could still be somewhere in the Hall," I said.

"So could Lucas," said Penny. "And you can bet someone is watching us, to see if we're getting too close to the truth."

A thought struck her. She strode over to the window, pulled back the curtains, and looked out at the grounds.

"Are you checking to see if the statues are creeping up on the house?" I said.

"You honestly didn't get a bad feeling from those awful-looking things?" said Penny, not taking her eyes off the grounds.

"No," I said firmly.

"Then I didn't either," said Penny.

She closed the curtains, turned her back on the window, removed her big black hat and sailed it across the room. It landed neatly on one of the bed-posts, and Penny shot me a triumphant *I meant to do that* look. I applauded politely. Penny strode over to the bed, threw herself onto the thick mattress, and bounced up and down for a while.

"Now this is more like it!"

"Make yourself comfortable," I said. "We won't be getting

much sleep later on. Glenbury Hall strikes me as the kind of place that only really comes alive once night falls."

"Are we talking about furtive people scurrying up and down the corridor on their way to secret assignations?" said Penny. "Or ghosts and ghoulies strutting their supernatural stuff?"

"A lot of that has to be misdirection," I said. "Somebody trying to hide something from us."

"They don't have a ghost of a chance," Penny said cheerfully.

The phone rang. I picked it up, and Arthur started talking without even introducing himself.

"Dinner will be served shortly, in the dining hall."

"I remember it, from our prowl 'round the ground floor," I said.

"You'll have to settle for a cold collation," said Arthur.

And then he put the phone down, before I could even raise the matter of desserts. He was going to have to learn some management skills, if he wanted to make a success of his new venture. I replaced the phone, and brought Penny up to speed.

"Don't expect anything special," she said. "Not if they could slap it together that quickly."

"A shared meal will give us a chance to get to know everyone," I said. "People reveal more of themselves, in a social setting."

"Do you see everyone in the Hall as suspects?" said Penny.

"Of course. Don't you?"

Penny sighed. "Just once, it would be nice to have someone around we could trust."

"Unfortunately, we're not in that kind of business."

"Do you think I could wear my big hat to dinner?" said Penny.

"I don't see why not," I said.

"I love my big hat."

"It suits you."

"I'm wearing it," Penny decided.

"Good for you," I said. "But there's no need for us to rush down. Let the others wait; we need to handicap the suspects."

Penny sat up on the bed, and smiled at me sweetly. "Are you going to rank them in order of general untrustworthiness, or by how much they've annoyed you?"

"I should start with the house," I said. "Glenbury Hall has so much character it's practically a suspect in its own right."

"A house that eats people," said Penny. "I keep expecting to open a door and find it full of teeth."

"Don't even go there."

Penny looked at me soberly. "Do you think Lucas could still be alive?"

"Depends on why he was taken," I said carefully. "And whether his abductor still sees him as valuable."

"Then we need to find him before they run out of reasons to keep him alive," said Penny.

"They can't do anything while we're here," I said, "for fear of attracting attention. Just by staying in the Hall, we're helping to keep Lucas safe."

"Unless he's already been killed."

"We have to assume he's still alive, until something proves he isn't." I sat down on the bed beside her. "Let's run through the suspects. Starting with Arthur and Marion. It's obvious they're keeping some things to themselves. Though they could just be worried about their new business getting a bad reputation."

"Wouldn't surprise me if they were keeping things from each other," said Penny. "Though it's obvious who wears the trousers in that marriage."

"People can always surprise you."

Penny smiled. "You should know."

I thought for a moment. "Ellen tried to tell us something, before Marion shut her down. But that was probably to do with what she saw on her laptop, rather than Lucas' disappearance."

"Catherine definitely has her own agenda," said Penny. "And she was a close friend of Arthur's parents, who, according to Marion, were truly awful people."

"As long as Catherine keeps talking, we can't get a word in to ask her questions," I said.

"Like why she ended up living in a town so close to the Hall," said Penny. "Is she guarding something in the Hall? Or protecting it?"

"And why did Arthur reach out to her, when he was in trouble?" I said. "Why not bring in a lawyer, or an accountant?"

Penny shrugged. "Sometimes a boy's best friend is his auntie."

"That leaves us with Wendy," I said. "The unexpected arrival. Why would she make such a long journey, over someone she barely knew? I'm not buying all that righteous indignation about being cheated out of her weekend."

"And why was she so determined to spend the night here?" said Penny.

"Perhaps she's looking for something," I said.

"Like what?" said Penny.

"Whatever Lucas had in his suitcases? Or, what he came here to find."

Penny leaned against my shoulder, and we sat companionably together, staring at nothing.

"What if it turns out the house really has taken Lucas?" Penny said finally.

"Then we just keep hitting it until it gives him back," I said. "But when you get right down to it...this whole mystery turns on Lucas going missing somewhere between the reception desk and his room. Because there's only one staircase connecting the two floors, and Arthur insists he was watching it all the time. So really, there's only a disappearance and a mystery because Arthur says there is."

"Then he must be involved in Lucas going missing, mustn't he?" said Penny.

"But what possible motive could he have for lying?" I said, frowning. "He didn't know Lucas, never met him before he turned up at reception. I suppose it's possible Arthur and Marion could be covering up something.... Maybe Lucas had some kind of fatal accident, and they decided to make the body disappear rather than have it upset their grand opening."

"Like the old story," said Penny. "Where a young couple books into a foreign hotel and the wife goes for a walk, but when she comes back the hotel manager denies ever seeing her or her husband. I think it turns out the husband had the plague, and everyone was desperate to hush it up rather than ruin the hotel's reputation."

"But I haven't found a trace of blood or violence anywhere in this house," I said.

"Maybe Lucas saw a ghost!" Penny said brightly. "And died of shock."

"Okay..." I said. "You are reaching now."

"Catherine made Glenbury Hall sound like the most haunted house in England," said Penny. "But if it was, I would have heard of it."

I looked at her sternly. "Have you been watching that *Mostly Haunted* show again?"

"Only in a spirit of irony," said Penny.

She bounced up off the bed, grabbed her black hat from the bedpost, and crammed it on the back of her head. She studied herself critically in the room's one decent-sized mirror, and then spun away to smile brightly at me.

"Shall we go down to dinner? I could eat."

The Glenbury dining hall was a huge room with a high ceiling, that had seemed dark and gloomy the first time I saw it. Now electric light from a chandelier gleamed richly on the wood-panelled walls. A long mahogany table stretched from one end of the hall to the other. It looked like it had been made to seat at least thirty people and still allow them plenty of elbow room.

A willow-pattern china service had been set out at the far end of the table, where everyone else was already seated. They'd been talking as we entered, but fell silent so Arthur and Marion, Ellen, Catherine, and Wendy could all present Penny and me with variations on the same look: *We've been waiting for you to turn up, so we could get started.* I smiled easily back, and Penny held her head high so everyone could admire her hat. I noticed Wendy wasn't wearing her Panama, and that Marion no longer had her scarf. Her dark shaven head gleamed brightly under the chandelier's light.

Interestingly, no one was seated at the head of the table. As current head of the Glenbury family, Arthur would have been entitled to take the place of honour, but instead he sat to one side, next to his wife. Marion rose from her seat the moment Penny and I sat down.

"I'll get dinner," she said shortly.

Arthur started to get up, only to sit right back down again when Marion gave him a look.

"I don't need any help," she said. "You're the host; entertain our guests."

She swept out of the dining hall through a nearby side door. Arthur smiled apologetically around the table.

"Welcome to the dining hall. It was originally designed to accommodate much larger gatherings, but I'm sure we can make the old place convivial enough, if we just put our minds to it."

I wasn't so sure. The room had no windows, and the walls were lined with portraits of dead ancestors staring grimly down at us, because no one ever smiles in a portrait. Faded gaps showed where the more valuable paintings had been removed and sold. It seemed to me that wherever I went in the Hall, I was constantly faced with reminders of the current family's desperate need for money. I had to wonder whether that might have had something to do with Lucas Carr vanishing...

I suddenly realised that all of us were seated directly underneath the chandelier. The original candles had been replaced by electric lights, but I couldn't help noticing a few of the bulbs weren't working. I also remembered how the chandelier had come crashing down in *Phantom of the Opera*. I felt like edging further down the table, but didn't want to have to explain why.

"You should have seen this dining hall as it used to be," Catherine said expansively. "Back in the Glenburys' glory days, this table would have been packed with colourful and important people. Sparkling conversation, roaring bonhomie, and all the best that life had to offer. Personal accounts from those days made the Glenbury gatherings sound like heaven on earth. Or possibly hell, given some of the family's proclivities. Either way, you can bet it was one hell of a party."

Arthur looked around, as though trying to see the dining hall through Catherine's eyes. In the end he just shrugged, and smiled apologetically around the table.

"The dining hall is on the list of rooms to be restored and upgraded, but it will have to wait its turn."

I heard the trundling of small wheels approaching, and then the side door slammed open as Marion returned, pushing a hostess trolley ahead of her. It was loaded down with food, and we all made appreciative noises on the grounds that Marion might take our meal away again if we didn't. Arthur was quickly up on his feet, to help his wife dispense dinner. Which turned out to be assorted cold meats, straight out of a tin, and a salad, only recently emptied out of bags from the supermarket. As dinners went this one didn't go far, but at least there was lots of it, and Arthur and Marion took a certain satisfaction in piling the food on our plates. Marion finally sat down, and we all tucked in with a good appetite.

Arthur produced two dusty wine bottles from the depths of the trolley, along with enough glasses to go round.

"I found this particularly fine vintage lurking at the back of the wine cellar," he said proudly. "Most of the good stuff was sold off long ago, but I think you'll find this makes a hearty addition to a simple meal. Bottled sunshine, in a hall full of shadows."

He uncorked the first bottle with a certain ceremony, and poured a little into a glass. He savoured the bouquet, took a sip and smiled appreciatively, and then set about pouring for the rest of us.

"I don't drink much wine," I said. "Any really good vintage would be wasted on me. I have no palate."

"Really?" said Ellen. "You know, you speak perfectly clearly."

There was a pause as we all looked at her, and then Ellen grinned broadly. Quiet laughter rose up around the table, and Marion nodded approvingly to her daughter, pleased at her attempt to lighten the atmosphere. Arthur sat down beside Marion, and drank half his glass in one go before addressing himself to his meal. As we ate, surprisingly it was Wendy who opened the conversation. She nodded to Marion, and gestured at the dining hall.

"How are you enjoying living in this marvellous old house?"

"This extremely draughty house," Marion said flatly. "You wouldn't believe the trouble we've had with heating. I suppose the Hall is very impressive, but I can't say I care much about it, except as something we can use to make money. Isn't that right, dear?"

She looked pointedly at Arthur, but he just nodded. Marion pushed her food around the plate with her fork, not taking her gaze off her husband as she addressed the table in general.

"Arthur and I have been together for more than twenty years. Through ups and downs, good times and bad. He seemed like such a good catch when I first met him."

"How did you meet?" Penny said politely.

"At a party in London," said Marion. "Just one of those mixers, where you go to meet people outside of work."

Arthur smiled at her. "I almost didn't go. I had a lot of work on. But if I hadn't gone, I would never have met you."

They shared a smile, and Marion reached out to take his hand in hers.

"You were doing so well, back then," she said. She stared around the table, almost defiantly. "But the City ate him up and spat him out."

Arthur had nothing to say. Catherine stirred uncomfortably, and turned away to smile at Wendy.

"What do you do for a living, when you're not being part of the Historical Society?"

"Legal secretary," said Wendy, around a mouthful of lettuce. She chewed determinedly for a moment, and then swallowed. "Civil law, not criminal; never anything interesting. History brings a little colour into my grey life."

"What made you pick the Ravensbrook Society?" I said.

"I found them online," said Wendy. "I was just jumping from one link to another, to see where they might take me, and then I found the Society's site ... and felt like I'd come home. They were interested in the same things as me—all the incredible events and people from a fascinating period—and their sheer enthusiasm just reached out and grabbed me." She smiled around the table, almost shyly. "I've always been taken with the romance of history. People were bigger and more colourful then, the causes more vital." She smiled suddenly at Arthur. "And speaking of the past; you don't remember me, do you?"

"I'm afraid not," Arthur said politely. "Should I?"

"We worked together in London," said Wendy. "Your company brought me in to cope with the legal complications of a new account they were handling, the Biederbook Transfer, and it took both of us to make sense of the mess they'd got themselves into."

Arthur smiled suddenly. "Of course! The Biederbook bond issue! I remember that. We spent weeks wading through the paperwork, trying to figure out what was going on."

"You remember the paperwork, but you don't remember me?" said Wendy.

"Sorry," said Arthur, and he sounded like he meant it. "I've never been good with names, or faces."

"I remember," said Wendy, and they both laughed.

"It was a long time ago," said Arthur.

"We spent a lot of time together," said Wendy. "In and out

of work. Do you remember, Arthur? The streets of London were considered so dangerous back then the company insisted we attend self-defence classes?"

"Oh yes . . ." said Arthur. "I was really bad at those."

"I wasn't!" Wendy said proudly. "I could still put a mugger down, with one good rabbit-punch!"

Looking at her squat and solid frame, I could quite believe it.

Arthur realised Marion was sitting very still beside him, and moved quickly to bring her into the conversation.

"The Biederbook affair was my first big success with the company, and Wendy helped make it possible."

"We did it together," said Wendy.

Arthur realised Marion was looking at him coolly. "This was before we met, of course."

"So," said Marion. "Your relationship never went anywhere."

"I wouldn't call it a relationship, exactly," Arthur said quickly, sensing he was on dangerous ground. "We were just colleagues. For a time."

"I left when the work was completed," said Wendy. "We never saw each other again."

"But you still remembered him," said Marion.

"I remembered the name," said Wendy.

"Well, that's London for you!" Arthur said brightly. "People coming and going all the time . . ."

"The Glenbury name struck a bell, when the Society booked this weekend at the Hall," said Wendy. "I did some research, and discovered you were the same man I'd worked with, back in the day."

"So you didn't just come here because you were told not to?" said Marion, with the air of someone moving a chess piece into place. "Or because of the insult to your Historical

Society. You came here to renew your acquaintance with my husband."

Wendy met her gaze unflinchingly. "I thought Arthur might need my help, yes."

"As a legal secretary, or a friend?" I said.

"Both," said Wendy.

"I'm fine," Arthur said loudly. "I don't need any help."

The tone of his voice put an end to the conversation, and everyone developed a new interest in their food. Though I got the impression Marion would be returning to the subject, once she and Arthur were alone. I also noticed that Ellen had been paying close attention to what her parents had been saying, and now seemed more than usually thoughtful. I nudged Penny with my elbow and nodded to Ellen, and Penny immediately picked up the ball.

"How are you settling in, Ellen?" Penny said cheerfully. "Are you making new friends in town? How about boyfriends?"

Ellen scowled, and while she kept her gaze fixed on Penny she was obviously addressing the whole table.

"I had to leave all my friends in London, after my parents took me out of school and dragged me all the way here, against my will. I don't have any friends now, let alone boyfriends, because the few times I tried going into town everyone treated me like a freak. Just because I'm a Glenbury."

She broke off, her voice failing, right on the edge of angry tears.

"Were they rude to you?" said Penny.

"It was worse than that," said Ellen. "They just ignored me. Like I wasn't even there."

"The townspeople will come around," Arthur said weakly. "Once they understand we're not like the ogres in the old stories..."

"No, they won't!" said Ellen. "They'll never change! I hate the town and I hate this house and I hate you!"

She jumped to her feet and stormed out of the room, leaving an embarrassed silence behind her.

"Teenagers..." Arthur said finally, trying for a light touch and not coming within a mile of it.

"She'll get over it," Marion said firmly.

Catherine made a determined attempt to change the atmosphere. She told us funny stories about the history of the house, dropping names and incidents as though she'd known the people personally. But then she started a story about Arthur's father, her good friend Paul, and the problems he had with a television set in the Hall. She made it sound quite amusing, until Arthur suddenly interrupted her, raising his voice to drown hers out.

"That's not how it happened," he said harshly. "Or at least, not what I heard. Admittedly, I didn't always listen when my father tried to tell me things, because I wanted nothing to do with my family. I just wanted to get away, and make a new life for myself. I ran off to London the moment I was old enough..."

And then he stopped, quite abruptly, and wouldn't say anymore.

"I have to say, I'm impressed by the breadth of your knowledge, Catherine," said Wendy, trying to save the moment. "We should have booked you as a guest speaker."

"And I'm sure we look forward to having the Society back with us again," Marion said quickly. "As soon as the current unfortunate situation has been cleared up."

Catherine made a valiant effort to change the subject again. "I used to love dining in here, with Paul and Mary and all our friends. There were enough guests to fill the whole table, back then. Everything was so bright and cheerful, and such good company. . . . I'm sure this room could be made to rise like a phoenix from its ashes, once everything has been properly restored."

"That is the plan," said Marion.

Catherine turned to me and Penny. "You're being very quiet, my dears. Why don't you tell us something about your job? It must be very exciting."

"I'm afraid I have to invoke the magic word Security," I said. "Penny and I aren't allowed to talk about what we do."

Everyone nodded understandingly, but I could see a certain amount of suspicion in everyone's eyes, as they tried to work out how much they could trust Penny and me. Because they just knew we didn't have their best interests at heart.

Penny smiled brightly at Arthur. "What was the trouble your father had with his television? You said earlier on that he saw something which disturbed him."

Arthur hesitated, frowning unhappily.

"It was a long time ago. I was only a child . . ."

"But you've never forgotten, have you?" I said, playing a hunch. "It left its mark on you."

Arthur looked at me steadily. "You're very observant."

"Part of the job," I said.

"I never trusted any television set after that," said Arthur. "When I was a child, I would refuse to be left alone in a room with one."

"Did you ever see the things your father saw?" said Penny.

"No," said Arthur. "It was father's private room. He said . . . the set showed him scenes from the past."

"Like the timeslip in the grounds?" said Penny.

"I suppose so," said Arthur. "And sometimes . . . the television would talk to him, and tell him things."

"What kind of things?" I said.

"Horrible things . . ."

We were all staring at Arthur now, taking in the strain on his face, and the sweat beading on his forehead. He didn't look at us, his eyes lost in the past.

"Father said . . . the voices told him things he didn't want to hear. About himself, and the family, and what lay ahead. And sometimes they would offer to change things, to save him from what was coming, if he would do something for them. I saw him leave the television room, once. He didn't see me. He looked like he'd been crying. It's a hard thing, for a child to see his father looking genuinely frightened.

"Things improved after he moved the television to a different room. He stopped seeing things, hearing things. He had the door to the old room locked, and then nailed shut. I thought, so that whatever was in the room wouldn't be able to get out and come after him. But he was never the same, afterwards."

Marion looked at him, lost for words. It was obvious he'd never told her any of this before, and she wasn't sure how to react.

"You always said your father made things up," she said finally. "That he would often tell you horrid stories, just to put a scare into you."

"That didn't mean some of them weren't true," said Arthur.

He pushed his plate away, though he'd barely touched his food. He drained the wine in his glass and refilled it to the brim. Marion looked quickly round the table.

"I would like to make it very clear that in all the time I've been at the Hall, we have never had any problems with the television reception."

She busied herself with her meal, clattering her cutlery loudly, as though that had put an end to the matter. I cleared my throat, to draw everyone's attention back to me.

"This may sound like an obvious question, Arthur, but I have to ask...Are there are hidden doors, or secret passageways, in Glenbury Hall? Priest holes and the like?"

Arthur seemed to rally, now we were back to discussing practical things. He put his glass down, and even managed a small smile.

"You think Mr. Carr could have disappeared through a hole in the wall, into some secret tunnel? Sorry to disappoint you, but there's nothing like that in Glenbury Hall. I spent ages searching when I was a child, and never found anything. Feel free to bang on the walls and check for yourself, if you like."

"What is a priest hole?" said Marion.

Wendy quickly stepped in, narrowly beating out Catherine, so she could show off her expertise.

"When King Henry VIII broke with the pope and established his own Protestant Church, certain aristocratic families refused to give up their Catholic faith, even though practicing it was now considered treason. They continued to hold secret masses in their homes, attended by priests travelling incognito, with specially constructed secret rooms for the priest to hide in, in case the king's agents came looking."

"But there wouldn't have been anything like that here," said Catherine. "The Glenburys were always fiercely Protestant."

"I bow to your superior knowledge," said Wendy. And she actually did bow to Catherine, who bowed in return, before they both gave in to giggles.

Penny smiled at Arthur. "It sounds like you had some fun at least, when you were a child; searching the house for secret passageways..."

"No!" said Arthur, catching us all by surprise with the

violence of his reply. "I hated this house. Only bad things happen, in Glenbury Hall. And I hated having to leave London, to come back to this awful place that was never a home. I've had nightmares my whole life about living here. But I had to come back, because this is my last chance to support my family."

Marion seemed honestly shocked by his outburst. She tried to take Arthur's hand again, but he jerked it away.

"I knew you had bad memories of this place," she said carefully. "But all of that's in the past now..."

"No," said Arthur. "It's always with me."

Marion seemed lost. "Why did you never tell me any of this before?"

"It's not an easy thing to talk about," said Arthur. "I often felt I was competing with the house for my father's attention, and the house always won. When he wasn't filling the Hall with people who were far more important to him than I ever was, I'd see him wandering the corridors, looking for family treasures to sell. He inherited enough money that he could have lived out his life perfectly comfortably, but he squandered it trying to find evidence we were descended from Ravensbrook's supposed illegitimate son. All so my father could lay claim to the aristocratic life he wanted so badly. *It doesn't matter whether you have money,* I heard him say to my mother, *as long as you have the right connections.* But he could never prove anything."

Penny turned to Catherine. "Paul was your friend. Did you know anything about this?"

Catherine was already shaking her head. For the first time she seemed uncomfortable, even unsettled.

"When I knew Paul and Mary, we only ever concentrated on our personal interests. It was a very intense relationship, very focused. They never once talked to me about this Royal fixation. Eventually I had to leave, and after that we never talked again . . ."

"Why did you go away?" said Arthur. "I never got a proper explanation. One day you just weren't around anymore, and when I asked my mother why all she would say was, there'd been an argument."

He looked accusingly at Catherine, and she took a moment before she replied, choosing her words carefully. She looked around the table at the rest of us, perhaps because that was easier than facing Arthur.

"You have to remember," she said slowly. "We were all so much younger then. Trying desperately to lead a different kind of life from our repressed parents. It was all about being rebellious, and embracing the sensual life, free from all the old restrictions. We tried every kind of drug, and philosophy, and sex; endlessly hungry for new experiences, and greedy for new sensations. Trying to liberate our minds, and set our souls free.

"Back in the seventies, emotion and conscience were never supposed to get in the way of everyone having a good time. You gave your body freely, but never your heart. But of course it was never that simple. Paul and I . . ." She braced herself, a little old lady used up by time and years, before she made herself turn to meet Arthur's gaze. It was obvious that each new confession was taking its toll. "In the end, I put your father in the position of having to choose between your mother and me, only to find he never wanted that. So I had to leave. For all our sakes."

Arthur sat stunned in his chair, shocked into silence. Marion shot a quick look at Ellen's empty chair, as though relieved her daughter wasn't there to hear this. Catherine smiled tiredly at Arthur.

"I know. It's always difficult, to discover your parents were people in their own right, with their own emotional needs. But it's important you understand that we were all very fond of each other. I miss both of them so much..."

For a moment I thought Catherine might break down into tears, but she was made of sterner stuff. She sat up straight, threw off her melancholy with a shrug, and smiled determinedly around the table.

"I never knew anything about this obsession with the aristocracy. Paul concealed a lot of things, for his own reasons."

"It's the house," Arthur said quietly. "It gets inside your head."

"If you hate this house so much," I said, "why did you come back? You let it stand empty for years, rather than have anything to do with it."

"I had nowhere else to go," said Arthur. "I had to do something to support my family, after I'd failed them so badly in the City."

Marion grabbed hold of his hand and wouldn't let him pull away, forcing him to look at her.

"You didn't fail us; it was the company that let you down. None of what happened in London was your fault."

Arthur shook his head. "I still feel guilty, that I wasn't a better provider for you and Ellen. I always swore to myself I would be a better husband and father than my father ever was. I let Ellen down, and you. I'll never forgive myself for that."

"You don't get to forgive you," said Marion. "That's my job. You came back to a place you hated and feared, because you wouldn't let your family down. And I have never been prouder of you."

They stared into each other's eyes for a long moment. Marion smiled, and Arthur smiled back. Marion let go of his hand and looked around the table, suddenly all business again.

"It's late, and it's been a long and trying day for all of us. I see everyone has finished their meal, so I suggest we retire now and get a good night's sleep. And then we can attack the problem of Mr. Carr's disappearance with new strength, first thing in the morning."

We all nodded our agreement, and got up from the table.

"Arthur and I will clear up," said Marion, before any of us could offer. "You can go up to your rooms."

It was almost an instruction, and I had to wonder if there was some reason why she was so keen to get us out of the way. But there was no point in asking; Marion would only ever tell us what she felt like telling us, and Arthur would only ever say what Marion wanted him to. I gave him a stern look anyway.

"Be sure you lock the doors," I said. "And as many of the shutters and windows as you can."

"Of course," said Arthur. "And I won't forget to set the burglar alarms. But really, no one from around here would dare visit the Hall at night."

"No one from around here," I said.

Catherine smiled sweetly at everyone. "Sleep well," she said, with just a hint of mischief. "And if you should happen to hear any unusual noises in the night . . ."

"It's probably the plumbing," said Marion.

❖ CHAPTER FIVE ❖
MOVEMENTS IN THE DARK

BACK IN OUR ROOM, Penny and I settled down on the bed together, ready to stand, or rather lie, guard the whole night long if that was what it took. We left the lights on, without either of us raising the issue. I liked to think it was all about being ready for anything, and being able to see what we were doing while we did it, but something about Glenbury Hall had left both of us feeling rather more cautious than usual.

A house doesn't have to be haunted, to be dangerous.

Penny and I had already taken it in turns to visit the communal bathroom. I listened carefully before I went out into the corridor, because I really didn't feel like queuing. I never know what to say in those circumstances. The facilities turned out to be adequate, though a sign above the old-fashioned toilet saying *Please allow the cistern time to react* didn't exactly inspire confidence.

After a while, I heard Marion and Arthur coming up the stairs. There was no mistaking Marion's heavy insistent footsteps, followed by Arthur's more hesitant tread. I listened carefully, in case they might feel like saying something revealing, but it seemed they weren't talking to each other. I had a feeling I knew what it was they weren't talking about, but even though I listened carefully I didn't hear Arthur so much as hesitate outside Wendy's door. He followed Marion into their room, and I heard the door close and lock behind them. After that, it was very still and very quiet in Glenbury Hall.

Time passed. Nothing disturbed the long, slow silence of the night.

"It's not exactly warm in here," Penny said finally. "Do you suppose that wall radiator is actually working?"

"If we're still here tomorrow night, I'll inquire about a hot water bottle," I said.

Penny looked at me sharply. "You really think we could be here that long?"

"Wouldn't surprise me," I said. "We've searched the entire house and questioned everyone in it, but we still don't have a single idea as to how Lucas Carr disappeared."

Penny thought about it, and then shrugged. "Didn't they use to have bed-warmers, back in the old days?"

"I don't think you're allowed to call servants that anymore," I said.

"Idiot. I meant those long-handled pans you could put hot coals in, to warm up a bed before anyone got in. We used to have some standing on display in Belcourt Manor."

"Presumably because they were antiques," I said. "And therefore worth money. Guess where I'm going with this . . ."

Penny stared thoughtfully at the ceiling. "Do you think Arthur and Marion really are as broke as they make out?"

I shrugged. "Marion does have the look of a woman who hoped for better things, and is not taking her disappointment gracefully."

"London's business community has always believed in Darwinian economics: red in tooth and claw," said Penny.

"I'm still not sure why Arthur came back to a house he hated, to run a business he clearly isn't interested in," I said. "Marion must have a really firm grip on him, to keep his nose pressed to the grindstone."

Penny stretched slowly, and then crossed her ankles, trying to get settled.

"I don't think he hates this house," she said slowly. "I think he's afraid of it."

"Because of the ghosts?" I said. "Or because now he can't get away from the memories of what his parents did to him? I get the feeling a lot more happened here than he's willing to talk about."

"Arthur's father sounds like complete pond scum," said Penny. "And yet Catherine has such fond memories of him."

"Yes..." I said. "Who would have thought such a sweet old thing would turn out to have such an interesting past?"

"Or that she would be the only person to have spent serious time in this house, and come away apparently entirely unscathed," Penny said thoughtfully. "You have to wonder what happened to all the other people who partied here, with Paul and Mary Glenbury. Did they emerge safe and sound, full of happy memories of sweaty times, or are they all still in therapy?"

"Catherine was very firm, that she never saw any ghosts here," I said.

"Probably too busy frolicking with one and all," said Penny.

I had to smile. "Is frolicking an actual word?"

"In Catherine's case, almost certainly," said Penny. "Maybe that's what protected her from the Curse of Glenbury Hall."

"Oh please," I said. "Isn't this house gothic enough as it is? The last thing we need now is a young woman in a nightie running across the grounds, glancing back at a single lit window."

"I used to devour those paperbacks when I was a teenager," said Penny.

"Somehow, I am not surprised."

"Beast," Penny said calmly. "And finally, on top of everything else . . . Wendy knew Arthur, back in London. Didn't see that one coming. Do you think she's still holding a torch for him, after all these years?"

"Hard to believe Arthur could inspire that kind of devotion," I said. "But Marion seemed ready enough to believe it."

"I think it's very romantic," Penny said firmly.

"It could just be a cover story," I said. "To distract us from Wendy's real motives."

Penny stirred restlessly. "But if she's not here for the Society, and she's not here for Arthur . . . what else could have brought her all the way out here, to Glenbury Hall?"

"Good question," I said.

We lay snuggled together on the big double bed, staring at nothing, while our minds ran in circles, going nowhere.

"What do you think Arthur's father saw, on that haunted television set?" Penny said finally.

"I'm not sure we can trust anything about that story," I said. "It comes from two different sources, who can't even agree on the basics of what happened. Catherine thought she was just telling us an amusing anecdote."

"But you saw how much the story upset Arthur, even after all these years," said Penny.

"Don't you find it odd," I said, "that the television went back to normal, once it had been moved to another room? I would have expected the set itself to have been the source of the trouble, not the room."

"Except that this is Glenbury Hall," said Penny, "where you can't trust anything. And Arthur did say his father could have made the whole thing up."

"Except, nailing up a room does seem a long way to go to back up a practical joke," I said.

Penny scowled. "What did Catherine see in that man?"

"We can't always choose who we give our hearts to," I said.

And then I broke off, as Penny suddenly sat up and stared around the room.

"Ishmael! Did you hear that?"

"No," I said, not moving. "And I'm pretty sure I would have, if there had been anything."

Penny scowled, as she sank slowly back onto the bed.

"I could have sworn I heard.... Maybe it's this room. There's just something about it that grates on my nerves. Though I couldn't tell you what, or why."

I took my time looking around. The furniture was seriously ugly, and whoever painted the walls that particular shade of yellow was not only colour blind but probably harbouring a terrible grudge against all humanity... but otherwise the room seemed perfectly normal. And perfectly safe. The curtains at the window were closed against the night, while the wind muttered moodily in the chimney, unable to get to us. The door was locked, and I had the only pass key.

I turned back to Penny, and she saw what I was going to say. She shook her head stubbornly.

"There has to be something wrong with this room; it's where Lucas Carr disappeared."

"Assuming he got this far," I said.

"I have a very definite feeling that he did," said Penny. "And that something bad happened to him, right here, in this room."

"If it did," I said, "there's nothing we can do about it now."

"You think he's dead, don't you?"

"I can't see any version of events that makes sense, if he isn't."

"It's not just this room," Penny said slowly. "It's the whole house. Glenbury Hall isn't anything like the House on Widows Hill; that place radiated strangeness from the first moment we set eyes on it."

"And with good reason," I said.

"The Hall feels more as though it's trying to appear normal, and failing, because it can't hide its true nature."

I considered my words carefully. "Whatever it is you're feeling . . . I'm not picking up anything. There is nothing about this room that makes me feel even a little bit threatened, or scared."

"You're never scared," said Penny.

"I can be," I said. "I just hide it so as not to worry you."

"That's sweet."

"Well," I said. "I'm only human."

Penny looked at me thoughtfully. "Except that you're not. For all your time in this world, you're still an outsider looking in at the rest of us. Maybe that's why you're not picking up the atmosphere that's spooking the rest of us."

"I am human, in every way that counts," I said carefully. "And usually I'm the one who notices things that the rest of you don't."

"Perhaps you're just too rational, to be completely human," said Penny.

"That's a terrible thing to say about your own species," I said solemnly.

We shared a smile, but it didn't last. Penny's scowl deepened as she glared around the room.

"It feels like simply by being here, we've walked into a trap. Just like Lucas."

I had to raise an eyebrow. "You think his disappearance was planned?"

"Don't you?" said Penny. "How else could he have vanished so completely, with not a single clue to explain it? Unless someone had put a hell of a lot of thought into how to disappear him."

"But why would anyone want to abduct Lucas?" I said. "He didn't know anything. The Colonel was very firm on that."

"The Colonel doesn't always tell us everything," said Penny.

I nodded slowly, acknowledging the point. "But if Lucas' kidnapping was planned in advance... why do it here?"

"Because it's so far from anywhere, and because they could use the Hall's bad reputation as a distraction."

"Not bad..." I said thoughtfully. "But that argument only works if Lucas knew something valuable. And I think the Colonel would have told us, if that was the case."

"What if... the Hall called to Lucas?" said Penny. "Reached out across all the miles, to get inside his head and influence him, like that old story about the siren in the well."

"But again, why would it want to?" I said. "Lucas wasn't anyone special."

"He brought us here, didn't he?" said Penny.

"Let's not over-complicate the situation," I said. "Lucas only came to the Hall to enjoy a weekend of scholarly fun with his fellow historians..."

"Did he?" said Penny. "You heard Wendy; Lucas hated travelling, and had difficulties when it came to meeting new people. Yet something compelled him to uproot himself, and travel all the way here."

"All right; what are you suggesting?"

"I don't know," said Penny. "Maybe just that there's more to this situation than meets the eye."

"Wouldn't be the first time." I looked at her carefully. "What is it about this house that's getting to you?"

Penny took her time answering. "We have been in far more dangerous places than this. We've faced all kind of weird threats, and kicked their arses. But this house feels... different. As though centuries of evil and ill-will had soaked into the wood and stone of Glenbury Hall, and poisoned every part of it."

She looked at me to see how I was taking this, but all I could do was shrug.

"You'll feel better once we've started some serious sleuthing. A few solid clues will give you a whole new view on things."

"You don't believe in clues. For you it's always all about the suspects, and their motives."

"We work with what we have," I said. I shifted my weight restlessly, and the mattress made low complaining noises. "Let's give the others a little more time to get their heads down, and then we'll nip out into the corridor and do a little discreet prowling."

"What if somebody else is already out there, sneaking around?"

"Then we follow them," I said. "At a respectful distance. Observe where they go and what they do, and hope it leads to something useful."

"Who do you think will leave their room?" said Penny.

"Wouldn't surprise me if they all did," I said. "They'll probably end up tripping over each other in the dark."

"Marion did seem very keen that we should all get to bed early," said Penny.

"But on the other hand, none of the others objected to an early night," I said.

Penny turned her head on the pillow, so she could meet my gaze squarely.

"Does it ever bother you, that you're always looking for the worst in people?"

"No," I said. "Most of the time it comes under the heading of self-defence. Get them, before they can drop a piano on you. So I look for the worst, and hope to be pleasantly surprised."

"And are you?"

I smiled at her. "Sometimes. But, there's nothing like an old dark house for bringing out the sinister in people."

"Catherine believes that like calls to like," said Penny. "And evil calls to evil."

"We need facts," I said firmly. "Good solid evidence.... Right now, we are so mired in theories and possibilities that we're just spinning our wheels, unable to get any traction. Normal motives don't seem to make sense, in a setting like this. Still ... I have no doubt that when we finally get to the bottom of things, it will all make perfect sense."

"I really would like to believe that," said Penny. "But what if Arthur is right, and the Hall honestly can get inside your head? What if it can make you think and do things you wouldn't even consider anywhere else?"

"Anyone trying to get inside my head does so at their own risk," I said calmly. "I wouldn't go in there without a chair and a whip."

Penny laughed, because she knew I wasn't joking.

Time passed. Penny dozed off, and made low snoring and snuffling noises. The Hall made all the sounds you'd expect from an old house settling in the night. Creaks and groans, a clump of soot falling down the chimney, and a brief water hammer in the pipes downstairs. A gusting wind swept around the Hall, and out across the grounds. I still couldn't hear any of the usual nocturnal birds or wildlife ... as though they had more sense than to go anywhere near Glenbury Hall.

I concentrated, listening for the sound of a door unlocking and opening, followed by surreptitious footsteps on the landing or creeping down the stairs ... but there was nothing. The Glenburys and their guests slumbered peacefully in their beds. The clearest thing I could hear was Penny's slow breathing beside me, as familiar to me as my own. I nudged her in the side and she surfaced reluctantly, muttering slurred words from a dream language. She yawned and stretched, and looked at me reproachfully.

"I only closed my eyes for a moment. Is it time to go walkabout?"

"Not yet," I said. "I was thinking ... there's something we should do first."

Penny smiled at me dazzlingly. "Darling, have we got time? Shall I put my big hat back on? You know you like that."

"I think we need to turn off the light," I said.

Penny stared at me for a long moment. "Why?"

"It could be shining past the cracks in our door, and spilling out into the corridor," I said steadily. "Letting the others know that we are still awake."

"You have got to be kidding," said Penny. "You really think anyone would notice that, from inside their rooms? We don't all have alien-issued eyes."

"If they have their lights off, ours could stand out in the dark," I said. "It's the first thing I'd look for."

"Yes, but you are an experienced secret agent and extremely weird," said Penny. She looked at me accusingly. "Did you wake me up because you were you worried I might freak out, if you just went ahead and did it?"

"You're my partner," I said. "I run all my decisions past

you. It would only be for a while, to lure anyone who might be watching into a false sense of security."

"You worry about the strangest things, Ishmael."

"And I'm usually right." I looked at her carefully. "Are you worried, that you might freak out in the dark?"

She snorted loudly. "The house isn't getting to me that much."

I wasn't entirely sure I believed that. I could feel the tension in her. But she just shrugged quickly, and knuckled grumpily at her eyes.

"Oh, go ahead then. Get on with it then."

There was no switch or pull cord near the bed. I swung my legs over the side and padded quickly over to the switch by the door. I turned the light off, and it was suddenly very dark. I could just make out a shimmer of moonlight past a crack in the drawn curtains, and I used that to find my way back to the bed. Penny made a startled sound as I dropped onto the bed beside her, and punched me in the arm.

"Give me some warning next time! I'm blind as a bat in this darkness."

"I'll get you some echolocation equipment for Christmas."

"You buy me the sweetest things."

She snuggled up against me again, a warm and friendly presence in the night, and I held her close as I kept a watchful gaze on the dim shapes of the furniture, so I would know if anything moved or suddenly wasn't where it should be.

"I can feel the Hall around me," Penny said quietly. "Not the people in their rooms, but the house itself. As though the Hall is listening to our every movement, just waiting for us to do something unwise and leave ourselves vulnerable, so it can pounce on us."

"It's just a house," I said.

"Is it?" said Penny. "What if the Glenburys did something here, long ago, to change the very nature of the Hall?"

"Concentrate on the people," I said firmly. "People are always the most dangerous elements in any situation."

Penny sighed slowly. "Any idea what time it is?"

"Ten to twelve," I said.

There was a pause.

"You didn't even look at your watch, did you?" said Penny.

"I didn't need to. I always know what time it is."

"Alien. Come on; I've had enough of lying around here, waiting for something to happen. I say we go out into the corridor and make something happen."

I smiled into the darkness. "Sounds like a plan to me."

We got up off the bed. I managed it easily because I could see what I was doing, but it took Penny several tries before she could even figure out where the edge of the bed was. I put a hand on her arm to steady her, and she snatched it away.

"I told you; give me some warning! I nearly jumped out of my skin!"

"But you knew it had to be me," I said reasonably. "I'm the only other person in the room."

"I wish I could believe that," she muttered. "But I keep getting this feeling that we're not alone in here."

I remembered Catherine talking about guests at the Hall who became convinced there were more people in a room than they could account for. There was no one but Penny and me. I was sure of that. Unless ... there was something in the dark that not even my senses could detect.

"Follow me to the door," I said. "And we'll take a look outside. Unless you need to use the chamber-pot first."

"The only use I have for that thing is to smash it over someone's head."

In the end Penny allowed me to take her by the elbow and steer her over to the door. We pressed our ears against the wood, and listened carefully.

"I'm not hearing anything," Penny said finally. "How about you, space boy?"

"Not a thing, spy girl," I said. "No, wait a minute. I think... there might be footsteps, somewhere down the corridor."

"Who do you think it is?" said Penny. "Catherine, out looking for ghosts? Or Wendy, looking for answers?"

"It could be Ellen, waiting to meet some boyfriend she invited over from town," I said. "Her performance at dinner could have been just a cover, so no one would try to stop her jumping the bones of some local boy she knew her parents wouldn't approve of."

"That's sort of sweet," said Penny. "In a sweaty, hormonal, teenage sort of way. Young lust would actually make a nice change from some of the possibilities we've been considering."

"Or it could be Arthur and Marion out there," I said. "Setting the stage for a special ghostly performance, to justify the Hall's reputation."

"You think they'd play tricks on us?" said Penny.

"What better way to attract guests to a failing business, than a dramatic haunting witnessed by a whole bunch of impeccable witnesses? Arthur and Marion could end up with so many new bookings they'd have to beat off the enthusiasts with an ectoplasmic stick."

"What if it isn't any of those people?" said Penny.

"I suppose it could always be Lucas Carr, come back to explain himself."

"You know what? I would really like that," said Penny. "We could take it in turns to slam him up against a wall and ask him pointed questions about what the hell he's been playing at."

"He could have escaped from some secret room where he'd been held prisoner," I said, and then smiled into the darkness. "Unless he's come back as a ghost, to join the spectral throng infesting Glenbury Hall."

"Don't even go there," said Penny.

Something in her voice made me turn my head to look at her. She was just a dim shape in the gloom, standing very still.

"This house really is getting to you, isn't it?"

"Yes," said Penny. "It is. And no, I don't know why. We've gone charging headlong into worse situations than this, armed with nothing more than a really bad attitude. I think it's just that the whole place feels wrong. Some old houses do go feral, and turn on their occupants. That's an established fact."

"In your world, maybe. Do you want to stay here, while I go and check out the lay of the land?"

"You even try that, and I will trip you up and walk right over you," said Penny. "You know you need me, to guard your back. Are you still hearing the footsteps?"

"No," I said. "They stopped, while we were talking. But I'm not sure when . . ."

"Maybe the house is getting to you as well," Penny said sweetly.

"That'll be the day," I said. "Or the night."

I reached out to open the door and then stopped.

"Hold it," I said quietly.

"What is it?" said Penny.

"I don't know," I said. "It just suddenly feels like . . . we're not alone."

"If there is someone in the corridor, we need to get out there and jump on them, before they get away!" said Penny.

I turned my back on the door, and stared into the darkness filling the room. "Whatever it is, it's in here with us. Listen! Did you hear that?"

Penny moved in close beside me. I could feel her arm tensing with anticipation, where it pressed against mine.

"I can't hear anything. What did you hear?"

"A kind of . . . scratching," I said.

"And you think this sound is coming from inside the room?"

"I'm not sure," I said. "It might have come from inside the wall."

I gestured at the wall to our right, and then realised Penny couldn't see the movement. I put a hand on her arm, and quietly turned her to face the wall. Her bicep bulged under my grip, as her hand closed into a fist. We both stood very still, listening hard. The silence and the darkness had a weight and a power all their own. And then the scratching started up again. Quiet, but very distinct, like claws, or long fingernails, scraping against the wood of the wall. I could just make out Penny nodding quickly, as she heard it too. The long, slow scraping continued, and something in the sound make me think of fingernails grown long in the grave, scraping against the underside of a coffin lid. I pushed the thought aside, and made myself concentrate on exactly where the sound was coming from. And then it broke off, and all I could hear was Penny's elevated breathing beside me.

"It's stopped," she said quietly.

"I know."

"What do you think it was? And don't say rats in the walls."

"There are bound to be some," I said, in my most reasonable voice. "In a house this old, this far out in the countryside."

"I heard rats when I was growing up in Belcourt Manor," said Penny. "Rats don't make noises like that. There was something . . . deliberate, about that sound. As though whatever was making it wanted to be heard."

She stopped talking, as the scratching sound started up again; only this time it was coming from the left-hand wall.

Heavier now, as though something was trying to claw its way through the wood of the wall, to get to us. I started to put myself between Penny and the sound, but she elbowed me aside and swept her hand back and forth until she found the side table by the door. She picked it up, and I heard the phone fall to the floor. Penny hefted the table, getting a feel for the weight of it.

"Try to remember that I'm here with you, when you start flailing around with that thing," I said.

"You can see what I'm doing, in this darkness?"

"Of course."

"Can you see what's making the noises?"

"No," I said. "I think it's outside the room and trying to get in."

"Let it," said Penny. "I've got its welcoming present right here."

The scratching stopped, as suddenly as it began.

"Has it broken through?" Penny said softly.

"I don't think so."

I concentrated as hard as I could, and still I couldn't see or hear or feel anything in the room with us. I took a cautious step forward, and Penny was immediately there with me, holding the side table out before her. The scratching sounds hadn't struck me as particularly threatening, but I was still ready to jump on whatever was causing them with both feet, the moment it showed itself.

The scratching started up again; short rhythmic strokes this time, coming from directly above us. Penny and I tilted our heads back. It sounded as though something was trying to dig its way through the ceiling.

"What's above us?" said Penny, her voice barely a whisper.

"I don't know," I said, just as quietly. "This is the top floor of the house. I don't think there are any attics."

"Maybe one of the gargoyles has got restless."

"Do gargoyles have claws?" I said, just to be saying something.

"No idea. And I really don't want to find out the hard way."

"Give me the improvised weapon," I said.

Penny handed me the side table, and I threw it at the ceiling, right where the scratching sound was loudest. The table hit hard, with a flat solid sound, and fell back again. I caught the table, put it to one side, and then listened hard. The scratching had stopped. Penny and I stood close together, straining our hearing against the dark, but the sounds didn't start up again.

"What the hell was that?" Penny said finally.

"Definitely not a ghost," I said. "Unless it was in urgent need of a manicure."

"But what was the point in just . . . making noises?"

"Someone, or something, was trying to scare us," I said.

"Why?" said Penny.

"Perhaps they thought they could intimidate us into leaving the Hall," I said. "Because they're worried we might find out something. Which of course implies that there is something to be found out. Or maybe they just thought it was funny."

"It didn't feel funny," said Penny. "It felt like a threat."

"Yes," I said. "It did. But if whatever it was had really wanted to get into the room, why didn't they just kick in the door?"

"I'm more concerned about how they were able to move around so quickly," said Penny. "From one wall to the other, and then on the ceiling . . . I didn't hear anything moving; did you?"

"No," I said. "And I should have."

I thought hard, considering the possibilities, but all my

mind could manage was an image of some huge horrid insect, scuttling around the outside of the room.

"At least it's over now," said Penny. "We're safe."

"I don't think so," I said.

"What?" said Penny.

"Mr. Scratchy might be gone," I said quietly, "but I have a strong feeling there's something else, watching us."

Penny stood very still. When she finally spoke her voice was so low only I could have heard it.

"You think something might have got into the room, while we were distracted?"

"I don't see how," I said.

"I'm not seeing or hearing anything," said Penny. "But if you say someone's here, I believe you."

"Look at the window," I said quietly. "Straight ahead of us."

"I can't see a damn thing in this darkness. Can't we turn on the light?"

"We don't want to scare it off," I said.

"We don't?"

"Not until we can get our hands on it. I can just make out a shape, at the window."

"Good," said Penny.

"Not necessarily," I said. "I'm not hearing a heartbeat, or any breathing."

"Really didn't want to hear that," said Penny. "Okay, point me at it. I am definitely in the mood to hit something."

I moved slowly forward across the room. Penny stuck close beside me, keeping her shoulder pressed against mine so she could always be sure where I was. I kept my gaze fixed on the window.

"What exactly are you seeing?" Penny whispered.

"A silhouette of a shape, on the other side of the curtains."

"What kind of shape?"

"Sort of human."

"Only sort of?"

"You don't get much in the way of detail, from a silhouette."

"All right, don't get tetchy. How do you want to handle this?"

"I think you should hang back, while I go check it out," I said.

I could sense Penny glaring at me, even if I couldn't see it.

"I am not being left out, now something is finally happening!"

"Think about it," I said steadily. "If this thing is on the other side of the curtains, that means it has to be outside the window. And we're on the top floor. So how did it get there? If this is something out of the ordinary, it makes sense for me to have first crack at it."

"I hate it when you're sensible," said Penny. "All right... you're up. But if it does turn out to be just a Peeping Tom on a ladder, feel free to punch them repeatedly in the head."

"Sounds like a plan to me," I said.

I padded forward, and the floorboards under my feet didn't make a single sound. I've had a lot of practice, when it comes to moving and not being heard. The closer I got to the curtains, the more distinct the silhouette became. It seemed to be crouching, perched on the outside windowsill. I had no idea how it was keeping its balance. It wasn't moving, not even a little. Just a dark human shape, holding itself inhumanly still, and not making even the smallest sound.

Despite myself, I couldn't help but remember Catherine's story about the statues in the grounds creeping up to the house, to stare in through the windows and see what the people were doing. I had no idea how a statue could end up outside a top-floor window, but I was ready to turn its head into rubble if I could just get close enough.

I eased to a halt before the curtains, took a firm hold on the material with both hands, and then hauled the curtains apart with one swift movement. Moonlight poured into the room, but there was no shape anywhere. Just an uninterrupted view, out across the grounds. I pressed my face against the window and stared out at the statues shimmering in the moonlight. I counted them quickly, to reassure myself they were all present and accounted for, and exactly where they should be. And then I felt a little annoyed with myself, for even considering the possibility that they might not be.

I took a deep breath. The scratching sounds could have been rats. The silhouette could have been just a trick of the eye, produced by the paranoid atmosphere. But I had been in scarier situations than this, and I'd always been able to trust my senses before. Unless...there was something in, or perhaps even under Glenbury Hall, that was affecting my senses. Something not of this world. Did the Colonel have some reason to suspect that? Was that the real reason why he'd sent us here?

Penny came forward to join me, moving more easily now the room was full of moonlight. She squeezed in beside me, peered out the window, and then looked at me. She took in the expression on my face, and put a comforting hand on my arm.

"What did you see, Ishmael?"

"Just a shape," I said.

"Where did it go?"

"I don't know. I don't see how it could have gone anywhere."

Penny searched for something practical to say. "It could have been someone spying on us. Maybe they went back down a ladder?"

I threw the window open as far as it would go, and leaned out into the night. Penny made an exasperated noise and grabbed the back of my belt with both hands, to keep me from falling. I looked up and down the front of the house, but there was no sign of a ladder anywhere. And there was definitely no one out in the grounds. Penny tugged hard on my belt, to make it clear she thought I'd been out there long enough, so I let her pull me back inside the room. And then I stopped, as something caught my eye.

"What is it?" said Penny.

"Look at this," I said, nodding to the windowsill.

"What am I supposed to be looking at?"

"Those scuff marks."

"Okay..." said Penny. "I suppose that could be scuff marks. You think they mean something?"

"They look recent," I said.

"And that makes them a clue?"

"Could be. I'll have to think about it."

"Well, while you're doing that could we please close the window?" said Penny. "Only it is getting a bit cold in here."

I shut the window and went to close the curtains, but Penny stopped me.

"I feel better with some light in the room," she said. "Particularly if there really was something out there."

"I saw something," I said.

"And it's not like you, to see things that aren't there."

"No," I said. "It isn't."

"Maybe one of the gargoyles climbed down from the roof."

I gave Penny a hard look. "I think we would have heard something like that."

"Not if it's a supernatural thing," said Penny. "They follow their own rules."

"Even Catherine didn't believe that the gargoyles get up and move around," I said carefully.

Penny's mouth tightened into a flat line.

"Is a gargoyle climbing down to peer in our window really any odder than some of the things we've encountered on our other cases?"

"Yes," I said firmly. "You have to draw the line somewhere, or you'd never know what to believe. Come on. Let's go out into the corridor and do something impulsive. You know that always makes you feel better."

"I am in the mood to take out my frustrations on anyone who looks even a little bit guilty," Penny admitted.

"If anyone gives us a hard time," I said, "I will knock them down, and you can put the boot in."

"Hell with that," said Penny. "I'll knock them down and you can put the boot in."

"I can live with that," I said.

We went back to the door, and I eased it open. The wood made only the faintest of creaking noises, and the hinges were surprisingly quiet. All the way down the long corridor, shafts of moonlight poured in through the gabled windows...but the shadows were still very deep and very dark. There was no one about, and everything seemed perfectly quiet. I stepped out into the corridor, and Penny was there with me in a moment. I pulled the door to, but didn't completely close it. Just in case we needed to dive back into our room in a hurry. When you're about to head off into dangerous territory, it always pays to have your exit route planned.

Penny stared down the corridor, narrowing her eyes against the shadows.

"We should have brought the flashlight from the car."

"It would only ruin your night vision," I said. "Take a moment, and give your eyes a chance to adjust."

I was struck by how much longer the corridor seemed, compared to when we'd walked it in daylight. Everything seemed strange and unfamiliar, as though we'd strayed into unknown territory, where anything could happen.

I smiled quietly to myself, as I let my mind range freely through the possibilities. What if... the Hall had been built over an ancient elven burial ground,; or there was a crashed alien starship buried deep under the well? What if the entire house was a doorway to another reality, where all the rules were different? If you're going to think really weird thoughts, you might as well go the whole hog. I pushed them all firmly to one side and set off down the corridor, to see what there was to see. Because that was what I did. And Penny was right there beside me, because that was what she did.

We moved through the gloom like ghosts, neither of us making a sound on the bare wooden floorboards. And my first thought was, if we can do this, so could somebody else. We kept to the shadows, avoiding the moonlight, just in case someone was watching. After a while, I eased to a halt. Penny stopped with me and leaned in close, so she could murmur in my ear.

"What is it, Ishmael? What can you see?"

"I'm not seeing anything," I said quietly. "I'd swear this corridor was completely empty. But I'm sure I just heard footsteps again, from somewhere up ahead."

"Human footsteps?" said Penny.

"I think we can rule out statues and gargoyles," I said.

"Of course," said Penny. "They're much heavier, so their footsteps would be louder."

I didn't look at her. I didn't want to know whether she was joking. I kept my gaze fixed on the shadows ahead of us. They seemed deeper and darker than ever.

"The footsteps seemed to just start up out of nowhere, and

then stop again," I said. "And there was something ... not quite right, about them."

"Okay ..." said Penny. "Glad to hear it's not just me who's freaking out. Let's run right at them, and see what happens."

I stabbed a finger at a movement further down the corridor. A dark figure had just emerged from the shadows. A human shape, though it took me a moment to be sure of that because it was down on its hands and knees. The head was hanging low, so I couldn't even get a glimpse of its face. The thing headed towards us with slow, deliberate movements, as though it was horribly tired, or in great pain. The figure was definitely there, a solid physical presence, I could hear the slow scrapings of its hands and knees against the floorboards.

And I remembered the barman saying, *It crawls* ...

It felt like I was in the presence of something not of this world, only able to exist in our reality through its own force of will. A threatening presence, come to do us harm. I realised I'd moved instinctively to place myself in front of Penny, and that thought was enough to put me back in a practical frame of mind. The crawling thing might be creepy as hell, but when in doubt ... get your hands on the threat, and see if you can shake some answers out of it.

I charged down the corridor, running straight at the figure. It lurched sideways, and disappeared into a wall. I yelled back at Penny.

"Turn on the lights!"

"I don't know where the switch is!" said Penny.

"Find it!"

I couldn't hear the sounds the figure had been making anymore. When I reached the spot where I'd last seen it, I crashed to a halt and looked quickly around, but there was no trace of the crawling shape anywhere. Penny finally found the switch, and bright lights flooded the corridor from end to end. It was completely empty, and where the deep dark shadow had been there was just a featureless length of wall. And no sign anywhere to suggest where the figure could have gone. I struck the wall with my fist, and the sound came back flat and solid.

I hurried on down the corridor, throwing open each door as I came to it, but every room was empty, with nowhere obvious for anything to hide. And besides, I was sure I would have heard a door opening and closing. As if to confirm that, doors started banging open behind me, and I looked back to see Marion standing in the doorway to her room, wrapped in an elegant silk robe. I thought she looked surprisingly neat and tidy, for someone who'd just been roused from her sleep.

"Who is making all that noise?" she said loudly. "Did I hear someone running up and down the corridor?"

"It's only me," I said.

She glared at me. "Mr. Jones. I might have known."

Wendy stepped out into the corridor, wearing an over-sized dressing gown and fluffy slippers. She didn't seem the least bit scared. Her hands had clenched into fists, and she looked ready to tackle anything.

"What the bloody hell is going on?" she said fiercely.

Before I could answer her, the door to the communal bathroom swung open and Arthur stepped out into the corridor, wearing baggy striped pyjamas. He blinked confusedly around him, before looking to Marion.

"Are you all right?"

"Of course I'm all right!" she said sharply. "Wait. Where's Ellen?"

We all looked round, but there was no sign of the teenage girl. Arthur hurried down the corridor and knocked loudly on Ellen's door, calling her name. Her voice came back immediately, as though she'd been standing on the other side of the door, just waiting for someone to come to her.

"I'm all right, Dad. But I'm not coming out. My door is locked and it's going to stay that way."

"Nothing bad is going on out here," said Arthur. The look on his face contradicted his reassuring tone. "But if you are feeling... upset, you could always come and spend the night with your mother and me. If you want."

There was a pause as Ellen thought about it, but when she finally answered her voice was flat but firm.

"No."

Arthur just nodded, as though he hadn't expected anything else. "Then stay where you are, sweetie, and don't come out till the morning. I'm sure everything will seem better, in the morning."

He waited, to see if there might be an answer. When it became clear he wasn't going to get one, he turned away and came back to join the rest of us.

"Teenagers," he said, trying to smile.

Penny came hurrying along the corridor to join me, and Marion glared at both of us.

"What are you doing out of your room? Why all this commotion?"

"Crashing about, at this hour of the morning," said Wendy, glowering heavily. "I'd only just dropped off!"

"I thought I heard someone moving about," I said steadily. "And when I came out into the corridor, I saw a shape emerging from the shadows. It was some kind of figure, down on all fours, heading towards me. When I tried to get closer... it disappeared into the wall."

"*It crawls*..." said Arthur. "No one's seen that manifestation in more than fifty years!"

Marion glared him into silence, and then turned a cold gaze on me.

"Are you saying we have an intruder in the house?"

"That's not possible," Arthur said immediately. "I set the burglar alarms myself, before I came up. Front door and back. And if anyone had broken a window to get in, we would have heard. Those old windows are really thick glass, and take a lot of breaking. There couldn't have been an intruder."

Marion looked at me scornfully. "Chasing ghosts, at your age." She switched her accusing stare to Penny. "Did you see this figure too?"

"No," said Penny. "But if Ishmael said he saw someone, I'm sure he did."

And then we all looked round sharply as a piercing scream issued from Catherine's bedroom, and we suddenly realised she was the only one we hadn't heard from. Wendy headed for Catherine's door, calling out her name. She was closer to it than me, but I still got there first. I rattled the handle, but the door was locked. I banged on it with my fist, hard enough to make the wood jump in its frame.

"Catherine! This is Ishmael Jones; what's wrong?"

She didn't answer, but her scream broke off, replaced by harsh tears. Wendy forced herself in beside me, and raised her voice.

"Catherine, this is Wendy. Please; open the door and let us in."

The sobbing didn't stop. Wendy glared at me.

"Do something!"

I already had the pass key in my hand. I unlocked the door, threw it back and burst into the room, with Wendy right behind me. I found the light switch by the door, and turned it on.

Catherine was sitting bolt upright in bed, in over-sized

flower-patterned pyjamas. Her back was pressed against the headboard, as though she was trying to retreat through it. She didn't even look at me, shaking all over from the force of her tears. Wendy hurried past me, and sat down on the bed beside Catherine. She reached out a comforting hand, and Catherine clutched it in both of hers. She tried to say something, but her voice was still choked with tears.

"You're all right, dear," Wendy said soothingly. "You're fine, you're not hurt, and I'm right here with you. Anyone gives you any trouble, I will kick them through a wall. Can you tell me what happened?"

Catherine's tears began to slow, and she swallowed hard. When she finally spoke, her voice was high and strained, but she seemed more in control of herself.

"Someone was in my room. Even though I'd locked my door."

"When was this?" I said. "Just now?"

Catherine shook her head jerkily. "No. Some time back. I woke up, and there was a figure standing at the foot of my bed. It didn't move, or say anything; it just stood there, staring at me."

"Was it a man?" said Wendy. "Could you see what he looked like?"

Catherine shuddered briefly. "It was so dark... All I could see was a shape. Human, but... It was the way it just stood there... I was so scared! And then suddenly it was moving, coming round the end of the bed, and I sat up and scrambled backwards, thinking it was coming for me, but it just walked into the wall and was gone! And all I could do was sit here, trembling, until I heard people talking in the corridor, and then I couldn't hold it in anymore."

She tried to smile, but couldn't quite manage it. "Screaming like a girl, at my time of life."

"Can you remember any details about this figure?" I said.

Wendy glared at me. "This can wait! She's in shock!"

"It's best to ask now," I said, "while the memories are still fresh."

Catherine was already shaking her head. "The room was too dark. But there was something in the way it stood, the way it moved, that made me think it wasn't ... completely human."

I moved quickly around the room, checking behind every piece of furniture, while Wendy stayed with Catherine. I even knelt down and peered underneath the bed, just in case. I got up again, and smiled reassuringly at Catherine.

"There's no one here now. You're perfectly safe."

"Would you mind taking a look inside the wardrobe?" Catherine said timidly. "I know I saw the figure disappear through the wall, so there can't be anything hiding in there ... But I always thought something might be, when I was a child."

"Not a problem," I said.

I opened the wardrobe's doors and pushed them all way back, so Catherine could see there was nothing inside apart from a few clothes on hangers.

"Check the window," said Wendy. "He might have got in that way."

It didn't seem the right time to mention the shape I'd seen at my window. I went over to take a look. Marion and Arthur were peering in through the open door, and I heard Marion sniff dismissively.

"We're on the top floor," she said, not even bothering to lower her voice. "Whoever it was would need a really long ladder. Or maybe he abseiled down from the roof?"

I pulled back the curtains, opened the window and looked out, and then closed the windows and the curtains, and turned back to smile reassuringly at Catherine.

"No ladder," I said. "And nothing to indicate the window was forced. I think you just had a bad dream, Catherine. That's what comes from telling too many ghost stories, with perhaps too much wine at dinner."

Catherine shook her head stubbornly. "There was someone in here..."

"Of course there was," said Wendy, glaring at me defiantly.

"Then where is this intruder?" said Arthur.

"He walked through the wall," said Catherine, in the kind of voice that made it clear she didn't expect to be believed, but had to say it anyway because that was what happened. She shook her head slowly. "This house is full of things that got left behind, or won't go away. Echoes of distant crimes that have never been forgiven. The past isn't as far away as it should be, in Glenbury Hall." She shuddered suddenly, and I saw her knuckles whiten where she gripped Wendy's hand. "I don't think the Hall likes me anymore."

It had occurred to me that Catherine might have faked her close encounter with a tall, dark stranger to give more substance to her spooky stories, but I didn't think she was a good enough actor to fake that much shock. Wendy looked around, and spotted a dressing gown draped across the foot of the bed. She prised her hand out of Catherine's, grabbed the dressing gown and draped it over Catherine's shoulders. It seemed to help. Catherine pulled the gown around her, and sat up a little straighter.

"I thought I wanted to see a ghost," she said, "but it wasn't anything like what I expected. No sense of awe and wonder, no feeling of meeting something that walked in eternity. It was just a piece of the night that had come alive, and wanted to hurt me. I felt so helpless! Like it could do anything it wanted to me, and there was nothing I could have done to stop it..."

The tears threatened to make a comeback, but Wendy patted her comfortingly on the shoulder, and the moment passed. Catherine managed a small smile for Wendy, and then looked at me steadily, to make it clear that while she might have made a scene, she was back in control now.

Marion and Arthur were still watching from the doorway. I walked straight at them until they had no choice but to back away, and then I joined them outside in the corridor. I started to close the door behind me, but Catherine cried out.

"Please; don't!"

"Hush, Cath," said Wendy. "I'm here."

"And I'll be right here in the corridor, Catherine," I said. "I'll leave the door open so you can see me."

Penny came striding quickly down the corridor to join us. She met my gaze, and shook her head.

"I've walked the whole length of the corridor," she said bluntly. "I couldn't find any trace of an intruder."

"Then it must have been a false alarm," I said to Marion and Arthur. "And I was just jumping at shadows. That's what comes of paying too much attention to ghost stories. But given the state we're in, I think it might be best if we all returned to our rooms, locked the doors, and didn't come out again till morning. We're all too on edge right now, and ready to see anything. We don't want anyone getting hurt, do we?"

"What if I need to use the bathroom again?" said Arthur.

"You've got one of those chamber-pots, haven't you?" I said. "I have a feeling we're all going to get very familiar with those before morning."

"Oh ick," said Penny.

Marion drew herself up to her full height, and stood on her dignity. "In all the time I've lived in this house, I have never experienced anything like this."

"None of us did," said Arthur. And then he fixed me and Penny with a speculative look. "Until you people turned up."

"You mean: until Lucas Carr disappeared," I said. "Good night, everyone."

Marion sniffed loudly, spun on her heel, and stalked back to her room. Arthur started after her, and then hesitated. He went back to Ellen's door, knocked quietly, and announced himself.

"I'm not coming out!" Ellen said loudly.

"You don't have to," said Arthur. "We've decided we're all going to stay locked in our rooms till morning. Just for everyone's peace of mind. We'll get together for breakfast."

"I don't like it here," said Ellen. "Please, Dad; can't we go home?"

"We are home, Ellen."

"I mean, home in London."

"I'm sorry, Ellen," said Arthur. "We can't do that."

He waited, but she didn't have anything more to say. Arthur's shoulders slumped, and he turned away and went back to his room. The door closed behind him, and I heard a key turn in the lock.

"What the hell is going on here?" Penny said quietly.

"I think someone wanted to make a supernatural impression," I said.

"Someone? Or something?" said Penny. "People don't just appear and disappear."

"Lucas Carr did," I said.

"I really didn't see or hear anything in the corridor," Penny said carefully. "Not even when you went chasing off after it."

"What I saw, with my better than average eyes, seemed entirely real and solid," I said. "Not even a little bit ghostly. Right up to the point when it suddenly wasn't there anymore."

"It couldn't have been anyone we knew," said Penny,

"because the whole household was present and accounted for. In a quite startling variety of bed wear. So who did you see, and where did they go?"

"Good questions," I said. "Maybe it went to wherever Lucas Carr is." I looked back through Catherine's open door. She and Wendy were still sitting together on the bed. I gave them my best encouraging smile. "How are you feeling, Catherine?"

She managed a small but genuine smile. "I feel such a fool, screaming like that. Upsetting everyone. I think you're right. It was just a dream."

She sounded like she was trying to convince herself, as much as anyone else.

"You'll be perfectly safe now," I said. "Just keep your door locked. Everything will make much more sense once it's daylight."

Catherine nodded. "Of course. I'm sure you're right."

"And no more thinking about ghosts," I said sternly.

"I was fine with them, as long as they were just stories," said Catherine. "But stories aren't supposed to appear in your room at the dead of night."

Wendy patted her hand, got up off the bed, and came over to stand before me.

"I'm going to stay with Catherine," she said quietly. "She's in no state to be left on her own. The last thing we need is her crying out again once we're all settled."

"Keep the door locked till morning," I said, "and you'll be fine."

"Of course we will," said Wendy.

She shut the door in my face, and locked it. I heard her raised voice, speaking cheerfully to Catherine.

"Pull back those covers, dear, and budge up. There's plenty of room for both of us to get comfortable."

✢ ✢ ✢

Penny and I went back to our room. I turned on the light, and then paused in the doorway, looking back down the corridor. Whatever I'd seen had got away from me, and I wasn't used to that. I decided I'd leave the lights on in the corridor, in case I found it necessary to sneak out again and do a little more prowling around. Just because I'd set the rules didn't mean I had to obey them.

I closed the door, and locked it. Penny was moving quickly around the room, checking everything was as it should be, in case someone had sneaked in while we were distracted.

"If there was anyone in here," I said, just a bit reproachfully, "I would know."

"It's not that I don't trust your incredible senses," said Penny. "It's just that I don't trust anything about this house." She sat down on the edge of the bed, and shook her head slowly. "Part of me wants to search every room in the Hall, and not stop until I've found something I can hit. But if there is something here, it probably knows this house a lot better than we do. It could jump out on us from anywhere." She stopped, and looked at me steadily. "Would you think less of me, if I asked you to leave the light on for the rest of the night?"

"Something is definitely going on," I said. "And a light would be helpful, so we can be sure to see anyone sneaking up on us."

"Well done, Ishmael," said Penny. "A calm and sensible reason, for doing what we want to do anyway."

"Get some sleep," I said. "I'll sit beside you, and keep watch."

She just nodded.

And so I sat there, all through the long marches of the night and into the morning, while Penny slumbered fitfully beside me. There were no more incidents or strange noises, and no footsteps anywhere.

✤ CHAPTER SIX ✤
FIGHTING YOUR CORNER

BREAKFAST THE NEXT MORNING was something of a subdued affair. It was morning and it was light, and we were all together, but that was the best you could say for it.

Penny and I sat at our usual places, while Arthur and Marion bustled around the dining hall table, dispensing food from the ubiquitous hostess trolley. They didn't have anything to say. I looked around the table, trying to work out why everyone still seemed so affected by the previous night's events. I saw the crawling ghost, but they didn't. Catherine saw a dark figure in her room, but no one else did. So why were they all so ready to lock themselves in their rooms all night? And why, now it was morning and the adventures of last night were safely over, did they still look like someone had sneaked up behind them and hit them over the head with a two-by-four?

Marion and Arthur had turned on the electric chandelier, perhaps hoping its bright light would help cheer the place up and keep the shadows from gathering. But instead, the flat, characterless light added a stark and artificial aspect to the windowless room, as though we were all trapped in a waking nightmare, just waiting for the next awful thing to happen.

Catherine and Wendy sat close together, chatting as cheerfully as they could manage about everything except what had made such an impression on them the night before. They argued over the Hall's history, over who had hogged most of the blankets in the early hours, and about what they were going to do once breakfast was over. But there was a definite forced quality to their light and cheery voices. Like whistling in a graveyard, to keep the bad things at bay.

Ellen sat stiffly in her chair, pouting sullenly at her plate and saying nothing; the picture of a teenage girl forced to be somewhere she didn't want to be. She went out of her way to make it clear she was ignoring everyone, but they were all too taken up with their own problems to notice.

Arthur and Marion put even more effort into bustling around, as though that would help them pretend the gloomy atmosphere in the dining hall wasn't happening. They had prepared a generous breakfast for their guests: sausage and bacon, scrambled eggs and baked beans, and heaps of fried bread. Presumably hoping it would distract us from the unpleasantness of the night before.

"Ah," I said, as the plate in front of me was piled high with traditional goodness. "The Full English. For when you feel like giving your digestive system a real challenge."

Nobody laughed, or even smiled. They were too busy staring glumly at their plates. There didn't seem to be much of an appetite for the fare provided, and while no one actually pushed it away and demanded a croissant, there was a lot of pushing the food around their plate before anyone actually tried anything. I just got stuck in. I've always said there's nothing like mysterious experiences in the night to give you a good appetite. Penny approached her breakfast in a more ladylike manner, cutting her fried bread up into neat little squares before popping them into her mouth one at a time. Everyone else watched us eat with a mixture of shock and awe. Wendy watched me pile up the meat on my fork, and actually shuddered.

"Animal!"

"More than one, if I'm any judge," I said cheerfully. "How is everyone feeling, this bright and glorious morning?"

"It's not natural to be so exuberant, this early in the morning," said Catherine.

"Oh, I quite agree," I said. "I'm not normally a morning person."

"This is true," said Penny. "Usually, all Ishmael can manage first thing is a cup of black coffee and the occasional grunt."

"But there's nothing like coming face to face with the creatures of the night, to make you feel full of life in the morning," I said happily.

"If he's going to be like this all day, I'm going back to bed," said Wendy.

"Oh hush dear, and eat your nice breakfast," said Catherine. "Think of all the fun things we have planned for today..."

Ellen was still refusing to engage with the whole breakfast scene. She sat stiffly in her chair with her arms defiantly folded, and scowled at her parents.

"I can't believe you did this to me! You know I'm a Vegan!"

"I thought that was last week," Marion said briskly. "You change your mind so often, dear. I can remember when you wouldn't eat anything but pizza, even though it did terrible things to your bowel movements."

"Mother!" said Ellen, caught between mortification and outrage.

"Try the fried bread," Arthur said encouragingly. "You can't get more Vegan than bread."

Ellen studied the burned slices suspiciously. "What were they fried in? Did it originally come from something that used to run around a field and make noises?"

"Well, not for long," said Arthur.

"And I don't see my herbal tea anywhere," said Ellen, just a bit dangerously.

"We've run out," said Marion. "You'll just have to slum it with coffee, like the rest of us."

"Caffeine is good for you," said Arthur. "It's practically a food group."

I had to wonder what Arthur had to be so cheerful about. Lucas Carr was still missing, seriously weird things were prowling around the Hall at night, and his business was still under threat. But the man's smile seemed genuine enough, particularly when his gaze met Marion's, and then she would manage a brief smile of her own. I shrugged internally, and concentrated on my breakfast. Out of the corner of my eye, I could see Wendy was still staring at me disapprovingly. I chewed cheerfully in her direction, and her scowl deepened.

"I don't think you're taking the situation seriously enough, Mr. Jones."

"I'm hungry," I said, in my most reasonable tone.

Penny cut in quickly, flashing Wendy her brightest smile.

"Did you and Catherine manage to get some sleep, after we left?"

"Eventually," said Wendy. "We sat up talking for quite a while."

"What about?" I said.

"Girl talk," said Wendy.

I looked to Catherine for confirmation, but she just nodded. She'd found a grilled tomato she liked, and had separated it from the rest of her breakfast so she could cut it up with surgical precision. Wendy glared at her own plate like a vampire faced with a stake smeared with garlic.

Arthur and Marion finally finished their serving duties, and sat down together at the end of the table. They made a point of shaking out the monogrammed serviettes that the rest of us had ignored, tucked them in place, and then set about their breakfasts as though determined to prove how good they were. I looked to Penny, because she was always so much better at breaking the conversational ice than me. She smiled determinedly around the table.

"The Hall seems so much more cheerful this morning. When I was lying in bed last night, I had trouble getting to sleep because of the wind howling around the Hall. It reminded me of how isolated we are, all the way out here. Such a spooky sound. . . . Like something trying to find a way in, so it could get at us."

"It was just the wind," Wendy said firmly.

I looked to Catherine, who was taking small cautious bites of her tomato, as though checking whether it really was what it appeared to be.

"Any old stories about the howling of the wind that comes to mind, Catherine?" I said. "A family banshee, perhaps?"

Wendy couldn't help herself. "Banshees are nothing to do with the wind. You're thinking of wendigos."

"I don't think I am," I said.

"My point," said Penny, "is that we are all alone out here. No one's going to turn up to help us. We have to sort this business out for ourselves, and that means working together."

She beamed encouragingly round the table, but no one had anything to say. They all kept their gazes fixed on their breakfast, whether they wanted it or not, so they wouldn't have to look at Penny or me.

"I do feel better, now it's daylight," said Catherine. Her voice and her hands were entirely steady. "The events of last night feel like they happened to someone else. Even though I know someone, or something, definitely did appear in my room."

"There was no intruder," Arthur said stubbornly. "It simply wasn't possible for anyone to have got into the house."

"I don't believe anybody did," said Catherine. "Whatever I saw, I think it was already here."

"Will you stop talking about ghosts as though they're real!" said Marion, glaring around the table, and then fixing her gaze on Catherine. "We only invited you here because Arthur was so sure you'd be able to help us. But so far, you haven't done a single thing to justify your presence."

"That's a bit harsh . . ." said Wendy, but Catherine cut her off with a gesture, and Wendy subsided, still bristling. Catherine nodded courteously to Marion.

"I'm sorry I haven't been able to contribute more," Catherine said calmly, apparently entirely unmoved by Marion's tone. "But there are things happening in the Hall that no one can help you with. This house knows all there is to know, about the darkest aspects of the human heart. The crimes and sins committed by the Glenbury family still linger in the Hall's rooms and corridors; never forgotten, and never forgiven."

The simple certainty in her voice held everyone's attention, but no one seemed to have anything to say in response.

"There must be something you can do," Arthur said finally.

"I am an historian," said Catherine. "So Wendy and I will take a turn around the Hall after breakfast, and see if we can dig up some fascinating facts you can use to lure in more visitors."

Wendy quickly cut in. "Proper historical evidence, to back up stories that have never been properly confirmed. Like... just how far into the Hall did Lord Ravensbrook get, before he vanished?"

No one around the table seemed particularly impressed.

"Does that really make a difference?" said Penny.

"The body was never found," said Catherine. "Working out exactly where Ravensbrook fell, or was pushed, should make a good starting place for a proper scientific search."

"The discovery of Lord Ravensbrook's body would be a major historical find," said Wendy. "Enough to put Glenbury Hall on the map. In a good way."

"Best of luck, trying to dig up something new," said Arthur. "I remember all sorts of people turning up at the Hall when I was a child, self-proclaimed experts in history, folklore, and all the alternative sciences. My parents would let them try their luck, if they seemed sufficiently amusing, or if they could pay. I used to watch from the sidelines as the ghost hunters and legend breakers went tramping round the Hall, probing the shadows with portable radar devices, bloodhounds on leashes, even dowsing rods.

"Not that it did them any of them any good. Interestingly... There were some areas in the Hall where the radar equipment simply wouldn't function, where the dogs would tuck their tails between their legs and back away, howling miserably, and where dowsing rods would snap in half in the dowser's hands. And they weren't even the same areas."

"You must all keep yourselves busy, as you see fit," Marion said briskly. "Arthur and I have a lot of cleaning up to be getting on with. There's never any end to the work that needs doing, to restore the Hall to its proper state."

Arthur smiled at Ellen. "Maybe you'd like to help us? Just for something to do."

She shook her head immediately. "I'm going to stay in my room."

"Of course you are," said Marion. "You're a teenager." She turned a cold gaze on me. "Can I ask what the two of you will you be doing on your second day of hanging around the Hall and not actually contributing anything?"

"I thought we'd take a bit of a stroll," I said easily. "See if we can spot something we might have missed yesterday. And then I thought we'd have a nice little chat with everyone, and see if that might give us something new to think about."

Wendy sniffed loudly.

"You do want us to find out what happened to Lucas Carr, don't you?" said Penny.

"Of course I do!" said Wendy. "He was my friend. Or at least, he might have been, if we'd ever got to meet in person. But I have this terrible feeling he's become just another of the Hall's mysteries. Another question with no answer. Catherine and I have a better chance of finding Lord Ravensbrook, than you two have of finding Lucas Carr."

"It sounds like you're coming round to my way of thinking," Catherine said amusedly. "That there are powers at work in this house beyond mortal understanding."

Wendy let loose with one of her sudden barks of laughter. "I don't think I'd go that far."

"If you want answers," I said, "you have to ask the right questions."

"But what if no one knows anything?" said Catherine.

"Someone always knows something," I said. "Even if they don't know that they know it."

Wendy scowled at me. "It is far too early in the morning for sentences like that."

"But we really don't know anything about what's going on," said Arthur.

I fixed him with a thoughtful gaze, and he shifted uncomfortably in his chair.

"You must have some opinion as to what happened to Lucas Carr?" I said easily.

"Nothing you'd find helpful," he said.

"Try me."

"The Hall took him," said Arthur.

"Nonsense!" Marion said immediately. "There is nothing at all to suggest that Mr. Carr was snatched away by the fairies, or abducted by some unknown force. . . . It's far more likely he chose to slip away, for reasons of his own. Or that someone took him, for reasons of their own. Those are the only options that make sense, and neither of them has anything to do with us." She fixed me with her hardest stare. "You are here to get to the truth about what happened, aren't you?"

"Are you sure that's what you want?" I said.

Marion seemed a little taken aback at being challenged so bluntly, and it took her a moment to recover.

"Of course!" she said finally. "Why wouldn't I? Arthur and I need to know what happened, if we're to put all of this behind us and open up for business again."

"We'll get you the truth," I said. "Every last bit of it. Whether you want to hear it or not."

Arthur smiled bravely. "The truth shall set you free."

"That has not always been my experience," I said.

"Marion and I have been talking about this," Arthur said carefully. "And it seems to us that we might be able to turn this situation to our advantage. Whether you find Mr. Carr or not, we can always spin the story of his disappearance into a real money-maker."

Ellen's head came up sharply. "That's a bit cold, isn't it, Dad?"

"It's just business, dear," said Marion. "History is all very well when it comes to attracting visitors, but there's nothing like a new urban legend to pull in the punters. Well, not exactly urban, but you know what I mean."

"I thought you didn't believe in the weird stuff?" I said.

"You don't have to believe in something to turn a profit from it," said Marion. "Old-timey ghost stories are one thing; an urban legend in the making, that's something else. People eat that stuff up with spoons, these days. And they will pay good money for a chance to get in on the ground floor." She smiled at her daughter, who was looking at her with something like shock. "Oh come on, Ellen; you spend enough time checking out those weird sites on your laptop to know what I'm talking about."

"Don't you care what happened to Mr. Carr?" said Ellen.

"Well, of course we care, darling," said Arthur. "But we have to be practical about this."

"Every inch a Glenbury . . ." said Wendy. "Always ready to make money out of someone else's suffering."

Arthur looked cut to the quick. He tried to say something, but the words wouldn't come. Marion jumped in quickly.

"I never even met Mr. Carr, so pardon me if his going missing doesn't exactly break my heart. And you only knew him from a distance, Ms. Goldsmith, so spare me the moral outrage. If Carr can be found, all well and good. If he reappears with an interesting story to justify his absence, even better. But if he insists on not being found, then it's up to me, and Arthur, to make the best of it."

"The family must come first," Arthur said to Ellen. And then he grinned suddenly. "You know what they say: if your horse throws you . . . shoot the ungrateful beast in the head and get yourself a better mount."

"Dad!" said Ellen, caught between outrage and laughter.

"It's not like we're talking about a real horse," Arthur said easily. "No actual horses were harmed in the making of this metaphor."

"Do you think Lucas Carr is dead?" I said bluntly.

"Don't you?" said Arthur, lobbing the ball back into my court.

"It's a possibility," I said.

"Then where's the body?" said Marion, with the air of someone slapping down a trump. "If it was still somewhere in the Hall, I think someone would have tripped over the damned thing by now."

"A great many people have gone missing, in and around Glenbury Hall," said Catherine. "None of the bodies have ever been found."

"But they didn't have me looking for them," I said.

"And what makes you so special, Mr. Jones?" said Wendy.

"Ah," I said. "That would be telling."

"In the old days," said Catherine, "people in the surrounding towns used to believe the Glenburys kept a demon from Hell imprisoned in a cellar under the Hall. Something that had to be kept fed."

"There are no cellars under Glenbury Hall," Marion said crushingly. "We checked. Isn't that right, Arthur?"

He nodded amiably. "For whatever reason, the original Glenburys decided they didn't want to dig down into the ground. Possibly something to do with the old shrine, and the well. I've seen the original plans for the Hall, and it was never intended that there should be any cellars. Even the family wine cellar is just a separate room at the back of the ground floor. However . . ." He paused, and looked around the table, as though wondering whether he could trust us with a family secret. "For a while, it was believed that there were rooms in the Hall which only certain members of the

Glenbury family could be allowed to know about. Because something was kept locked up in them, that the world could never be allowed to know about."

"Are you talking about what happened in the nineteen twenties?" said Catherine. "That was just a story, wasn't it?"

"What story is this?" said Wendy, frowning.

"Supposedly, back then a group of Bright Young Things were partying at the Hall," said Arthur, "and someone raised the notion of these hidden rooms. The head of the family was away, so someone got the idea to send everyone round the Hall, and have them hang a towel out of every window. After this was done, they all went outside, and saw immediately that there were two windows with no towels. At which point the head of the family returned, lost his temper big time, and kicked all the Bright Young Things out. And that was that."

Ellen sat forward in her chair, fascinated. "Is this something that actually happened?"

Arthur smiled at her. "So they say. But people say a lot of things about Glenbury Hall."

"Is there any reason to believe that these hidden rooms actually exist?" said Penny.

"Because Lucas Carr might be in one of them?" said Arthur. He shook his head firmly. "I have been all over this house, and never once found a door I couldn't open or a room I couldn't enter. Just like I never found a hidden door or a sliding panel."

"But did you ever try hanging towels out of all the windows?" said Ellen.

Arthur shook his head solemnly. "And ruin a perfectly good legend? Sometimes a good story . . . is just a good story."

"Of course," said Catherine. "There are lots of stories about the Glenburys, none of them to their credit." She thought for a moment, before continuing. "The Hall is supposed to be packed full of ghosts because it's the scene of so many deaths and disappearances. Glenburys who never got to leave the Hall; victims who never got to go home. So many lost voices in the night. Lucas may have become just the latest in a long line of spirits trapped in this house. I've been wondering whether the figure I saw in my room might actually have been Lucas' spirit, come back to tell me what happened to him. And I didn't listen."

"You were upset," said Wendy. "You can't be sure about anything you saw."

"I saw something," said Catherine.

"Last night," Penny said carefully, "you seemed very certain that this figure meant you harm."

"I was frightened," said Catherine. "Too confused to understand what was really going on. I'd hate to think I let Lucas down..."

"Why would he come back to visit you?" said Arthur.

"Because I'm the one who believes in ghosts," said Catherine.

"This faith in spirits and spectral visitors is all very sweet," said Wendy, "but you can't let your beliefs get in the way of common sense."

"If Lucas wants to talk to me, I have a duty to listen," said Catherine.

"What if it all happened so quickly, he doesn't know who's responsible?" said Arthur. "Maybe he came back to find out what happened."

"Oh please," said Marion. "Don't encourage her."

"So you think Lucas definitely is dead, Catherine?" I said. "Not just missing?"

"Stories don't tend to have happy endings, in Glenbury Hall," said Catherine.

"Stop it!" said Ellen.

She brought both hands slamming down on the table, with such force that the crockery jumped. We all turned to look at her. Ellen glared around the table, furious that we were taking seriously things she didn't want to have to think about.

"This whole business is just creepy!" she said loudly. "Arguing over whether a man is dead or not, and how to make money out of him. It's disgusting, and I don't want anything to do with it. I wish we'd never come to this horrible place." She glared from her mother to her father and back again. "If you won't send me back to London, I'll go on my own."

"You're not old enough to make that decision," said Marion.

"Try me," said Ellen. "I can walk out the door and down the road, and just start hitching. Someone will give me a lift, and then all I have to do is keep going until I get back to London. I have friends who'll put me up. What will you do then; drag me back here in chains?"

"I would never do anything like that!"

We all turned to look at Arthur. He was staring at his daughter with something like horror, and I think everyone was surprised by the vehemence in his voice. Father and daughter stared at each other, and Arthur was the one who looked away first. Ellen smiled triumphantly, and it suddenly occurred to me to wonder whether Ellen could be the one behind everything that was happening. Could she have been trying to sabotage the family business all along, so her parents would have no choice but to go back to London? So Ellen could have her old life back, and all her old friends. She was supposed to be in her room most of the time. . . . But if no one ever saw her, she could have been anywhere. Doing anything. How far would Ellen go, to get what she wanted?

Wendy cleared her throat loudly, and when we turned to look at her, she smiled determinedly at Catherine.

"I think we should concentrate on problems we have a real chance of solving. Like discovering what happened to the missing Lord Ravensbrook. It's time we started our search, Cath."

Catherine nodded quickly, happy for a chance to talk about something else.

"I say we start at the lobby, and work our way out." She looked apologetically at me and Penny. "I should have done that with you yesterday, instead of just reeling off ghost stories and legends. I didn't tell you a single useful thing, did I?"

"They were very interesting stories," Penny said tactfully.

"But did they have anything to do with the history that shaped this house?" said Wendy.

"You can't separate the Hall's ghosts from its history," said Catherine. "Here, ghosts are history."

"You are never going to get me to believe any of that nonsense," said Wendy.

Catherine smiled at her sadly. "Unfortunately, the Hall doesn't care what you believe."

"You need to immerse yourself in some hard facts and figures, Cath," Wendy said sternly. "Get some solid history under your belt. There's nothing like facts, to help you deal with fancies."

"How will any of that help us find Lucas?" I said.

"Understanding the Hall and its history is vital, if you want to get to grips with what's really going on here," said Wendy.

"And you think you've got it all worked out?" Penny said politely.

Wendy sat back in her chair, and smiled smugly. "I've been

giving the matter a lot of thought, and I don't think the situation is nearly as complicated as some people would like us to believe. Give Cath and me some time to go exploring, and I think we might dig up some very useful answers to questions no one else has thought to ask."

"What if you don't?" said Arthur.

"Then all we need to do is wait for tonight," said Catherine, "and see if Lucas turns up in my room again. If he does, I can ask him how he died."

Arthur looked at Wendy. "Lucas was supposed to be your friend. Perhaps he'll turn up in your room."

Wendy stared at him, lost for words.

"Lucas wouldn't go to Wendy," said Catherine. "She doesn't believe in ghosts."

"I would like to see Lucas," Wendy said quietly. "Alive and well, with a good story to tell. I still believe that's possible. I have to believe that's possible."

"Much more likely, than believing this house is haunted," said Marion.

"The Hall is haunted by history," said Catherine.

"Oh please," said Wendy.

"The past is always with you, at Glenbury Hall," said Arthur. "It never lets go of you."

"Good," said Marion. "Then we can sell it to the punters, at so much a head." She smiled determinedly down the table. "Would anyone care for some more breakfast?"

Wendy and Catherine quickly pushed back their seats and rose to their feet, abandoning their plates even though there was still quite a lot of food left on them. Ellen drained her coffee, slammed the cup down, and got to her feet. I looked at Penny, and we stood up too. Marion didn't even try to hide her annoyance.

"After all the trouble we went to, Arthur," she said loudly, "to make sure everyone started the day with a proper breakfast."

Arthur smiled. "To be fair, dear, I was the one who actually cooked everything. You just supervised, and made suggestions. You never did have much of a flair for the culinary arts."

Ellen smiled suddenly. "You could burn water, Mother."

"Then maybe you should help us prepare the midday meal," said Marion.

"I'm going back to my room," Ellen said immediately.

"Not until you've helped with the washing up, you're not," said Marion.

Ellen looked at the door, clearly trying to decide whether to make a run for it. And then she glanced at her mother, and saw just as clearly that Marion was quite prepared to chase after her and rugby tackle her to the floor. Ellen's shoulders slumped, and her face went into full pout mode.

"Oh all right. If I must."

She slouched to her feet and reluctantly started helping Arthur and Marion clear plates from the table, while Catherine and Wendy made their way out of the dining hall, chatting happily together.

"I refuse to have my faith in the nature of reality shaken, just because a few things are happening that I don't completely understand," Wendy said loudly. "I think I have a very good idea as to what's really going on here. All I need is a few pieces of solid evidence to back me up. I am going to get to the bottom of this, and nothing is going to stop me!"

"Good for you, dear," said Catherine. "When you find out, be sure to let me know. I'd hate to think I missed it."

They swept out the door, still talking. I looked at Arthur and Marion and Ellen, who looked at each other and made an obvious agreement not to say anything while Penny and I were still in the room. Interestingly, the mood in the room seemed to have lightened, now the group had broken up. I shrugged, nodded to Penny, and we left the dining hall.

By the time we got to the lobby, there was no sign of Wendy and Catherine. They'd already taken themselves off somewhere else. It was all very quiet, and very calm. Bright sunlight spilled in through the lozenged windows, with dust motes swirling in the golden beams.

"Do we have to search the ground floor again?" said Penny. "We've seen all there is to see, and most of it wasn't worth seeing."

"There have to be lots of places we haven't properly examined yet," I said, gesturing grandly at the doors stretching away before us. "Think of the possibilities!"

"I think the people here have more to offer us than a bunch of empty rooms," said Penny.

I nodded. "All right; let's question everyone. And get them to tell us all the things they don't want to tell us."

"Who should we start with?" said Penny.

"I think Ellen is our best bet."

"You see her as the weakest link?"

"Maybe," I said. "But mostly, I want to hear about the strange things she's been seeing on her laptop."

"Because it could be connected to what Arthur's father saw on his television set?" said Penny.

"Be a hell of a coincidence if it wasn't," I said.

"Let us not forget that Ellen is an isolated and frightened teenage girl," Penny said sternly. "You'd better leave most of the talking to me."

"My plan exactly," I said.

"Of course, first we have to separate Ellen from her very protective parents."

I had to smile. "I will bet you that she's already given them the slip, and disappeared back to her room."

Penny laughed. "No bet."

Back in the dining hall, Arthur and Marion were still busy scraping unwanted food off plates and into a bucket. There was no sign of Ellen anywhere. When I asked where she was, Marion just shook her head.

"Oh, she's gone. Vanished the moment I took my eyes off her."

"She always was strong willed," said Arthur. "I wonder which of us she got that from? But she's never been happy about all this supernatural stuff. She probably just feels safer in her room."

"That girl is more frightened of hard work than she ever was of ghosts," said Marion.

"Do you mind if we ask her a few questions?" said Penny.

"You go right ahead," said Marion. "See if you can get a straight answer out of her. That would be one more than I ever managed."

"She's at an awkward age," said Arthur.

"Ellen has always been at an awkward age," said Marion.

Arthur surprised me then, by fixing me with a hard unwavering stare. "I don't want Ellen upset. If you're going to talk to her, I want her treated with respect."

"Of course," I said. "That's what we do."

Penny and I went upstairs, and I knocked politely on Ellen's door. There was no response, so I said her name loudly. She replied immediately, her voice coming clearly through the door, as though she was standing right on the other side of it.

"Yes? Who is it?"

"Ishmael and Penny," I said. "We just want to talk to you about a few things."

"We did clear it with your parents," said Penny.

"Go away," said Ellen. "I don't want to talk to anyone."

"We're not anyone," I said. "We're security experts. And I'm afraid we do need to talk to you."

"I don't care. I'm not unlocking my door."

"I have a passkey," I said.

There was a pause. "You wouldn't dare!"

"Try me."

There was another pause.

"Bully," said Ellen. "All right. Come on in, if you're going to."

It didn't take me long to realise she had no intention of unlocking the door herself, just to make a point, so I unlocked the door and we went in. Ellen was sitting at a work desk, with her closed laptop before her. Suggesting she had just been looking at something she didn't want us to know about. Though given that she was a teenage girl, that could cover an awful lot of ground.

Ellen scowled at Penny and me impartially. "What do you want? I'm busy."

"Really?" I said politely. "Doing what?"

Ellen glanced at her laptop, and then scowled at us again. "Homework."

"What subject?" said Penny. "Maybe we can help."

Ellen just shrugged.

"We need to ask you about the strange things you've been seeing on your laptop," I said.

Ellen smiled broadly and actually relaxed a little. "Really? That's why you're here? I made all of that up, to put pressure on my parents to get us out of this awful place! I thought since everyone else was making such a fuss about ghosts, I might as well join in."

I sighed, internally. Ellen suddenly stopped smiling.

"You won't tell my parents, will you? I mean, I'll only deny it all anyway."

"Just answer a few questions, and we'll pretend this little chat never happened," I said.

"Deal," said Ellen. "What questions?"

"You really should have asked that first," said Penny.

"Rats," said Ellen. "Oh hell, get on with it."

"You were here when Lucas Carr came up the stairs and went to his room," I said. "Are you sure you didn't hear anything?"

"I had my headphones on," said Ellen. "Listening to my music. I like it loud."

Her answer had a certain rehearsed quality, as though she'd been coached in what to say by her parents.

"So..." I said. "You didn't see anything weird on your laptop. Have you seen anything unusual in the Hall?"

Ellen shook her head firmly. "No. And I don't believe anyone else has either. It's all jumping at shadows, and people seeing what they expect to see."

"You said this house was creepy," said Penny.

"Well it is! There's been all kinds of gruesome murders here! I've been on all the sites..."

For a moment enthusiasm drove the sullenness away, but then Ellen realised she was being cooperative and shut down again, sinking back into her default scowl and sulk.

"Why didn't you want to come out of your room last night?" I said. "If you don't believe there are any ghosts in Glenbury Hall, what was there to be frightened of?"

Ellen folded her arms stubbornly, in a gesture she'd probably picked up from her mother. "Because none of this is anything to do with me, and I am not going to get involved."

She gave me her best cold stare, and then switched it to Penny, defying either of us to get anything else out of her. Even if she did know something, she wouldn't tell us. Because we were adults and therefore the enemy. I nodded to Ellen.

"Have fun with your homework."

We'd only just shut Ellen's door behind us when I heard a key turn in the lock. I gave Penny a look, and we moved off down the corridor a way before we said anything, just in case Ellen was still standing and listening on the other side of her door.

"Can we be sure that she made up all that stuff about the laptop?" said Penny. "She sounded very convincing at the time."

"I think Ellen would say anything that she thought might get her out of here," I said. "Remember; she only volunteered her story after she'd heard about the television."

I set off down the corridor, and Penny strolled easily along beside me. It all looked very open and harmless in the bright morning sunshine, and the few shadows huddled in the corners and kept to themselves. After a while, Penny shot me a thoughtful look.

"Are we headed anywhere in particular, Ishmael?"

"I thought we'd take a close look at the spot where I saw the crawling figure," I said. "Are you sure you didn't see anything?"

"It was very dark," Penny said apologetically. "And I don't have your eyes. By the time I'd turned on the lights—"

"It had disappeared into the wall," I said.

"Like Catherine's visitor," said Penny.

"The similarity had not escaped me."

"What exactly did your figure look like?" said Penny.

"It was down on its hands and knees," I said slowly. "And

it moved like it was crippled, or in great pain. It kept its head well down, so I couldn't get a look at its face."

"Did it strike you as dangerous?" said Penny.

"More . . . disturbing," I said.

"And you think it might have been one of the Hall's ghosts?"

"I don't know," I said. "I would have sworn it was completely real and solid; right up to the point where it suddenly vanished."

"What would a ghost be doing, on its hands and knees?" said Penny.

"I don't know," I said. "Looking for a contact lens?"

"That makes about as much sense as anything else around here," said Penny.

We finally reached the spot where I saw the crawling figure lurch into a shadow by the wall, and disappear in a moment. I knelt down and looked the wall over carefully, and then tapped on the wooden panelling, listening for any indication of a hollow space. The wall gave every indication of being completely solid.

"According to Arthur, he banged on walls all over this house when he was a child," said Penny. "And never found a thing."

"I don't think we should necessarily trust everything Arthur comes out with," I said, pressing an ear against the wood to hear better.

"What reason would he have to lie?"

"If we knew that, we'd know a lot more than we do now." I sat back, and looked thoughtfully at the wall.

"Don't we need a reason, to assume someone is lying?" said Penny.

"Not in this house," I said. "And not with this case. I'm starting to wonder whether something in the Hall is messing with people's heads. Making them see and hear things that aren't necessarily there."

"Does that include me?" said Penny.

"I'm afraid so."

"But not you?"

"No."

"Even though you saw the crawling thing?"

"Yes."

"Because you're ... different?"

"Possibly."

"Okay ..." said Penny. "This is a new level of paranoia, Ishmael, even for you."

"Paranoids are just people who are paying attention," I said.

I banged on the wall as hard as I could, but still couldn't detect even a hint of a space behind it. I ran my hands over the delicate wooden scrollwork, searching for hidden levers and secret triggers, anything that might open a concealed door. But despite all my efforts I couldn't persuade anything to move, so I got to my feet and kicked moodily at the wall.

"If there had been a sliding panel here," I said, "I'd have had a simple and straightforward explanation as to how the crawling figure could have disappeared."

"But there isn't," said Penny. "So you don't."

"They did build secret rooms well, back in the day," I said. "Because it could mean death for the whole family if they were found harbouring a priest. I am seriously tempted to tear this whole wall apart."

"I don't think Arthur and Marion would take kindly to that," said Penny.

"Let's go talk to them some more."

We made our way back along the corridor, and down the stairs. No matter how carefully I walked, the sound of my feet on the bare steps still boomed out like thunder. Penny shot me a meaningful look.

"Yes, I know," I said. "But...when you get right down to it, Arthur's testimony is still all we have to tell us what happened to Lucas after he arrived."

"But Arthur doesn't have any reason to lie," Penny said patiently. "And Marion did back him up. She swore Lucas wasn't in his room, and that he hadn't gone to the rear of the Hall when she was there. They'd have to be in this together, and I can't help feeling Marion would have insisted on a more convincing story. Sometimes she seems actually embarrassed, that the story she's having to tell makes no sense. And she hasn't wavered one bit in her refusal to believe any of the ghostly stories attached to Glenbury Hall. Even after everything that happened last night."

I stopped suddenly, as we reached the foot of the stairs.

"You've just realised something," said Penny. "What?"

"Something struck me as odd, last night," I said. "When Arthur stepped out of the bathroom."

"Was it his pyjamas?" said Penny. "They were seriously ugly."

"No," I said. "It wasn't something I saw...it was something I've only just realised I didn't hear. There was no sound of the toilet flushing when Arthur opened the bathroom door."

"Maybe he did that before he came out..."

"No," I said. "I would have heard."

Penny looked at me. "Really? Through a closed door?"

"You'd be amazed at some of the things I have to pretend I don't hear."

"Oh ick," said Penny. "Well...Maybe he was in a hurry, to get out into the corridor and find out what was going on?"

"But then I would have smelled the urine in the bowl..."

"Not listening!" Penny said loudly. "Fingers in ears not listening!"

"I can hear Arthur and Marion arguing," I said. "Shall we go and eavesdrop?"

"Let's do that," said Penny. "I could use something else to think about."

I followed the voices to a kitchen at the rear of the Hall, and then gestured for Penny to stop. Arthur's and Marion's voices came clearly to us through the half-open door.

"I think we've cooperated more than enough with those security people," said Arthur. "Neither of them is listening to what we're telling them."

"We have to tell them something," said Marion.

"No, we don't," said Arthur. "Whatever we say, they'll find some way to turn it against us. They don't give a damn about our problems. They just want someone they can blame, so they can put it in their report and claim their job is over. And we have to be the most obvious suspects."

"Why would they want to accuse us?" said Marion.

"Because I was the last person to see Lucas Carr alive," said Arthur. "Because you didn't seem upset enough over his disappearance. And because they probably don't get paid unless they can point the finger at someone."

"But if we don't cooperate," said Marion, "this whole mess will just drag on and on! We need them to sign off on some kind of solution, so we can put this nonsense behind us and get our guests back. You know there's no way in hell the bank will agree to a further extension on our loans!"

"I hadn't forgotten," said Arthur.

There was a long pause before Marion spoke again, in a voice that didn't do a very good job of trying to sound casual.

"So this Wendy person turning up here was a complete surprise to you?"

"Of course it was," Arthur said wearily. "I didn't even recognise the woman! She had to remind me we'd even worked together."

"It's just that it does seem very suspicious, her arriving at the Hall even though you'd phoned and told her not to come."

"Yes," said Arthur. "It does seem very suspicious."

I could almost hear Marion's ears pricking up. "You think she might have something to do with Carr going missing?"

"She knew him from the Society," said Arthur. "Which makes her the only person here who had any kind of history with Carr. Wait a minute . . . Did you just hear something, out in the passage?"

Penny and I breezed into the kitchen as though we'd just happened to be going that way. The fittings turned out to be surprisingly modern, with white-tiled walls and gleaming appliances. Arthur was bent over a large metal sink with his sleeves rolled up, working his way through the washing up, while Marion stood back and watched him do it. A cigarette drooped from one corner of her mouth, and she quickly removed it.

"I'm allowed one a day! For my nerves. In moments of crisis."

"She is cutting down," said Arthur, turning away from the sink and wiping his hands on a stripey tea towel. "She's doing very well. Or at least she was, until all this happened."

"It's a stress thing," said Marion.

She stubbed the cigarette out on the steel draining board, to prove she didn't really need it, and then didn't seem to know what to do with her hands. She folded her arms and stared coldly at me and Penny.

"Well? What do you want? We're busy."

"Just wanted to say sorry about that business in the corridor last night," I said easily.

Marion sniffed loudly. "I couldn't help noticing that everything calmed down, the moment you were back in your room."

"Did you really see someone?" said Arthur.

"I saw something," I said.

"I often saw strange figures creeping up and down that corridor, back when I was a child," said Arthur. "Of course, that was usually just my parents' friends, bed-hopping. But even after all of that stopped, I still heard movements in the early hours, when no one was supposed to be about."

"Did you ever take a look, to see who it was?" I said.

He shook his head quickly. "I never left my bedroom, once it got dark."

"Weren't you curious?" said Penny.

"I was more afraid I might catch something's attention," Arthur said quietly. "If this Hall teaches you anything, it's to keep your head down and not be noticed."

Marion saw he was getting upset, and moved protectively closer to him.

"Have you finished talking to Ellen?" she said, quickly changing the subject.

"We had a few words," I said. "She does seem very determined to get back to London."

"She misses her friends," said Arthur. "I knew the move was going to be hard on her, but then, it was hard on all of us."

"She understands," said Marion. "Deep down. Where it counts."

"I never wanted to bring her here," said Arthur. "I know better than anyone that the Hall is no place for the young. But there wasn't anywhere else we could send her. The rest of my family is dead, and Marion's family never approved of our marriage."

"Hell with them," said Marion.

She shared a smile with Arthur, and then looked longingly at the cigarette she'd stubbed out on the sink. Arthur quietly moved to block her view, and Marion fixed Penny and me with a cold glare.

"Ellen will settle down fast enough, once this nonsense is over. I'm sure I can get her interested in helping out with the business, until it's time for her to go off to university."

"Even though she doesn't like hard work?" I said.

Marion smiled briefly. "This is a working family. We all do what we have to."

"You said earlier, that you thought you could use the mystery of Lucas' disappearance to bring in more guests," said Penny.

Marion shrugged. "Life hands you lemons; make lemonade. And then charge extra for the straw."

"So you could say, you had a vested interest in Lucas going missing," I said.

Arthur looked like he couldn't believe what he was hearing. "You can't honestly believe we'd kill a man, just to help our business!"

"Of course not. But you might make a deal with him," I said. "Have him pretend to disappear, just long enough to build up a mystery. And then Lucas could reappear later, with a convincing explanation, and you would have a story you could use to boost your business."

"I never met the man, before he appeared in reception," Arthur said flatly.

"But you were in contact with him," I said.

"Only a few e-mails," said Arthur. "When he booked in for the weekend. I never even spoke to him on the phone."

"And I would never have gone along with any such scheme," Marion said flatly. She was so close to Arthur now she was practically in his pocket. "Partly because it's a stupid idea, but mostly because we would have been bound to get found out, and then we'd be a laughingstock. All we have to sell is the Hall's history, and our reputation."

I kept my gaze fixed on Arthur. Because even though I'd openly accused him of crime and conspiracy, he didn't seem the least bit bothered.

"All right," I said. "We'll leave that, for the time being. Arthur, did Lucas say anything to you when he was booking in, that might help explain why he went missing?"

Arthur made a point of thinking about it. "I remember he wasn't much of a one for pleasantries, or small talk. Didn't get half a dozen words out of him, until I saw he was interested in the lobby display, and raised the subject of Lord Ravensbrook's disappearance. After that he wouldn't shut up. He kept going on and on about how important his presentation was going to be. He seemed to think it would cause quite a stir in the Historical Society."

"Did he say what his paper was about?" said Penny.

"No," said Arthur. "Only that it concerned Lord Ravensbrook. I got the feeling he didn't want to give me any details in case I said something to the other guests, and spoiled his surprise. Like I gave a damn..."

He stopped abruptly. "I'm sorry. I don't mean to sound uncaring. I am really worried, that he hasn't turned up yet. But the man seems to have gone out of his way to ruin my life, and my family's. If he does show up again, or you discover where he's been hiding himself all this time, he had better have a damned good reason for everything he's put us through."

Penny looked at Marion. "What do you think happened to Lucas Carr?"

"I think he arranged all of this himself," she said flatly. "He must have worked it all out in advance, to be able to pull off this vanishing act so smoothly. Maybe he needed to escape from his old life, and chose to do it here because he knew the Hall's reputation would make for the perfect cover. You go back to his company and check out his background, and I will bet you'll find he had good reason to disappear. Before he was found out."

Arthur smiled at her proudly. "You've been thinking about this."

Marion smiled back at him. "One of us had to."

"It's an interesting idea," I said. "Now, if you'll excuse us, Penny and I need to talk to Catherine and Wendy."

"You think they know something?" said Arthur.

"Wendy seemed to believe she'd worked something out," I said.

"Too clever for her own good, that one," said Marion.

Arthur sighed. "Don't start, Marion. Please."

"I'm just saying, I'll be glad when she's out of here."

Penny and I headed for the door. I waited till we were almost there, and then I stopped and looked back at Arthur and Marion.

"Just one more thing," I said. "Penny and I are going to need access to the Hall's roof at some point."

"The roof?" said Marion. "Why would you want to go up there?"

"I'm still trying to figure out how anyone could have got into Catherine's room last night," I said. "There was no ladder propped against the wall outside her window, but someone could have climbed down from the roof."

"There wasn't anyone in her room!" said Marion. "She just had a bad dream!"

"You really think a dream would affect someone that badly?" said Penny.

"Nightmares can walk around on their own, in Glenbury Hall," said Arthur.

Marion didn't even look at him. She was on a roll.

"How could anyone even get down from the roof, without being noticed?" she said sharply. "Swoop down out of the night, on a hang-glider?"

"I would like to see that," said Arthur.

"Is there a way to get to the roof, from the top-floor?" I said patiently.

"There must have been some way to get up there, in the past," said Arthur, "but I've no idea what it might have been. I suppose you could always climb out of a top-floor window, clamber up the wall and over the guttering, and then haul yourself up the rest of the way, but I wouldn't like to try it. It's a long drop, down to the grounds."

"And we can't give you permission to try anything like that," Maureen said quickly. "Our insurance would never cover it."

"You could always say you didn't know we were going to do it, until it was too late," I said.

Marion smiled at me coldly. "I don't suppose you'd sign a letter saying that?"

"Sorry," I said. "Security."

"If you do decide to climb up there, be careful," said Arthur. "No one's carried out any repairs on that roof for ages. You could plunge right through parts of it. You wouldn't believe the problems we have with leaks, when it rains."

"Oh, I think I would," I said.

We left the kitchen. Arthur and Marion barely waited for me to close the door behind us, before they started arguing again, over what they should and shouldn't have said in front of strangers. It didn't sound particularly interesting, so we left them to it and strolled off through the ground floor.

"Why are you so keen to get to the roof?" said Penny.

"Because it's the one place in the Hall we haven't checked," I said. "And it seems to me that it would make a great place to hide out, and watch over the rest of us. If there is a secret way up and down, it could explain a lot."

Penny nodded. "So; Catherine and Wendy...Do you want to split them up, so we can question them separately?"

"I'm not sure we could," I said. "Wendy has become very protective, where Catherine is concerned."

"There's something going on there," said Penny. "Do you suppose Wendy fancies Catherine?"

"Wendy said she came here because she used to be close to Arthur," I said.

"But like you said, that could just be a cover," said Penny. "Any idea where we should start looking for them?"

I pointed to a narrow passageway. "They're down that way."

"You and your ears," said Penny. "Can you hear what they're talking about?"

"They're arguing over a painting," I said. "Rather heatedly."

"Historians," said Penny. "Who knew there'd be so much to argue about, over things that have already happened."

We ended up in a side room that looked like it might have been a parlour, long ago. It was a fair size, with bulky furniture lurking under dust sheets that clearly hadn't been disturbed in some time. Catherine and Wendy were standing in front of a painting hanging over a disused fireplace, a large if faded portrait of a harsh-faced individual in an outfit similar to the one on the dummy in the lobby display.

Catherine and Wendy's argument seemed to have descended into *Yes it is/No it isn't*, with neither woman prepared to give an inch. They were glaring right into each other's faces, and didn't so much as glance round when Penny and I entered the room. In the end, I had to clear my throat loudly to let them know we were there. They quickly took a step back from each other, and pulled their dignity about them. They seemed more angry at being interrupted, than over being caught arguing so fiercely. Wendy hit Penny and me with her best challenging stare.

"Yes?"

"What's all this fuss about?" said Penny.

"No fuss, dear," Catherine said quickly. "Just a friendly dispute between scholars. I maintain that this is a portrait of Alexander Glenbury, head of the family when Lord Ravensbrook paid his unfortunate visit to the Hall."

"The one who was supposed to be Ravensbrook's illegitimate son?" I said.

"Exactly," said Catherine. "Though of course, there was never a shred of evidence, just reported gossip from the period."

"But this can't be Alexander!" said Wendy, unable to stay quiet any longer. "Look at the style of the painting; it's all wrong! This has to date from at least a generation later!"

"Couldn't you just ask Arthur?" said Penny. "It's his family."

"Arthur decided long ago that he wasn't interested in his family history," said Catherine. "And after everything his parents put him through, you can't blame the poor lamb."

"Paul and Mary Glenbury," I said. "Your very close friends."

"They were fun people to be around," Catherine said stiffly. "Just not very good when it came to raising a child."

"There are things about Arthur's parents that you're not telling us," I said.

"There are lots of things I'm not telling you about that

period of my life," said Catherine. "Because they're none of your business."

"Exactly!" said Wendy, moving protectively closer to Catherine. "You stand up for your rights, dear. They don't have the authority to interrogate you like this!"

"We have to ask questions to get answers," I said.

Wendy just kept up her intimidating glare. "What do you want with us, Jones?"

"Please," I said. "Call me Ishmael."

"I'd rather die," said Wendy.

"Perhaps you'd rather answer questions separately," said Penny.

"You just want to get Cath on your own so you can bully her into talking about things she doesn't want to talk about!" said Wendy.

"We don't do that," said Penny.

"Oh please," said Wendy. "I know how *Good cop/Bad cop* works. I watch television."

"I can speak for myself, dear," Catherine said firmly. "I don't need my hand held."

Wendy looked a little hurt.

"Do you need your hand held, Wendy?" I said.

She looked astonished at the very idea, and fixed me with a contemptuous stare.

"Of course not."

"You said earlier that you came here to offer help and support to Arthur," I said. "But since you arrived you've hardly spent any time with him."

Wendy sniffed. "Because his wife won't let me anywhere near him. You must have noticed. And right now, I think Catherine needs my help more."

"I'm not made out of porcelain, dear," said Catherine.

"This house has a way of finding people's weak spots, and

then taking advantage of them," said Wendy. "You must have felt that."

"Of course," said Catherine. "But I've recovered now, from what happened last night. I was just caught by surprise, that's all. I've been telling ghost stories about Glenbury Hall for so long I'd started taking them for granted."

"Do you still want to see a ghost?" said Penny.

"Oh yes," said Catherine. "More than ever."

"Good for you, girl," said Wendy.

"I thought you didn't believe in ghosts?" said Penny.

"I don't," said Wendy. "I just like to see people standing up for what they believe in."

"What do you think Catherine saw last night?" I said.

"A stone tape recording," said Wendy. "That's when an extreme circumstance in the past imprints itself on its surroundings, and then plays itself back in the present."

I looked at her, and she bristled defensively.

"That's science," said Wendy. "Not superstition."

"Let's talk about Lucas Carr," I said.

"Must we?" said Wendy.

"That is why we're here," said Penny.

"I wonder if he will appear in my room tonight," said Catherine. "If that was his ghost I saw . . ."

"Let's stick to the facts," I said. "Wendy: what kind of person was Lucas?"

"I already told you," said Wendy. "My only contact with the man was through the Society's web site. He was always very chatty, in his posts. Very friendly and engaging . . . And extremely enthusiastic when it came to discussing the history of Glenbury Hall. He could be quite insightful, when discussing other people's theories. And often very helpful. He would go out of his way to support other members, recommending useful sources, and where to look for them."

"Was he popular, with the rest of the Society?" said Penny.

"Mostly," said Wendy. "He had his particular hobby-horses, that he didn't like to be challenged on."

"Such as?" I said.

"Matters of historical detail," said Wendy. "Nothing that would mean anything to you. The trouble with history is that only so much of it is based on proper contemporary sources, or matters of official record. A lot of it derives from conflicting accounts, set down by people with their own personal and political axes to grind. Sometimes all you can do is choose one account over another, for reasons that seem good to you."

"Did Lucas have any enemies, in the Society?" said Penny. "People who disagreed with his choices?"

"There were arguments," said Wendy. "But it was always friendly. Discussing our theories, and debating what is factual and what isn't, is what the Society is all about! Fighting your corner is part of the fun! That's why we were looking forward to finally meeting in person, this weekend."

"You said over breakfast, that you had an idea as to what's really going on here," said Penny. "Is there anything you'd like to share with us, Wendy?"

Wendy's face shut down, and she looked coldly at Penny. "I have nothing to say, at this time."

"Even though it could help us find your missing friend?" I said.

Wendy shook her head stubbornly. "It's all a matter of who I can trust. And I haven't decided that yet."

"Not even me?" said Catherine. She tried to make it sound like she was joking, but she really wasn't.

Wendy looked at her steadily. "Walls have ears, Cath. Especially in a house like this."

"But there are still questions that need to be answered," I

said. "To start with; I don't believe there ever was anything between you and Arthur. You tried to imply there was a close relationship, back in London, but he honestly didn't remember you until you reminded him of the work you'd done together. And even then, he only remembered the work, not you. In all the time you've been here, you've made no real attempt to get close to him, or provide the personal and professional support you offered. And while Marion definitely is suspicious of you, she hasn't done anything to keep you away from her husband. Because she hasn't needed to. I think you used the implied relationship to explain why you travelled all the way here, when actually you had a whole different reason for needing to be here."

"Really?" said Wendy, meeting my gaze unflinchingly. "And what might that have been?"

"Well," I said. "Since you're clearly not going to tell me, I'll just have to work it out for myself."

Penny grinned at Catherine. "Watch him work. He's really very good at this."

"It has to be something to do with Lucas Carr," I said. "You are the only one here who had any real relationship with the man. I think you worked with Lucas on his presentation paper. Perhaps helped him find some of the sources, for whatever big revelation he was going to make. But when you were told he'd disappeared, and that he wouldn't be able to make his big announcement after all, you couldn't let that happen. Not after all the hard work you'd put into it. So you came here not just to find out what happened to Lucas, but what happened to the proof he must have brought with him, to back up his big reveal about Lord Ravensbrook. How am I doing?"

"Go on," said Wendy, neither confirming nor denying.

"When Lucas arrived, he wouldn't allow Arthur to take

his suitcases," I said thoughtfully. "And I also noticed that you wouldn't let him touch your case. So I'm guessing you brought some of your source material for the paper with you. What would I find, Wendy, if I searched your suitcase?"

"I am not giving you permission to do that!" Wendy said immediately.

"I don't need your permission," I said. "I'm not the police. But let's move on. . . . At breakfast this morning, you couldn't wait to begin your search for Lord Ravensbrook so you could find where his body is hidden. Which leads me to think you expect to find something with his body. Some proof that would back up what you think you know about the true nature of his disappearance. Since Lucas' evidence vanished with him, you could take this other proof and use it to make your own big announcement. And take all the credit for yourself."

"That's not how it is!" said Wendy.

"Then tell me," I said. "How is it, really?"

Wendy took a deep breath. Her back remained straight, and her voice was entirely steady.

"All right, yes; I helped Lucas research his paper. I'd found some very interesting references to an old document that would shed a whole new light on what really happened to Lord Ravensbrook. I told Lucas, and he was able to track down the document itself. He was going to show it to the Society, when he made his big announcement. I believe Lucas was murdered here, to stop him revealing the truth. I need to find Lord Ravensbrook's body, and what should be with it, so I can make Lucas' announcement for him. So he won't have died for nothing."

Catherine looked at her, horrified. "Have you been using me as a distraction, because Arthur didn't work out? To keep everyone from noticing what you were really after?"

Wendy turned quickly to look at her. "No, Cath! I wouldn't do that."

"Then why didn't you tell me any of this?"

Wendy reached out and took Catherine's hands in hers. Catherine didn't pull away, but she didn't look convinced either.

"You're the only one in this house I do trust, Cath," Wendy said steadily. "I couldn't tell you, because in this house you can never be sure who's listening."

And then Wendy stopped, and looked round suddenly. We all did, and there was Arthur, standing in the doorway. He blinked at us uncertainly.

"I heard raised voices. Everyone seems to be in such a bad mood this morning. . . . What's going on?"

"Didn't you hear?" said Wendy.

"I only just got here," said Arthur.

I wasn't too sure about that. I hadn't heard him approach, and I should have. But then, I had been concentrating on what Wendy was saying. Penny smiled brightly at Arthur.

"We've been arguing about whose portrait that is, over the fireplace. Do you know who it's supposed to be?"

"Of course," said Arthur. "That's my ancestor, Alexander Glenbury."

Catherine looked triumphantly at Wendy, who sighed and let go of her hands. She turned back to me.

"Look, Ishmael . . . Just leave me alone to get on with my work, and I will get to the bottom of what's really going on here. You'll never find out on your own."

"I wouldn't be too sure of that," I said. "Continue your search. But keep me posted."

Catherine cleared her throat politely. "Can I ask you something, Ishmael?"

"Of course," I said.

"Are you any nearer to working out how Mr. Carr could have vanished so completely?"

"Not yet," I said. "But we're getting there."

And then I led Penny out of the room, before Wendy could challenge us to fight our corner.

✦ CHAPTER SEVEN ✦
DAYLIGHT HORRORS

PENNY AND I went for a pleasant stroll through the ground floor. It was all splashed with early morning sunshine, though the odd shadow lurked in the background to remind us this was still Glenbury Hall. Doors stood invitingly open to every side, freely offering their rooms for inspection, as though to prove the house had nothing to hide. If anything, that made me even more suspicious.

"You're frowning again," said Penny.

"I'm just wondering why this case seems so determined to frustrate me at every turn," I said. "I can't even get a grip on what kind of a case this is. Are we investigating a disappearance, a kidnapping, or a murder? Are we surrounded by suspects, or a house full of ghosts? I'm starting to wonder whether we've been looking in the wrong direction all along, and Lucas just did a runner for reasons of his own, and vanished over the nearest horizon."

"That would explain why we haven't been able to find him," said Penny. "And why we haven't been able to establish a motive for any of the suspects."

"We certainly didn't learn anything useful from our little

talks," I said. "If anything, they seemed as baffled as we are as to what's going on."

"But why would Lucas want to run away?" said Penny. "He wasn't here long enough for the Hall's resident spooks to throw a scare into him."

"He might have worked up the nerve to get this far," I said, "only to discover that faced with the prospect of having to make a big speech to so many people, his courage failed him. And all he could think of was to get the hell out of here."

"Okay," said Penny. "I can see him sneaking out of the Hall, somehow, but why didn't he just call a taxi and go home? Why hasn't he contacted anyone, to let them know he's okay?"

"I don't think he has anyone to contact," I said.

"He must have known people at the Organisation."

"Maybe he was too embarrassed," I said. "And he might not have had a mobile phone. Not everyone does, even in this day and age. Perhaps he tried to walk back into town across the fields, and got lost. I'd hate to think he was still out there in the countryside."

"Someone would have found him by now," said Penny.

"You're right," I said. "Cancel the running away idea. It just shows how desperate I'm feeling, that I was even prepared to consider it."

"Arthur and Marion backed each other up," said Penny. "And so did Catherine and Wendy."

"First question, when it comes to alibis," I said. "Who benefits? The person being vouched for? Or the person doing the vouching?"

Penny frowned. "It's hard enough to find a motive for one person, let alone two people working together."

"If everyone was telling the truth, Carr's disappearance would be impossible," I said. "So someone has to be lying."

"But no one has any reason to lie!"

"Breathe," I said kindly. "Don't let it get to you. All we need is a moment's insight, and everything will drop neatly into place."

"Either that, or a really lucky break."

"Yes," I said. "One of those would help. Now; where were we?"

"The word impossible had just been used," said Penny. "And not in a good way."

"Like any conjuring trick, it only seems impossible as long as we don't know how it was done," I said.

"The only other suspect is Ellen," said Penny. "She did lie about seeing things on her laptop . . . but she doesn't have any obvious motive to lie about anything else."

"So where does that leave us?" I said.

"There's always the Hall," said Penny. "This house feels like it holds a grudge against anyone who dares stay in it."

"But then why did it only make Lucas disappear?" I said. "He was a stranger, on his first visit. Everyone else has spent far more time here, and none of them have disappeared."

Penny sighed. "I always hope that if you ask enough people enough questions, then the guilty party will be bound to incriminate themselves. You know: *Yes, I did it! I killed him and I'm glad, do you hear, glad! Because he deserved it!* And then they go on to spell it all out in detail, just to prove how clever they've been. But somehow, that never happens."

"The more people I talk to," I said, "the more I think this house holds all the answers."

"I assume you're not suggesting we interrogate the ghosties and ghoulies," Penny said carefully. "So . . . you're back to thinking about concealed doors in the panelling, hidden passageways, and secret rooms?"

"It has to be something like that," I said. "Lucas could be

imprisoned in a hidden room somewhere. Or his body could have been dumped in one. I'm thinking there must be a maze of secret passageways hidden away behind these walls, to allow someone to move around the house unseen and only emerge when no one's looking. It's the only answer that makes sense."

"Even though Arthur said flat out that there isn't anything like that, anywhere in the Hall?" said Penny. "I mean, he should know, given he spent most of his childhood trying to find them."

"So he says." I looked thoughtfully at Penny. "Have you noticed how Arthur always seems to have an answer for every question we put to him?"

"And you think that makes him look guilty?"

"It's usually the way to bet."

"It's far more likely that he and Marion got together and worked out what their answers were going to be, before we got here," said Penny. "She strikes me as the kind of woman who wouldn't want to leave anything to chance."

I shrugged. "You could say the same about everyone here. They all seem to have things they don't want to talk about."

"Which is situation entirely normal, for most of our cases," said Penny.

"I've been wondering if there might be some unknown extra person in the house," I said. "Hiding away in a secret room, and only emerging briefly to put the wind up people."

Penny looked at me sharply. "Could this unknown person be Lucas? Just messing with everyone, for his own reasons?"

I looked at her. "Why would Lucas want to do something like that?"

Penny smiled. "Beats the hell out of me."

"And how would Lucas even know where the secret rooms are?"

"Because he's an expert on the history of the Hall."

"Okay..." I said. "Put that one of the back burner, for now. I'll think about it." I gave the nearest wall my best suspicious look. "I can't believe I haven't been able to spot a single concealed door or sliding panel anywhere."

"You just want them to be here, because that would give you a simple answer as to what's going on," said Penny.

"Yes!" I said. "Exactly!"

"We don't get the kind of cases with simple answers," said Penny. "You must have noticed."

I nodded. "With a little encouragement, I think I could become seriously depressed."

"Nonsense," Penny said briskly. "You've got me."

"That does help," I said.

"And you know how you love it when an explanation finally comes together, and you get to lecture me on all the things I've missed."

I smiled. "Yes. I do enjoy that."

"One of these days, I'll get there before you."

"It's good to have dreams," I said.

We continued on our leisurely way through the ground floor, keeping an eye out for anything interesting. The further we progressed, the grimmer and more dilapidated everything seemed in the unforgiving glare of daylight. Every piece of furniture was old enough to be an antique, but covered with enough scrapes and scratches to explain why it hadn't been sold off. The wood-panelled walls were increasingly dull and dusty, and the few remaining historical items wouldn't have troubled any collector's dreams. It was like walking through a museum that no one gave a damn about anymore. Portraits on the walls stared disapprovingly as we passed by, as though appalled at the state their ancestral home had been allowed to fall into. I half expected them to make sardonic comments, or start gossiping behind our backs.

"This place is a mess," Penny said finally. "I can't believe Arthur and Marion really thought they were ready to open up their Hall to paying guests. Most of it looks like no one's been round with a feather duster for centuries."

I shrugged. "The first guests they let in were historians, who might have preferred to see the Hall this way. Untamed and untouched, preserved from the improvements of the modern world. There's no snob like your specialist scholar."

"Ishmael," said Penny. "Much as I am enjoying our little excursion, I have to ask: are we looking for anything in particular?"

"I think that comes under the heading of: we'll know it when we see it," I said. "Or possibly, when we don't see it."

Penny gave me a stern look. "There are times when I think you talk that way just to annoy me."

"Sometimes, it's the things that aren't where they should be, or the people who don't say or do the things you'd normally expect, that help to give the game away," I said patiently. "Remember what was wrong with the dog in the night? He didn't bark, because he recognised the intruder."

"So we have progressed from searching for clues, to looking for the absence of clues," said Penny. "Wonderful. Ishmael . . . We have no body, and no actual evidence of a crime, just someone who isn't where they're supposed to be. How can we solve a case, when we can't even be sure what the case is?"

"Look on the bright side," I said.

"What bright side?" said Penny, just a bit dangerously.

"It could be raining."

Penny smiled in spite of herself, and slipped her arm through mine. We moved deeper into the ground floor, accompanied only by the soft sounds of our footsteps and the occasional creak from the woodwork, disturbed by the vibrations of our passing. Like walking through a tomb that had been untroubled by the living for far too many years.

"Does this part of the house seem suspiciously quiet, to you?" said Penny, after a while.

"It's so quiet I can almost hear the death-watch beetle gnawing on the woodwork."

Penny looked at me. "Really?"

"I said almost."

Penny stared distractedly about her. "I don't like this house, even in broad daylight. There isn't a single part of it that feels friendly, or welcoming. And now . . . I am getting a very definite feeling that we are being watched."

I stopped, and Penny stopped with me. I looked up and down the corridor, listened carefully, and then shook my head.

"There's no one else in this part of the house. If there was, I'd know."

"I'm not talking about human eyes," said Penny.

I kept my voice carefully calm. "Are we back to talking about spooks and spirits and the walking not entirely deceased?"

"Whoever's watching us doesn't feel like people," Penny said stubbornly. "If you say we're alone here, I trust your weird alien senses. But something is watching us with bad intent. I can feel it, in my bones and in my water. I don't know, Ishmael . . . Maybe it's all these portraits! So many unfriendly gazes in one place."

She looked at me unhappily, knowing she wasn't making sense but trying to make me understand what she was feeling. To keep the peace, and because I trust Penny's instincts the same way she trusts my senses, I took a good look at the aristocratic mug shots staring sternly at us from out of the past. They all had the same expression: grim and dour, as though all human weaknesses had been scoured out of them by living in the Hall. Or by being Glenburys. I picked one at random, and strode over to stare it in the eye.

Some forgotten dignitary glowered back at me, in his best clothes and a truly ugly chain of office. The image was so dark and faded it might have been painted at midnight after someone blew out the candle. The eyes were just dark smudges, with no life or menace in them. I leaned in close, until my nose was practically touching the canvas and I could make out the individual brush-strokes. I turned back to Penny, and shrugged.

"It's just a painting. Like all the others. Whatever sins these people might have been responsible for in the past, they don't have any interest in us now."

Penny scowled around her. "But something is definitely here with us! It's like . . . when you can feel unfriendly eyes boring a hole into your back, in the middle of a crowded room."

I nodded. I knew that feeling.

Penny scowled up and down the passageway, banging one fist quietly against her hip.

"We have come up against some truly weird things in our time, Ishmael," she said slowly. "But nothing like this house . . . It feels like some kind of predator, just waiting for us to lower our guard . . ."

I chose my next words carefully. I could hear a real disquiet in Penny's voice. And she wasn't someone who disturbed easily.

"I am taking your suspicions seriously, Penny. But I can't do anything, until I see some evidence of a threat. Do you think the Hall is planning to abduct us next?"

"How could we hope to stop it, if it tried?" said Penny.

I decided it was time to play the frivolous card, and hopefully lighten the atmosphere.

"I suppose it would depend on how the house disposes of people," I said. "Are we talking concealed trapdoors in the floor, that suddenly drop open to deliver us into the house's stomach? Or perhaps there are disguised dimensional doors, that lead into some nightmarish other reality? Or perhaps there are things like giant trapdoor spiders, lying in wait?"

Penny didn't look particularly amused. "Am I to understand those are all real possible threats?"

"They are all things I've encountered on past cases," I admitted. "The important thing to remember is that I am still here and they, for the most part, are not."

"You have lived a seriously strange life, Ishmael. And yet you still refuse to believe in ghosts..."

I shrugged helplessly. "I'm sorry, Penny, but as far as I can tell Glenbury Hall is just a house. And as far as Lucas Carr is concerned, I am putting my money on a human culprit, with a very human grudge."

"So what do you think happened to him?" said Penny.

"Beats the hell out of me," I said.

And then we both looked round, as some way down the corridor a door swung slowly open on its own. The hinges creaked loudly, as though trying to attract our attention. Penny and I stood very still, watching the door carefully as it swung slowly back, leaving nothing but the gloom of an open doorway. The corridor was suddenly very still, and very quiet.

"Okay..." I said. "That isn't just an invitation, that's almost insultingly blatant. Step into my web, said the spider to the fly. The kettle's on."

"We are still going to check it out, though, aren't we?" said Penny.

"Of course," I said. "I love walking into traps! They always end up revealing so much useful information about whoever set them."

"Then feel free to take the lead," said Penny. "I will be right behind you."

"Because I make such an excellent human shield?"

"Got it in one," said Penny. "Be as broad as you can, there's a dear."

We set off cautiously down the corridor, watching and listening all the way, but nothing moved and nothing stirred, even in the deepest of the shadows. We finally came to a halt before the open doorway, but all I could see was the gloom of an empty room. I shoved the door all the way back, with such force it slammed deafeningly against the inner wall. The echoes took some time to die away. Penny actually jumped a little, and looked at me reproachfully. I nodded apologetically and then raised my voice, addressing the open doorway.

"Hello!" I said cheerfully. "Anybody there?"

Penny shook her head. "Do you really believe someone hiding in ambush would actually forget themselves enough to answer you?"

"I live in hope," I said.

I felt around inside the doorway for a light switch, but there didn't seem to be one. I stared into the gloom, but I couldn't even make out any furniture. The room gave every appearance of being completely empty. I entered slowly, one step at a time. Penny moved quickly into position beside me, ready for anything. Because the humour stopped the moment we were in enemy territory. It quickly became clear that the room consisted of nothing but bare walls and a scuffed floor. Drawn curtains covered the only window, blocking out the sunlight. We came to a halt in the middle of the room and looked around us, and nothing at all looked back.

"Ishmael," Penny said quietly. "If there's no one in here, who opened the door?"

"I suppose it's always possible that the doorframe could have become warped over time," I said. "So the door doesn't hang properly anymore, and the vibrations from our footsteps made it swing open. Remember Arthur's story, about the phantom footsteps on the top floor?"

Penny started to nod, and then sneezed explosively. She sniffed a few times, and then wrinkled her nose.

"It smells like something died in here."

"Probably just rats in the wainscotting," I said.

"Can't you smell it?"

"Too much dust in the air," I said. "It's hard for me to pick up anything."

"Then why aren't you sneezing?" said Penny.

"Please," I said. "I have my dignity to consider."

The door slammed shut behind us. I spun around, dived for the door and grabbed the handle, but it wouldn't turn. The door was locked. The room seemed suddenly that much darker.

"Could someone have sneaked down the corridor and locked us in?" said Penny. Her voice was entirely steady, but I could hear the tension in it.

"It isn't usually possible for anyone to sneak up on me," I said. "But I was concentrating on the room."

"Try the pass key," said Penny.

The key didn't want anything to do with the lock. I put it away again.

"The pass key was only ever intended for the renovated rooms on the top floor," I said.

Penny glared at the closed door. "Why would anyone want to lock us in here?"

"To throw a scare into us?"

Penny smiled briefly. "They don't know us very well, do they?"

"Maybe they just wanted us to be in a position where we'd have no choice but to call for help, and be rescued," I said. "To undermine our authority, and make us look like idiots."

"But we're on the ground floor," said Penny. "We could just smash the window and climb out."

"Please," I said. "Think of our dignity. And besides, I feel the need to make a statement."

I lashed out, and punched the steel lock so hard it flew right out of the wood, and dropped onto the corridor floor outside. I hauled the door back, strode out into the corridor, and looked quickly in both directions, but there was no one about. Penny emerged at her own speed, just to make it clear that being locked in a darkened room hadn't bothered her in the least. She looked at the smashed lock lying on the floor, some distance away.

"Show-off."

"I was in a bit of a mood," I admitted. "I hate being caught off guard. Still, if you can't punch the one you want, punch what's there."

Penny looked at the ragged gap in the door where the lock used to be, and smiled.

"Marion and Arthur really aren't going to like that."

"Tough," I said.

"What if they ask how you did it?" said Penny.

"I shall just smile and look mysterious," I said.

"You are very good at that."

"Years of practice."

We set off down the corridor again. If we had been locked up to prevent us from going any further, then whatever lay ahead was where I wanted to be. I finally stopped before one particular side door and considered it thoughtfully. Penny stopped beside me, and looked the door over carefully.

"What's so special about this room?"

"Arthur was here, not long ago," I said. "I can smell his scent, still hanging on the air."

"So?" said Penny. "It's his house. He and Marion have probably been all over it, checking out what needs doing."

"But this was just him," I said. "I'm not picking up any trace of Marion."

I tried the handle, and it turned easily. I threw the door open, sending it flying back to slam against the inside wall. Someone once hid behind a door to ambush me, and I've never forgotten. The room was a decent size, with bright sunshine pouring in through a large window. The curtains had been neatly tied back. I took one last glance down the corridor, just in case someone was waiting for a chance to lock us in again, and then moved cautiously forward into the room. Penny stuck close beside me, peering eagerly around her.

The walls had been painted in bright primary colours, though they were somewhat faded now. A teacher's desk stood at the far end of the room, before a blackboard fixed to the wall. It had clearly been some time since anyone used it, but the room smelled as though it had been cleaned recently. One wall was lined with shelves crammed full of books, and Penny leaned in close to study the creased and battered spines.

"Basic school textbooks, all the usual subjects," she said. "And . . . a whole lot of children's fiction. Enid Blyton! I used to read her all the time when I was young. *Famous Five, Secret Seven.* . . . Ooh, *The Faraway Tree!* I loved that one!"

"A school room," I said. "And the only child in this house, in recent times, was Arthur."

Penny nodded approvingly at the room. "It seems his parents did do something for him."

"I wouldn't be too sure about that," I said.

I pointed to something half hidden by the teacher's desk. Penny frowned.

"What is that?"

We moved over to the desk and I pushed it to one side, revealing a metal cage just big enough to hold a medium-sized dog. The bars had been reinforced with steel mesh in places, and the entrance was held shut by a heavy steel padlock. I crouched down beside the cage, and studied it carefully.

"There's dried blood on the mesh, and on the door," I said. "Very old blood. Whatever was locked in here hurt itself, trying to get out."

"What is a cage doing in a school room?" said Penny. "Did Arthur have a pet?"

"No," said Arthur. "I was never allowed pets."

I straightened up and turned to face Arthur. He was standing stiffly in the doorway, as though unwilling to enter the room.

"Then what was this cage for?" I said.

"It was for me," said Arthur. "When I was bad."

Penny made a shocked sound. "Your parents locked you in a cage?"

"It seemed quite roomy when I was small," said Arthur. "Of course, it got more cramped as I grew older. They would take away my clothes and put me in, and leave me in the cage, all day and all night. No food, no drink, no chamber-pot. I think that was when I learned there was no point in crying. Because it didn't make me feel any better, and no one would come. I must have been a very bad child, that they had to put me in it so often."

His voice was perfectly calm, but his eyes were cold and far away.

"Did Catherine know about this?" said Penny.

"I don't believe so," said Arthur.

"How could parents do this to a child?" said Penny.

"They wanted me to behave," said Arthur. He stepped cautiously forward, and smiled briefly at the books on the shelves. "They didn't like me to have toys. I made too much noise, with toys. They liked it when I discovered books, because stories kept me quiet and out of their way. They didn't realise that books opened my eyes to the outside world. Somewhere I could escape to."

"How did you know to find us here, Arthur?" I said.

"I heard a door slam," said Arthur. "So I thought I'd better come and take a look. I was worried some ghostly force might have locked you in a room."

Penny looked at him. "Really?"

"Used to happen all the time, when I was a child," said Arthur.

I gestured at the cage. "Does Marion know about this?"

"No," he said. "It would only upset her."

"So you cleaned this room on your own," I said.

He shrugged. "Someone had to."

"Why is the cage still here?" said Penny.

"You can't just throw away your past, and pretend it never happened," said Arthur.

He turned abruptly, and left the room. Penny shook her head slowly.

"The more I learn about that man's parents, the more I want to find out where they're buried so I can dig them up and punch them in the face."

"And Catherine was their very close friend," I said. "I think we need to press her some more on that."

"Arthur said she didn't know about this."

"And you believe that?"

Penny scowled. "He's trying so hard to be a good father, so he won't be anything like his own. And he does seem genuinely fond of Catherine. The aunt he never had."

"The woman who went away," I said. "And left him with parents who locked him in a cage."

Penny shuddered briefly. "I'd hate to think that sweet little old lady could have had anything to do with this . . ."

"Always remember the first rule," I said. "Suspects lie. For all kinds of reasons. We can't trust anything they say, including Arthur. What he told us could just have been a story, designed to get us on his side."

Penny's mouth flattened into a tight line. "It didn't feel like a story. You saw his face. And there's still blood on that cage."

"Yes," I said. "There is."

"What are we going to do, Ishmael?"

"This isn't what we're here for," I said steadily. "The monsters responsible for what happened in this room have been dead for ages."

"Arthur was right. The past is always with you, in Glenbury Hall," said Penny. "The horrors don't go away, even when it's daylight."

We searched the room thoroughly, taking our time, but couldn't find anything useful, never mind interesting. And then I stopped, and lifted my head.

"What is it?" said Penny.

"Can you hear something?" I said.

"Yes . . ." said Penny. "What is that?"

I moved quickly over to the window, and Penny squeezed in beside me. We stared out across the open grounds, brightly illuminated by the morning sun. There was nothing to be seen, apart from the statues, but I could hear a large gathering of people all talking at once.

Penny grabbed my arm. "Ishmael! It's the timeslip! The people from the past, that the two women saw!"

"Then why can't we see anything?" I said.

"We're too far away," said Penny. "We need to get out into the grounds!"

She scrabbled at the latch, but the window wouldn't budge. I forced it open, and Penny threw a leg over the windowsill and was outside in a moment. I quickly followed her out, dropping down onto the grass beside her, but even as I looked around the sounds just stopped. The grounds stretched away before us, completely still and utterly silent.

"Where did everybody go?" said Penny.

"I don't think they were ever here," I said. "Someone just played a recording, to fool us."

Penny looked at me. "Why would they want to do that?"

"To lure us out here," I said.

"But there's no one here!"

I heard a slow scraping sound, of stone moving against stone. Despite myself, my first thought was to check out the statues, but none of them had stirred or changed their position. I concentrated, and realised the sound was coming from behind and above me. I turned around to look at the Hall just in time to see one of the stone gargoyles lean out from the roof, as though trying for a better look. And then it launched itself out from the roof, and plummeted down. Heading straight for Penny.

I threw myself forward, and shoved her back out of the way. That left me directly underneath the falling gargoyle, but Penny grabbed my arm as she fell backwards, and pulled me after her. We crashed to the ground in a tangle of limbs, and the gargoyle slammed into the earth. Penny and I took a moment to check we were both all right, and then scrambled to our feet. The gargoyle was barely a foot away, half buried in the ground by the force of its arrival.

"You saved my life," said Penny.

"You saved mine," I said.

Penny smiled dazzlingly. "That's what partners are for."

We looked up at the roof. None of the other gargoyles had moved, though there was an obvious gap where one of them used to be.

"That thing didn't just fall on its own," I said. "I heard definite scraping sounds, as it was forced from its setting."

"Somebody just tried to kill us," said Penny.

"Well you, anyway," I said. "Who would want to kill me?"

"Someone who'd met you?" said Penny.

We shared a smile. Brushes with death always bring out the frivolous in us.

"If someone is trying to kill us," I said, "that must mean we're getting close to something. I only wish I knew what it was."

We moved further out into the grounds, so we could get a better look at the Hall, and its roof. The gargoyles held their positions, ignoring the gap where one of them used to be. I couldn't see anyone moving around on the roof.

Catherine suddenly emerged from the front door, and came hurrying forward to join us.

"Are you all right, dears? I was just looking out the window when I saw a gargoyle go flying past!"

"We're fine," I said.

Catherine looked bemusedly at the half-buried stone figure. "How on earth could something that's been set in stone for so many years have broken loose?"

"We were wondering that," I said.

"Excuse me," said Penny. "But where's Wendy? Isn't she still with you?"

Catherine looked startled, as she realised her friend wasn't there. She looked back at the front door.

"She was with me when I saw that thing fall. I told her what I saw..."

She stared at the open door, as though expecting Wendy to come bustling through it at any moment. When that didn't happen, Catherine turned back to us, her face creased with worry.

"I don't understand. She was right behind me..."

"Let's go back inside," I said, "and see if we can find her."

On entering the lobby, the first thing we saw was Arthur heaving a large box onto a tottering pile of other boxes, next to the reception desk. He was breathing hard, his face glistening with sweat. He looked up, and seemed a little taken aback by the urgency in our faces. I strode over to the desk, while he quickly sat down behind it and did his best to look like the man in charge. And not someone who'd just worn himself out with a little manual labour.

"I was sorting through some old records," he said. "Can I help you with anything?"

"One of your gargoyles has fallen from the roof," I said. "It only just missed hitting Penny and me."

"Oh that's all we need!" said Arthur. "Our insurance isn't set up to cover things like that."

"Ishmael and I are fine, thank you," said Penny, just a bit pointedly.

"Of course you are," said Arthur. "Was the gargoyle damaged in the fall?"

Penny turned to me. "I take back every sympathetic thing I thought about him."

"I would," I said.

Catherine slapped her hand smartly on the desk, to attract Arthur's attention. He looked startled and a little put out, as though he'd already dismissed us so he could concentrate on more important things.

"Where is Wendy?" said Catherine.

"The last I saw, she was following you through the lobby," said Arthur. "And then she stopped, seemed to change her mind, and went up the stairs to the next floor."

"Why would she do that?" said Catherine.

"I don't know," said Arthur. "I did call after her, to see if everything was all right, but she didn't look back. Now if you'll excuse me, I have to go outside and take a look at the gargoyle, and the roof. See how bad the damage is. Though how we're going to put the thing back where it should be, without hiring a crane.... Oh, I don't even want to think about how much that's going to cost."

Catherine gave up on him and headed for the stairs. Penny and I went after her.

"Catherine?" said Penny. "Where are you going?"

"To Wendy's room, of course," said Catherine, starting up the stairs.

"I thought she was staying with you?" said Penny.

"That was last night," Catherine said impatiently. "I'm fine now."

"Something must have happened, to make her break off from following you," I said. "And it must have been important, to distract her from a falling gargoyle. Something that mattered to her.... Catherine! Does Wendy have anything in her room, that she would want to protect?"

Catherine didn't even glance back at me, as she threw her reply over her shoulder. She sounded irritated that I was bothering her with questions when she had far more important matters on her mind.

"How would I know what Wendy has in her room? Her things, I suppose. She didn't have much with her when she arrived. Just the one suitcase, as I recall."

We reached the top of the stairs, and then had to pause as Catherine leaned on the bannisters to get her breath back. I looked along the passageway, as I heard someone moving about. There was no one in sight, which meant they had to be in one of the other rooms. Catherine headed for Wendy's door, and Penny and I went after her.

Marion emerged from a room further down the corridor, and came hurrying forward. She went to pass us by with just a brief nod, but I stepped forward to block her way, so she had no choice but to stop and talk to us. She gave me a hard look, but did her best to sound calm and businesslike and not at all long-suffering.

"Is this really important, Mr. Jones? Only I do have a lot of work to be getting on with."

"It might be," I said. "We're looking for Wendy. Have you seen her recently?"

"No," said Marion. "But I did hear footsteps coming up the stairs not long ago, and a door open and close."

"Could you tell which room?" I said.

She looked at me. "Not from behind a closed door, no."

"Didn't you come out, to see who it was?" said Penny.

"Of course not," said Marion. "It was none of my business. You're all free to go wherever you want, as guests in the Hall." She turned her attention back to me. "I don't suppose you've seen my husband anywhere, have you?"

"He's working at the reception desk," I said.

"Well, what's he doing down there?" said Marion. "He knows he's supposed to be helping me clean these rooms out!

Honestly, you can't take your eyes off anyone in this family. I'd better go down and see what he thinks he's doing."

She stepped quickly around me, and bustled off down the stairs. The moment Marion was out of the way, Catherine knocked loudly on Wendy's door and called her name, but there was no response. She tried the handle, but the door was locked. Penny looked at me.

"I'm getting a bad feeling about this," she said quietly. "Doesn't it remind you of when Marion banged on Lucas' door, and didn't get an answer because he wasn't there?"

I nodded. "There's no way this is going to end well."

"Of course not," said Penny. "We're in Glenbury Hall."

I took Catherine by the shoulders and urged her gently but firmly to one side. I unlocked the door with my pass key, and pushed it open. Catherine all but elbowed me out of the way and rushed into the room, calling out to Wendy. Penny and I went in after her.

The room was empty. Catherine's voice trailed away, as it became clear no one was going to answer her. I looked around and pointed out Wendy's door key, lying on a side table by the door.

"She must have dropped it there when she came in," I said.

"At least we can be sure she did come in here," said Penny. "But she couldn't have come out again, because she would have needed that key to lock the door behind her, after she left."

"Then how did she leave?" I said. "There isn't any other door."

"Maybe she jumped out the window, to get away from something," said Penny.

"First, the window is closed," I said. "And second, we were out in the grounds. Even with everything that was going on, I think we would have noticed a falling historian."

Penny scowled. "I hate locked room mysteries."

We broke off, as Catherine tugged at my sleeve imploringly. Her face was pale, her eyes wide and lost.

"Wendy has to be in here somewhere..."

"I really don't think so, Catherine," I said.

She sat down suddenly on the side of the bed, as though all the strength had gone out of her. Penny and I moved quickly round the room, looking inside the wardrobe and behind all of the furniture. I even checked underneath the bed. The search didn't take long, and when it was over there was no trace of Wendy anywhere. I looked to Catherine, and shook my head. Her shoulders slumped, as though I'd taken away her last hope. Her lips moved, but no sound emerged, as though she was trying to frame a question but didn't know what to say. Penny and I moved a little away, so we could talk quietly.

"Another disappearance," I said.

"Just like Lucas," said Penny.

"What could have mattered so much to Wendy, that she would abandon her friend and rush up here?" I said. "Did she see something in the lobby, that made her believe someone might be messing with her things? And what could she have had in here, that anyone would want?"

"I'm not seeing her suitcase anywhere," said Penny. "The one that was supposed to have historical evidence in it."

"If it was here, I would have seen it," I said.

"This is following the same pattern as Lucas," said Penny. "Someone disappears under mysterious circumstances, and their luggage goes with them. Which would suggest the two events are connected."

"Or that someone wants us to think that," I said.

I looked around the room again, and then stopped abruptly as I spotted something lying on the floor next to the side table. I got down on one knee, and inspected my find carefully without touching it. Penny pressed in behind me, peering over my shoulder.

"What have you got there?"

"Something interesting," I said. I picked up the fallen cigarette butt and studied it carefully. Penny rested her chin on my shoulder, so she could look at it too.

"What is that doing here?"

"Good question," I said.

The butt was barely an inch long. I touched the burned end.

"Cold. No telling how long it's been here."

"Wendy didn't smoke," said Penny. "Did she?"

"I never saw her smoking," I said. "And I never smelt cigarette smoke on her clothes."

"So this could have been dropped by whoever took Wendy," said Penny.

"In this house, the only person who smokes cigarettes is Marion," I said.

"And she was up here, hiding in another room when we arrived," said Penny.

"If she was hiding, why did she come out?" I said.

"Because it would have looked bad if we found her?"

"Perhaps."

"But if Marion was in this room," said Penny, "how did she take Wendy, and leave the door key inside?"

"There's something not right about this cigarette butt," I said thoughtfully.

"What's not right?" said Penny.

"I don't know . . ."

"It's still a clue, isn't it?"

"Of course," I said kindly.

I tucked the cigarette butt carefully away in my jacket pocket, and got to my feet again.

"Wendy's gone," said Catherine.

Penny and I turned to look at her, sitting small and crushed on the side of Wendy's bed.

"The Hall took her," said Catherine. "Just like it did Lucas Carr. My friend is dead."

"We can't be sure of that," I said.

"I can," said Catherine. "I wonder if she'll come to visit me, in my room tonight..."

✠ CHAPTER EIGHT ✠
THE BODY OF EVIDENCE

PENNY SAT DOWN on the bed beside Catherine and put a comforting hand on her arm, but Catherine barely seemed to know she was there. Her eyes stared off into the distance, and whatever she was feeling she didn't feel like sharing.

I looked around the room, pleasantly lit by the sunshine pouring in through the window. And it occurred to me to wonder why both Lucas and Wendy had disappeared in broad daylight, rather than at night when everyone was affected by the spooky atmosphere. Did the disappearances have nothing to do with how the house made people feel?

I frowned as I concentrated on the problem. Why did Wendy have to disappear now? Had something significant changed between last night and this morning, that made it necessary for her to disappear? The only thing that had happened so far was the shared breakfast. Had Wendy done or said anything unusual? I thought back and remembered Wendy saying she had an idea as to what was really going on, and who was behind it. I nodded slowly. If I'd noticed that, someone else could have too, and taken it seriously enough that they thought they needed to remove Wendy before she could share her ideas.

Next problem: who would Wendy have invited to join her, in her room? It couldn't have been Catherine, because she was out in the grounds with Penny and me, so that just left Arthur, Marion, and Ellen. Unless there really was some other, unknown, person scurrying around the house.

The audio recreation of the timeslip, and the falling gargoyle, could have been intended to keep Penny and me occupied while the killer went after Wendy. But whoever was responsible must have been running around like a mad thing, activating the recording, forcing the gargoyle off the roof, separating Wendy from Catherine, and then attacking her in her room . . .

My head came up, as I smelled something new on the air. I turned around and stared directly at Ellen, catching her by surprise as she stood in the open doorway. The teenager had a hand raised to knock on the open door, but lowered it awkwardly as I looked at her.

"Can I help you with something?" I said.

"I heard someone banging on a door, and people yelling," she said. "What's going on?"

"You heard us?" I said. "Even past your headphones?"

She did her best to look down her nose at me. "I'm not always listening to my music."

I looked at her thoughtfully. "Did you hear Wendy come up the stairs, just now? And go into her room?"

"I heard someone," said Ellen.

"Did you hear anyone else?"

"Just my mother, moving about. She's been working up here for some time. And then a whole bunch of people came charging up the stairs . . ."

"Did you hear your mother come into this room, and talk to Wendy?" I said.

Ellen shrugged. "I wasn't paying attention. I was busy."

"How long have you been smoking cigarettes, Ellen?"

Her jaw actually dropped a little. "How did you know about that?"

"I can smell the cigarette smoke on your clothes," I said.

Ellen pouted unhappily. "All right . . . I picked up the habit from my mother, back in London. I sometimes sneak the odd cigarette from her pack, when I'm feeling a bit stressed. Please don't tell her. She's got enough to worry about."

"It's none of my business," I said.

"Then why did you bring it up?"

"Just being nosey," I said.

Ellen could have dropped the cigarette butt I'd found in Wendy's room . . . but why would Wendy let her in? It wasn't like they were close. I wasn't sure I'd heard them exchange a dozen words. I was also having trouble seeing Ellen overpower a woman who'd boasted about her self-defence skills. No. The only way this made sense was if Wendy trusted her attacker enough to turn her back on them.

Ellen cleared her throat meaningfully, and I realised I was still staring at her.

"Sorry," I said. "I was thinking."

"You haven't explained what's going on here," said Ellen, just a bit accusingly.

"Wendy has gone missing," I said.

Ellen's eyes widened. "She's been killed? Like Lucas Carr?"

"We don't know that she's dead," I said. "And keep your voice down. Catherine is feeling rather upset."

"But Wendy really could be dead?" said Ellen, still not lowering her voice. Or sounding particularly upset.

"It's a possibility," I said. "All we can be certain about is that Wendy isn't where she was supposed to be. Still, now you're here, you might as well make yourself useful."

Ellen immediately stopped being interested, and dropped back into her default sullen and put upon look. "I don't do useful. I'm a teenager. I'm excused."

"Not by me, you're not," I said. "I need you to escort Catherine downstairs, so your parents can look after her while Penny and I finishing searching the room."

"Oh," said Ellen. "Well . . . I can do that. I suppose."

I took her over to where Catherine was sitting slumped on the bed with Penny. Catherine didn't even look up as Ellen and I stood in front of her.

"Ellen's going to take you downstairs now, Catherine," I said.

"I can't leave," she said quietly. "Wendy might come back."

"I thought she was dead?" said Ellen. She looked at me accusingly. "You told me she was dead!"

"Don't you know by now, that doesn't mean anything in Glenbury Hall?" said Catherine. Animation returned to her face as she stared coldly at Ellen, who had the grace to look a little abashed. "Nothing is ever lost in this house. Everything comes back. I let Lucas down last night, when his spirit returned to me. I won't make the same mistake with Wendy."

"I don't think what you saw in your room last night was Lucas," I said. "And we don't know for sure yet that Wendy is dead. She might just have been taken, and in need of rescuing."

Catherine looked at me, her face showing the beginnings of hope, but it didn't last. She didn't believe me. Her shoulders slumped again and she stared at the floor, as though the world had become too much to deal with. Penny looked at me over Catherine's lowered head, and put her arm across Catherine's shoulders.

"You need to tell Arthur that he's lost another of his guests. He'll take it better, coming from you."

Catherine nodded, and made an effort to pull herself together. "Of course. You're quite right. Arthur needs to know that there's a new ghost in Glenbury Hall."

She got to her feet, ignoring Ellen's offered hand, and walked steadily out of the room. Ellen looked at Penny and me, shrugged, and hurried after Catherine. I listened as they descended the stairs, not speaking to each other, and then turned to Penny. I started to say something, but stopped suddenly as an idea occurred to me. I took out the cigarette butt, and studied it carefully.

"What are you looking for?" said Penny. "Fingerprints? DNA evidence?"

"My eyes aren't that good," I said.

Penny looked carefully at the stub, and then at me.

"Have you just deduced something, Ishmael?"

"Do you know, I think I have," I said. "This is a clue, after all. Just not the one I thought it was."

"Is there something unusual about the cigarette?" said Penny. "Have you recognised it as some rare foreign brand?"

"It's more what isn't there, that should be," I said.

"Don't start that again," said Penny. "Are you going to tell me what you've found, or not?"

"Not for the moment," I said. "I need to think about this some more."

"How am I supposed to help, if I don't have all the facts?"

"It's not a fact," I said. "Just the beginnings of a theory."

Penny nodded reluctantly. She knew I hated discussing my ideas until I was sure I had them pinned down. If only because some of the ideas I come up with can be so off the wall they'd made me look really dumb if I shared them. I put the cigarette butt back in my pocket.

"So!" Penny said brightly. "Do you want some help dismantling this room, until we find a secret door or a sliding panel?"

I looked at her. "You think there is one?"

"How else could someone have got Wendy out of a room locked from the inside?" said Penny.

"The search can wait," I said. "Right now, while Arthur and Marion are preoccupied with Catherine and Ellen, we are going up to the roof."

Penny frowned. "Because someone threw a gargoyle at us?"

"Because there has to be an access point somewhere on the top floor," I said. "Once we're on the roof, we should be able to spot the hidden entrance. And that should help us locate some of the others."

"How are we supposed to get to the roof?" said Penny. "I shouldn't think there's a ladder long enough anywhere in the Hall."

"We don't need a ladder," I said cheerfully. "Arthur already told us how to get up there."

Penny thought for a moment, and then her eyebrows shot up as she remembered.

"Wait just a minute! I am not climbing out of any top-floor window! I am a solver of mysteries, not a mountaineer!"

"Come on, Penny," I said persuasively. "Where's your sense of adventure?"

"I left it in the car," said Penny. "Tell you what: you go on up to the roof, while I go back to the Bentley and look for it."

I went over to the window. It opened easily, and I placed my hands on the thick wooden windowsill, bracing myself as I leaned right out so I could get a good look at the grounds. Once again Penny moved quickly in behind me and took a firm hold on my belt with both hands. I leaned out even further, and Penny grunted loudly.

"You are putting on weight."

"Think of it as a compliment to your cooking."

"I'm not that good a cook," said Penny.

"I don't think I'm going to say anything."

"Very wise."

The grounds stretched away before me, open and unoccupied. The statues ignored me, and I returned the compliment. I twisted around, ignoring some strained sounds from Penny as she took on more of my weight, and looked up. There was no gable on this window, so I had a clear view to the edge of the roof. It wasn't that far, and the old-fashioned black iron guttering looked to be well within reach. And straight above us was the wide gap left by the departure of the gargoyle. I smiled slowly, as I saw how easily the thing could be done.

"You can let go of my belt, Penny," I said.

"Are you sure?"

"Reasonably sure," I said. "I've had an idea."

"Oh, that's always dangerous," Penny said sadly.

She released her hold, and I stepped up onto the windowsill. I waited a moment, till I was sure the sill would support me, and then I eased myself out of the window and turned around. The wooden sill creaked loudly under my weight, but it felt sturdy enough. I took a firm hold on the window-frame, and flakes of old paint came away under my grip. I carefully estimated the distance to the guttering and the roof, did some quick mental calculations, and then called to Penny.

"Come out here and join me."

"I can see you just fine from where I am."

"Penny, I need you out here."

I could almost hear her scowling before she answered.

"I am really not happy about this, Ishmael. Wait a minute, while I take off my boots and hat."

I moved carefully over to the far edge of the windowsill, to make room for Penny, and after a moment she squeezed through the window and stepped cautiously out onto the sill. The old wood made loud protesting noises, but didn't crack or sink perceptively under our combined weight. Penny clung tightly to the window-frame, keeping her back turned to the grounds, and the long drop that led down to them. The gusting wind plucked loosely at our clothes and tousled our hair.

"There you go, Penny," I said. "Easy peasey."

"I want you to know that I hate you more than anything else in this world," she said, not looking at me. "Out of all the seriously dubious things you have talked me into doing on our various cases, this is quite definitely one of them. What now?"

"Brace yourself," I said. "And when you hit the roof, tuck and roll quickly to soak up the impact."

"*What?*"

Before Penny could realise what I was about to do and dive back through the window, I took a firm handful of the back of her clothes, pulled her away from the window and threw her at the roof. Penny made a loud unhappy noise as she went sailing through the air, soared inelegantly over the guttering, and crash-landed on the roof. Her voice cut off, but I heard her roll several times before coming to a halt. I then heard her call me a whole bunch of really unpleasant names, so I knew she was fine.

I measured the distance to the guttering, bent at the knees, and jumped. The strength in my leg muscles was more than equal to the task. I grabbed hold of the guttering and heaved myself up over it and onto the roof. I lowered a shoulder as I made contact with the flat surface, and rolled several times until I ended up lying on my back beside Penny. She punched me hard in the shoulder. I grinned at her, and she laughed despite herself.

"Even after all these years, you can still surprise me, Ishmael. Of course, that's not always a good thing."

"I have always believed in taking the direct route," I said solemnly.

"Just how strong are you, space boy?"

"Strong enough, spy girl."

I helped her up onto her feet, and she took a moment to tug at her dress and brush herself down.

"That was exciting and exhilarating," she said briskly. "And I never ever want to do it again. You had better find a secret door up here somewhere, because I am not climbing back down to that window. Not unless you have a parachute tucked away about your person."

"Have a little faith," I said.

We took a stroll around the flat roof, while the cold wind whipped around us. The broad open space was punctuated by crumbling chimney stacks, and surrounded by a low crenelated wall, interrupted here and there by scowling gargoyles. The roof occasionally found reason to mutter complainingly under our weight, but it seemed firm enough. I stepped carefully into the jagged gap left by the missing gargoyle, and Penny eased in beside me, clutching my arm firmly. From our high vantage point, we could look out across great open chequerboards of fields and make out The Smugglers Retreat and the town of Under Farthing. I tore my gaze away from the view and looked down at the ragged gap where the missing gargoyle had crouched and brooded for so many years.

"Looks like someone went to work here with a crowbar," I said. "See the scars on the stonework?"

Penny frowned. "How much time and effort would that take?"

"Depends on how loose the gargoyle was in its setting," I

said. "But given a crowbar, determination, and the right leverage, something of that weight should have toppled away quite easily."

"Do you think whoever it was really meant to kill us?" said Penny. "Or was it just a warning?"

"I think they would have been happy enough either way," I said.

I leaned forward and looked down at the grounds. Heights have never bothered me. The fallen gargoyle was still half buried in the earth. Maybe the Glenburys could pass it off as a conversation piece, like the old well. I thought about the heavy stone figure falling, and that led me to think of other things falling from this height. And what impacts they might have made, when they hit the ground. Ideas were beginning to come together in my mind.

I stepped back, and turned my attention to the flat roof. There was a lot of accumulated dirt and soot and bird droppings, but when I concentrated I could just make out a series of marks leading away from the gap in the wall. I pointed them out to Penny, but she shook her head.

"Sorry, Ishmael, I don't have your eyes. What are you seeing?"

"Looks like footprints," I said. "Recent ones too."

"Oh good," said Penny. "I'd hate to think I was thrown through the air for nothing."

I followed the trail to a trapdoor concealed behind a chimney. I knelt down beside the wooden door, and traced its outlines with a fingertip. When I checked my finger there was hardly any dust, indicating that someone had opened the trapdoor not long ago. There was a steel ring in the centre, but when I took a firm hold and pulled, the trapdoor wouldn't budge.

"I thought you were strong?" said Penny.

"I am," I said. "I think this thing is bolted shut, on the underside. Stand back, and give me some room to work."

Penny grinned. "Go for it, Ishmael. Show that thing who's boss."

She retreated a few steps, and I punched the trapdoor. The thick wood split jaggedly down the middle, and splinters flew threw in all directions. I grabbed the trapdoor's edges, tore the thing in half, and threw the pieces aside. Penny applauded wildly. I peered down into the opening, and discovered a metal-runged ladder dropping away into an undisturbed gloom. Penny moved in beside me, took one look at the ladder, and stepped back again, shaking her head firmly.

"That ladder does not look at all secure."

"Someone must have used it to get up here," I said reasonably. "Look, I'll go down first, and if the ladder doesn't fall apart you can come down after me."

"What if it does?" said Penny.

"Then jump down, and I'll catch you."

Penny smiled. "Of course you will."

I set off down the ladder.

Sunlight fell through the opening after me, but couldn't reach far enough to illuminate the flat metal rungs. I took it one step at a time, setting my feet carefully, but the rungs accepted my weight easily enough. I waited till I was past the halfway point, and then called up to Penny to follow me down. She scrambled down the ladder so quickly, I'd barely reached the bottom and stepped to one side before she dropped past the last few rungs to land beside me. Penny smiled brightly, and struck a graceful pose.

"Easy peasey!"

"You must learn to trust me on these things," I said.

"That'll be the day. Where are we?"

"Inside one of those hidden rooms Arthur was so sure didn't exist."

"Not very big, is it?" said Penny.

We were standing face to face in the middle of a room not much bigger than a closet, barely illuminated by the sunlight falling in from the roof. Something tugged at my attention. I sniffed at the air, and then pulled a face as I recognised a particular smell.

"What is it?" said Penny.

"A scent I've encountered before," I said. "But not something I expected to find here."

"What scent?" said Penny. "I'm not smelling anything."

"We need to find a way out of here," I said.

I ran my hands over each of the walls in turn, until finally my fingertips discovered the outlines of a door. I slammed my shoulder against it, and the door flew open. I stepped through the doorway with Penny crowding my heels, and just like that we were back in the top floor of the Hall. Penny looked back to study the wall we'd just come through, and shook her head.

"Why didn't we notice the door earlier?"

I closed the door, and then raised an eyebrow as its outlines disappeared into the woodwork. I nodded my admiration for the workmanship, and then opened the door again and examined its interior. I smiled slowly as a great many things became clear.

"Take a look at this," I said. "The door is a good three inches thick, and it's surrounded by a layer of solid stone. The original Glenburys added this extra insulation so anyone tapping on the walls wouldn't be able to hear anything. I'm guessing this room started out life as a priest hole, that the family couldn't afford to have found."

"Hold it," said Penny. "According to Catherine, the old Glenburys were famously Protestant."

"Nothing like a well-established reputation to hide the truth," I said. "And nothing like hidden doors and secret passageways to help someone move around this house unseen."

I didn't add *I told you so* but I was pretty sure Penny could tell I was thinking it.

"But there would have to be concealed doors opening onto rooms and corridors throughout the Hall," said Penny. "Why would the Glenburys need so many?"

"This whole area used to be prime smuggling territory," I said. "Remember the sign we saw, at The Smugglers Retreat? Smugglers dressed as skeletons, to scare people away? I think one of the reasons the Glenburys encouraged their bad reputation was to keep people at a distance, so they wouldn't see the smugglers and their goods coming and going. The Hall must have been a centre for storing smuggled merchandise, and the family added more and more secret rooms and passageways down the years, to hide their illegal wares from unexpected searches by the Revenue Men. That's why there's a trapdoor to the roof, so that in emergencies goods could be hidden where no one would think to look for them."

"No wonder Arthur couldn't find anything, when he was a child," said Penny.

"If you believe him," I said.

Penny looked at me sharply. "You think he was lying about that?"

"Someone's been lying from the start," I said. "It could be Arthur, or it might have been Marion. She could have discovered any number of hidden doors, during the renovations. And of course Ellen spends a lot of time up here, on her own. Maybe she found clues for where to look when she was surfing sites about the Hall on her laptop. And it is possible that Catherine knew all about them, given how much time she spent in this house when she was younger."

"So really . . . any one of them could be behind what's happening?" said Penny.

"Possibly more than one," I said. "I'm having trouble convincing myself that just one person could be responsible for everything that's happened."

"Could that be the reason for Wendy's disappearance?" said Penny. "A falling out among thieves?"

"Wouldn't surprise me," I said.

"But still, we come back to the original question," said Penny. "What could any of these people have had against Lucas Carr? A man none of them had ever laid eyes on before?"

"I'm still working on that," I said.

Perhaps because we were talking about death, I was reminded of the unusual scent I'd recognised in the secret room. I pulled the door open again, stuck my head into the room, and breathed deeply.

"Ishmael?" said Penny. "What are you doing?"

"I smelled something way out of the ordinary in this room," I said. "Something without a source. But if all these secret rooms really are connected by hidden passageways . . ."

I closed the door and set off down the corridor, drawing in deep breaths of air.

"Take it easy," said Penny, "or you'll hyperventilate."

"Hush," I said. "I'm concentrating."

I ranged back and forth across the corridor, checking out doors and walls at regular intervals, until finally I caught another trace of the scent. I put my cheek up against a section of the wall that appeared no different from any other, inhaled deeply, and then nodded to Penny.

"This is it."

"Another hidden room?" said Penny.

"And, just maybe, the answer to a great many questions."

I couldn't see the outlines of a hidden door anywhere, even though I knew what I was looking for. I banged on the panelling with my fist, hard enough to crack the wood, but I still couldn't hear any trace of the concealed room I knew had to be there. So I ran my hands carefully over the woodwork, checking out each of the carved details in turn. Tugging and turning all the curlicues, Tudor roses, and bas relief hunting scenes . . . until suddenly one inconspicuous candle holder turned ninety degrees in my hand, and a section of panelling slid silently to one side, revealing a large dark space. I took a deep breath, pulled a face at the smell, and shook my head.

"What is it, Ishmael?" Penny said quietly.

"The past," I said. "Catching up with the present." I stared into the dark. "There aren't going to be any electric lights in there. We need candles."

"Have we found something important?" said Penny.

"There's someone in this room," I said. "And he's been there for a very long time. I think I saw some candles in an old candelabra, on a table further down the corridor."

"Of course you saw them," said Penny. "You see everything."

She hurried back down the corridor, while I stood before the opening, staring into the dark and thinking dark thoughts. Penny quickly returned with a brass candelabra packed full of candles entirely untroubled by dribbles of wax. I produced a box of matches and carefully lit all of the candles.

"Who carries matches around these days?" said Penny.

"Old-fashioned people, like me," I said.

"You mean old."

"But still young at heart."

"Yeah," said Penny. "That's what old people always say."

"Hold the candles still."

When I was done, I stepped carefully into the dark opening, and Penny crowded in after me, holding the candelabra high to spread its light as far as possible.

The room was a fair size, with featureless walls and a low ceiling, packed full of accumulated antique junk. A storeroom for all the bits and pieces that people in the past had decided didn't matter anymore. Flickering candlelight sent shadows jumping across the walls as Penny and I waded through the ankle-deep mess, kicking aside broken pieces of furniture, cracked china, and discarded ornaments. In the middle of the room, a man was sitting stiffly in a tall-backed chair. Penny and I stopped before him, and the candlelight illuminated a face whose skin had been stretched unnaturally taut. Blackened lips drew back from yellowed teeth in a disturbing grin, and the eyes had been replaced with glass. Withered hands clutched at the arms of the chair, and old-fashioned clothes hung loosely around the man's shrivelled frame.

"He was stuffed, and then hidden away in this room," I said.

"How did you know he was here?" said Penny.

"I caught a whiff of the preservative chemicals in the room under the trapdoor," I said. "And then I smelled them again in the corridor, through a crack in the wall. The scent must have carried through a connecting passageway."

"I'm not even going to ask how you can recognise the chemicals needed to preserve a human body, just by the smell," said Penny.

"Best not to," I said.

Penny moved the candles closer, and shadows moved across the dead face like the dreams of old emotions.

"How long do you think he's been here?" said Penny.

"Centuries," I said. "You are looking at the missing Lord Ravensbrook."

Penny shook her head slowly. "You could still smell the preserving chemicals, after all these years?"

"The air in this room hasn't been disturbed in a long time," I said. "Until quite recently."

"You're sure this is Ravensbrook?" said Penny.

"The clothes are the same as those on the dummy in the lobby," I said. "And you might remember there was a small portrait included in the display. Even allowing for what the years and the chemicals have done to the face, it's still him."

"So this is where he disappeared to," said Penny. "But who put him here?"

"Look around," I said. "See if you can spot anything that might help us."

We searched through the antique miscellanea piled up on the floor, but none of it proved at all useful. Penny started toward a large wooden trunk pushed up against the far wall, but I put out an arm to block her way.

"Leave that, for the moment," I said. "It doesn't contain what we're looking for."

"How can you be sure?" said Penny.

"Trust the nose."

"Oh ick."

It finally occurred to me to search the clothes on the corpse. I had to move in close as I thrust my hands inside the scratchy clothes, and I heard Penny stir uncomfortably as I hunted through the various pockets, but the presence of the dead didn't bother me. At last I found a folded letter, tucked away inside the jacket. I stepped back, and Penny brought the candlelight in close. The paper was thick and discoloured with age, more like parchment, and it cracked loudly as I unfolded the letter, as though threatening to fall apart. I ended up with a single sheet of paper, covered with crabbed handwriting. The date at the top was the nineteenth of October, sixteen eighty-five, and the signature at the bottom was Alexander Glenbury.

"Head of the family, when Lord Ravensbrook paid his fateful visit to Glenbury Hall," I said. "This would appear to be a confession, left here with the murder victim for history to discover."

"What does he say?" said Penny, crowding in close.

"Alexander admits to killing Ravensbrook, because the lord refused to acknowledge him as his son, and make him his official heir. Apparently Alexander was older than the legitimate heir, and believed he should inherit the title. Ravensbrook refused to acknowledge him, and declared no bastard would ever become Lord Ravensbrook."

"Alexander killed his own father?" said Penny.

"There's more to it," I said. "According to this, Ravensbrook was killed on the orders of King James' agents, to prevent another rebellion. Alexander was paid a tidy sum to do the deed, but says he would have spared his father, if only he'd done the right thing by him. So pride as well as payment led to Lord Ravensbrook's death." I skimmed to the bottom of the page. "There's nothing in this confession to indicate any other member of the Glenburys was involved in the murder, but Alexander must have had support from someone. If only to help him haul the body all the way up here."

"But why did he stuff and preserve his father?" said Penny.

"As a trophy," I said. "Because like everyone else in this

part of the country, Alexander was a great one for the hunt. Remember all the stuffed and mounted heads on display at The Smugglers Retreat?"

Penny nodded slowly.

"Alexander doesn't say why he hid the body in this particular room," I said. "Maybe it had some special significance for the family. Or perhaps this was just where they dumped all the stuff they never wanted to see again. I'm guessing that hiding the body was designed to add to the mystery of Lord Ravensbrook's vanishing. No one would ask too many questions, if the disappearance could be linked to the Hall's evil reputation."

"But the body was evidence of a murder," said Penny. "Why take the risk of hanging on to it?"

"Maybe Alexander just couldn't let go of the man who should have been his father."

"That is twisted," said Penny.

"The Glenburys were a famously twisted family," I said.

Penny turned her back on the body, took a deep breath and looked around the room.

"It's a pity Wendy isn't here to see this. She would have loved it."

"She is here," I said.

Penny looked quickly around, as though half expecting to see Wendy sitting in a corner, tied up and gagged. I shook my head.

"It wasn't just Ravensbrook's body I smelled in here."

I took Penny over to the large wooden trunk and lifted the lid, and there was Wendy, crammed in tightly. Her neck had been broken, so that she seemed to be staring back over her shoulder. Her eyes were wide open, as though astonished that such a thing could happen to her. Penny looked at the body for a long moment.

"Why didn't you tell me about this before?"

"There was nothing we could do for her," I said. "And discovering the truth behind Ravensbrook's disappearance was far more important."

"Why?"

"Because his death is the key to everything that's happened recently."

Penny waited, but I had nothing more to say. She started to reach out a hand to Wendy, and then stopped herself. Because she knew there was nothing she could do for her.

"Wendy deserved a better end than this," she said quietly. "Not just dumped in here, with all the other stuff no one gave a damn about."

"She ended up surrounded by history," I said. "I think she would have liked that."

I closed the lid of the trunk on Wendy's staring eyes, and turned away.

"We can send someone up for her later," I said. "As soon as we're done with this case."

"Why does she have to wait?" said Penny.

"Because we don't want the killer to know that we know what he did with her," I said.

"Who did kill Wendy?" said Penny. "Do you know?"

"I'm almost ready to point the finger at who's behind all of this," I said. "But not yet. There are still a few loose ends I have to work on."

Penny knew better than to push me. She looked around the room, and shadows lurched across the walls and ceiling as she waved the candelabra back and forth. "Are you sure Lucas isn't here, as well? Maybe buried somewhere, under all of this stuff?"

"There are no more bodies here," I said. "I'd know."

"Do you think Lucas is dead?"

"Yes," I said. "There's no way the killer would have left him alive."

"Are we going to have to search all the hidden rooms in the Hall to find Lucas' body?"

"I don't think so," I said. "If I'm right about how he died, the killer didn't have time to plan anything. Wendy was only dumped here because Ravensbrook's last resting place must have been weighing on the killer's mind."

"Then where is Lucas?"

"Well," I said. "It's obvious, when you think about it. Where would you dispose of a body, if you were in a hurry and needed a place where you could be sure it would never be found?"

Penny glared at me. "You can be really irritating at times, you know that?"

"I know," I said. "I practice." I folded the letter carefully, and slipped it inside my jacket. "At least now we know why Lucas was killed."

"We do?" said Penny.

"Of course. Isn't it obvious?"

"I will slap you a good one, Ishmael, and it will hurt."

"Give me some time," I said, smiling. "I need to be sure I've worked this through properly, before I accuse anyone."

"The first time I set eyes on this house," Penny said sternly, "I told you it had to be riddled with secret rooms and passageways, because places like this always are."

I nodded to her, acknowledging the point. "So you did. I must listen to you more often."

Penny smiled dazzlingly. "And your admitting that has made my day."

We emerged from the hidden room and back into the top floor, stretching slowly as we straightened up again. Penny blew out the candles and set the candelabra down on the nearest table, while I carefully closed the sliding panel. No point in revealing that we knew about the hidden room.

"So," said Penny. "We've solved the mystery of Lord Ravensbrook's disappearance, and found Wendy's body. But I still can't see why anyone here would want to kill her. What danger could she possibly have posed anyone?"

She looked at me hopefully, but I shook my head.

"Still thinking."

"It's a wonder to me that Poirot's sidekicks didn't gang up on him and beat him to death with blunt instruments," said Penny. "Are you at least getting close? We do have someone trying to kill us."

"I did notice," I said. "I've worked out most of the how, but I'm still working on some of the why."

"What about all the ghosts and weird happenings?" said Penny.

"What about them?" I said politely.

"How do they tie in with what's been going on?"

"They don't," I said.

Penny made an exasperated sound. "This house is driving me crazy!"

I stared at her, and then grinned broadly. "And that's it! That is what this has all been about. The house of Glenbury. Not the Hall, but the line of descent, the family tree. You just gave me the final clue I needed. Put that together with Alexander's confession, and everything falls into place."

"It's good to know I provide some assistance," said Penny. "But how does any of that explain what happened to Lucas Carr? Do you know who killed him now?"

"Oh yes," I said. "But I think we should do this the old-fashioned way. You mentioned Poirot, and this is a murder mystery in an old manor house.... So I say we gather all the suspects together, talk them through who did what and why, and then you can observe and applaud respectfully as I prove who the guilty party is with my ruthless logic."

Penny sighed. "Are you about to tell me that there is nothing supernatural about Glenbury Hall, and that there's a perfectly rational explanation for all the weird stuff that's been happening?"

"Absolutely," I said.

"So there weren't any ghosts?"

"Not a one."

"And that thing you saw, crawling down the corridor on all fours?"

"Classic misdirection."

"But what about the awful atmosphere, and the bad feelings everyone's been getting?" said Penny.

"If enough people become convinced of something," I said carefully, "everyone starts believing. Unless you're an outsider, like me."

"That is what makes you so good at this," said Penny. "Come on; let's go downstairs and get this show on the road. I can't wait to hear you explain everything."

"I don't know about everything," I said. "Just enough to reveal the killer. And that is what we came here for."

❖ CHAPTER NINE ❖
THE PAST IS ALWAYS WITH YOU

I WAS READY TO GO DOWNSTAIRS, make my big speech and solve the mystery, but Penny insisted that first we had to return to Wendy's room, so she could retrieve the boots and hat she'd left there before we went up on the roof. Heaven forfend she should face the assembled company with bare feet and a bare head. So she strode along the corridor, humming happily to herself, while I followed patiently on behind. Because experience has taught me that there are some arguments you're never going to win.

Back in Wendy's room, Penny tugged on her boots, clapped her big black hat on the back of her head, and then posed in front of the room's only decent-sized mirror. This involved a certain amount of bobbing about and deforming herself, because the mirror wasn't big enough to show Penny as much of herself as she felt she needed to see. Experience had also taught me to just stand well back and let her get on with it. I felt like looking at my watch, but didn't. I knew it wouldn't make any difference.

"You look good," I said hopefully. "You always look good."

"Nicely said, sweetie," said Penny, not looking away from her reflection. "But I just can't decide whether I should wear the hat, or not. What do you think? It is a bit much, for such a solemn occasion?"

There is no correct answer, in situations like this. All you can do is plunge, and hope for the best.

"On anyone else, perhaps," I said. "But you can carry it off."

"I want to look my best for the denouement, darling. This is your big moment."

"Keep the hat," I said. "That hat is you."

"Of course," she said happily. "You're always right about these things."

I wasn't going to argue, if it got us out of the room. Penny turned her back on the mirror, and rewarded me with a brilliant smile. She slipped her arm through mine, and pressed it against her side.

"Let us now descend to the lower levels and razzle-dazzle the rubes! Do you have all your ducks in a row, and pointed in the right direction?"

"I have a theory," I said. "But not much in the way of evidence to back it up. Hopefully, if I spell it all out in enough detail the killer should confess. And maybe just this once they really will say *Yes, I did it, and I'm glad!*"

"I've always admired your optimism," said Penny.

We went back down the stairs, accompanied by the usual low thunder of feet on bare wooden steps, only to find that the lobby was completely deserted. I led Penny over to the historical display next to the desk. The dummy wearing Lord Ravensbrook's outfit looked a little disturbing, now we'd seen the real thing. I pointed out the small portrait, and Penny recognised enough in the face to nod her agreement.

"Told you it was him," I said.

"Yes, darling," said Penny. "But I thought you were in a hurry to get to the big confrontation? Why are we hanging around here?"

"Because this is where it all started," I said. "If it hadn't been for this display, no one would have had to die."

She waited hopefully, but I just smiled easily. Penny shook her head.

"Could you be any more enigmatic?"

"If you want."

"Don't push your luck, darling."

"Okay . . . Then allow me to point out a useful clue that you might have missed. Notice anything different about the display?"

Penny looked the small exhibition over carefully, and then fixed me with an impatient stare. "It all looks the same to me. What am I missing?"

"That's just it," I said. "Something is missing. Remember the audio drama of the timeslip gathering? The CD you were supposed to order in advance is now notable by its absence."

Penny smiled broadly, as she suddenly got it. "That's what we heard out in the grounds! Somebody played the audio recording, to lure us out there!"

"Got it in one," I said. "They must have concealed a speaker somewhere, and then activated it by remote control."

"I suppose we should be grateful they didn't decide to attack us with the farm implements," said Penny.

"Our killer isn't that direct," I said. "They much prefer sneaking around in the background."

Penny grinned again. "The scratching noises we heard last night; that was them, moving around in the hidden passageways surrounding our room!"

"Got it in one," I said.

Penny frowned. "Wasn't that . . . just a bit childish?"

"It worked, didn't it?" I turned away, and listened carefully. "I can hear people talking. They're all gathered together in the dining hall."

"How very convenient," said Penny. "It'll make a marvellous setting for your big speech. Is there anything I can do to help, once you're belabouring them with the truth?"

"Just watch my back."

"Don't I always?"

"And make sure nobody leaves."

"You think someone is going to make a break for it?"

"I would," I said.

We set off down the corridor. The day was wearing on, and sunlight falling through the windows had a pale exhausted look. When we finally reached the dining hall, I quietly signalled to Penny that we were going to stop outside the door so we could listen to what everyone was saying.

The door had been left half open, and a quick peek through the gap revealed Arthur and Marion at the far end of the table, sitting on either side of Catherine and trying to be supportive with their presence. Arthur looked concerned about Catherine's condition, but Marion mostly looked impatient, as though she couldn't understand why Catherine didn't just snap out of it. Ellen sat opposite them, shifting uncomfortably in her chair. She looked like she wanted to say something, but was too far out of her emotional depth to contribute anything useful.

"Would you like a cup of tea?" Marion said to Catherine. "I could make some. It's no trouble."

Catherine didn't even shake her head. She just sat staring down at her hands, clasped together in her lap. Her face was drawn and tired, and she looked her age and more.

"I don't think Catherine wants any tea," said Arthur.

"All right then!" said Marion. "You suggest something."

Arthur looked like he wanted to suggest Marion shut the hell up, but he didn't. Instead he kept his gaze fixed on Catherine, waiting for her to notice him. Ellen looked like she'd rather be anywhere else, clearly uncomfortable at being in the presence of older people being emotional, but she stayed where she was, held in place by the drama of the situation.

"I think you should go home, Catherine," said Arthur. "The Hall isn't good for you."

Catherine still wouldn't look at him, and when she spoke her voice was flat and tired.

"I don't like it here. But I can't leave."

"Why not?" said Marion.

"So Wendy's ghost will be able to find me, when she comes back," said Catherine. "Just like Lucas did. I have to ask Wendy who killed her."

Marion looked like she wanted to grab Catherine by the shoulders and give her a good shake, but managed to restrain herself.

"There are no ghosts in Glenbury Hall," she said firmly. "I have been living in this house for months, and I have never once seen anything out of the ordinary."

"You must have felt the atmosphere, Mother," said Ellen.

"There is a presence in the Hall," said Arthur. "We've all felt it. I'm worried we might have woken something, when we started making changes in the Hall. We've all heard something walking the corridors at night . . ."

"Have you actually seen anything?" said Marion.

"Not seen," said Arthur. "More like . . . sensed."

"I've felt all kinds of things I couldn't explain," said Ellen. "We're not alone in this house. We have to get out of here!"

"We are not going back to London!" Marion said loudly. "Stop being so selfish, Ellen! We all had to leave things behind, when we came here. Do you think you're the only one who misses their friends?" She stopped for a moment, breathing steadily as she brought herself back under control, and when she spoke again her voice was quiet but determined. "We can't go back, because we don't have the money to move again. All we have is this house, and the business. Either we make it work, or we go under."

"But living here is driving us crazy!" said Ellen, sounding just as determined as her mother. "How can you stand to live here?"

"You're all letting your imagination get the better of you!" said Marion. "Glenbury Hall is just an old house, with far too many stupid stories attached to it."

"A house where history isn't content to stay in the past," said Catherine. "Where people can just vanish into thin air, and no one knows how or why." She turned suddenly, to stare accusingly at Arthur. "Why weren't you more upset, when I told you Wendy was dead? She was your friend too."

"I barely remember the woman," said Arthur. "She might have thought we were close once, but we really weren't."

"And yet she came all the way from London, just so she could be supportive in your hour of need," said Marion.

"Don't start that again," Arthur said tiredly. "I promise you; she means nothing to me now." He turned his attention back to Catherine. "I don't think you should expect to see Wendy's ghost any time soon."

"Why not?" said Catherine. "Lucas came back."

"That was just a bad dream," Marion said impatiently.

"This house is full of bad dreams," said Catherine. "And some of them walk the Hall at night, desperate to be heard."

I decided I'd heard enough, and gave Penny the nod. We slammed the door open and strode into the dining hall. Everyone turned around in their seats to look at us.

"Please!" I said cheerfully. "No need for anyone to stand up!"

It didn't look like the thought had crossed any of their minds. I gestured for Penny to take up a position at the end of the table, so she could block any attempt to reach the door, and then I took my time strolling down the length of the room, so I could give everyone my best *I know something you don't* smile. They stared back at me, saying nothing. I came to a halt at the head of the table and drew myself up, but before so I could launch into my big speech Marion cut in.

"Have you found Wendy yet?"

"Yes," I said. "We found her body. Wendy has been murdered."

I deliberately kept it blunt so I could study their reactions. Catherine just nodded, as though I'd merely confirmed her worst suspicions. Ellen shrank back in her chair, as though she'd been hit. Arthur stared at me. And Marion looked even angrier.

"Another suspicious death at the Hall? Oh, that's all we need! How are we ever going to get this business off the ground if the guests keep on dying?"

"Probably not the best approach to be adopting just now, dear," Arthur murmured.

"To hell with that!" said Marion. "I'll speak how I like in my own house."

"Your house?" said Catherine. "Glenbury Hall was here centuries before you showed up, and it will still be here long after you're gone."

"Hold your tongue!" said Marion, infuriated enough to lash out at anyone. "We brought you in to help us, but you haven't contributed anything useful that I can see. I will not lose the Hall; not after everything we've put into it!"

Ellen sat up straight in her chair, as shock gave way to anger. "Two people have died in this house... and all you can think about is what that might mean for bookings?"

"Not now, dear," said Marion.

"Yes, now!" said Ellen, her voice rising dangerously. "Since when is running a business more important than people?"

Marion made an effort to be polite, since she was in the presence of outsiders. "What happened to Mr. Carr and Ms. Goldsmith is unfortunate, and very sad, but they were just visitors. Family comes first."

"Poor Wendy," Arthur said quietly. "She came so far to help me, to a place she'd always dreamed of visiting, and the Hall killed her."

"No," I said, and everyone's gaze snapped back to me. "It wasn't Glenbury Hall that killed Wendy. She was murdered by someone in the Hall."

A heavy silence fell across the table, as everyone stared at me. Marion was the first to recover.

"Are you saying she was killed by one of us?"

"There's no one else in the Hall," I said.

"You know who did it?" said Arthur. "You have proof?"

"Mostly theory," I said. "But with a certain amount of evidence to back it up."

They all looked quickly around the table, searching each other's faces for signs of guilt, and then turned reluctantly back to face me.

"Who was it?" said Catherine. "Who killed Wendy?"

"Have you worked out what happened to Mr. Carr, as well?" said Ellen.

"Yes," I said. "It's all connected."

"Do you know where Carr is?" said Arthur.

"I've got a pretty good idea," I said. "But let's start at the beginning, so I can walk you through what's really been going on at Glenbury Hall."

I took a moment, to rehearse my arguments. It was a complicated story, and I didn't want to leave anything out.

"It's taken me this long to get to the bottom of what's been happening," I said, "because the killer has been tap-dancing like crazy to distract me from realising there was only one person it could have been. It was you, Arthur. All along you've been saying you should never have come back to Glenbury Hall. To the house that poisoned your life. You did everything you could to escape from your abusive parents, and the weight of the Hall's history, but when your life in the City crashed and burned you had no choice but to return home. Even though you knew what being here would do to you."

Marion, Ellen, and Catherine stared at Arthur blankly. He looked calmly back at me, saying nothing, defying me to prove anything.

"All right," I said. "We'll do it the hard way, step by step."

As always, Marion jumped in to protect her husband. "You can't seriously believe that Arthur would kill anybody? It just isn't him!"

I didn't make the mistake of arguing with her. I just met her gaze steadily, until she looked away and settled angrily back in her chair. I took my time looking round the table. Ellen was looking to her father for reassurance, but he had his gaze fixed on me. Catherine had shrunk into herself when I announced that Wendy had been murdered, but now I was threatening the only member of the family she really cared about, she found new resources and sat up straight.

"It couldn't have been Arthur!" she said sharply. "I've known him since he was a child. He's not capable of anything like that. Tell them, Arthur."

He was still looking at me steadily, apparently entirely unconcerned by my accusation.

"What makes you think I'm the killer?"

Marion couldn't keep from cutting in again. "Have you forgotten that Arthur was at the reception desk when Carr disappeared?"

"No he wasn't," I said. "That's just what he wanted us to believe."

Marion turned on Arthur to order him to explain himself, but he wouldn't even look at her. Marion seemed suddenly lost, unsure what to say in the face of Arthur's refusal to defend himself. She looked around the table for help, but Ellen and Catherine were just as thrown as she was. In the end, all of them just sat there and looked to me to explain things.

"From the very beginning," I said, "it's been like dealing with a stage magician who keeps fooling you into looking the wrong way, so you won't see him setting up the trick. Arthur told us that Lucas Carr turned up at reception, signed in, and then went up the stairs on his own. Only to mysteriously vanish before he could reach his room. Lucas must have disappeared, because he never came back down the stairs, which Arthur was watching all the time. But there were no witnesses to support any of this. All we had was Arthur's word as to what happened.

"So; let me walk you through it. Step by step. Lucas definitely did arrive at reception. We have his signature in the book, which I sent to my people to verify. But this is what I believe happened next...

"Arthur escorted Lucas up the stairs, on the pretext of helping him with his heavy suitcases. He already told us how Lucas all but collapsed, carrying those very heavy cases into reception. But once the two of them were inside Lucas' room,

Arthur waited till Lucas turned his back on him; and then broke the man's neck with a rabbit punch. Which is why there was no spilled blood, or signs of violence, in his room. Wendy told us they were taught how to do that in London, at the self-defence classes their company ordered them to take."

"But Arthur was never any good at those!" said Marion, unable to contain herself.

"That's what he told us," I said. "But as in so many things, he wasn't being entirely truthful. Either way, when it mattered, the technique came back to him. Arthur then searched the suitcases until he found Lucas' presentation paper, and the documentation he'd brought to back it up. And then he destroyed them because of the threat they presented to him, and his family. I'm guessing he burned them; there are any number of open fireplaces in the Hall, where no one would notice a few ashes.

"Arthur was then faced with the problem of what to do with Lucas' body. He could have dumped it in one of the Hall's many secret rooms.... We'll get to those in a moment.... But once the Historical Society turned up, it was always possible they might know about the secret doors and sliding panels, so he had to dispose of the body somewhere he could be sure it would never be found. The one place at Glenbury Hall that has always been famous for accepting bodies in a way that guaranteed they would never be recovered. The old well, in the grounds. But he couldn't just carry Lucas' body down the stairs because there was always a chance Marion or Ellen might appear and see him.

"So Arthur opened the room's window, and threw the body out. I found recent scuff marks, on the windowsill. Arthur then closed the window, left the room, and locked the door behind him with his spare pass key. I always knew there had to be another. No hotel management would have just the one made, in case they lost it. So . . . Arthur hurried down the stairs, carefully bringing the small suitcase back down with him, so he could leave it by the reception desk and Marion would have a reason to go upstairs and check on Lucas. Pretty fast thinking for someone who hadn't planned to commit murder when he got up that morning.

"Next, Arthur went out the front door, and there was Lucas' body lying on the grass. The body made a shallow depression in the earth, where it hit. One of the first things I noticed, when I checked the grounds, was a small area of flattened grass and compressed earth right in front of the Hall. Later on, when Arthur tried to kill Penny and me by dropping a gargoyle on us, the heavy stone figure all but buried itself in the ground, and that made me think about things falling, and what affects the impacts would have. Probably still running on adrenaline, Arthur picked up the body, carried it over to the well, and dropped it in. That deep, dark place, that no one has ever got to the bottom of."

I stopped and looked at Arthur, to give him a chance to confirm what I'd been saying. He sat perfectly still in his chair, staring calmly back at me. Marion jumped in again.

"This is all nonsense! How could Arthur have managed all of this without being seen?"

"He knew you were busy working at the back of the house," I said. "And that Ellen was busy listening to her music. The only real risk he was taking was that some other members of the Historical Society might have turned up. But fortunately, Lucas had arrived a lot earlier than expected. I'm not sure what you did with the suitcases, Arthur. They had to vanish as well, to back up the strange nature of Lucas' disappearance. I'm assuming you just dumped them in one of the hidden rooms, till you could dispose of them properly later."

"There are no hidden rooms in Glenbury Hall!" Marion

said furiously. "No secret doors, and no sliding panels. We looked!"

"They're not easy to find," I said, "but they do exist." I nodded to Arthur. "After the gargoyle threw itself off the roof at Penny and me, I decided we needed to go up there and took a look around. You tried to put us off by making the only way up there sound too dangerous to try, but you had no idea what we were capable of."

"Neither did I," said Penny.

I looked at her politely. "Did you want to add something?"

"No, no, you carry on," said Penny. "I'm fascinated."

"Glad to hear it," I said, and turned back to face the others.

"Once we were on the roof, it didn't take us long to find a trapdoor that gave access to an old priest's hole on the top floor. That led us to another secret room, and what we found inside proved that Arthur was responsible for everything that's happened in the Hall."

"What did you find?" said Catherine.

"The answer to more than one mystery," I said. "Starting with: why did Arthur want to kill Lucas? A man he'd never even met before? It all comes down to the disappearance of Lord Ravensbrook." I produced the letter from my jacket and unfolded it to show them the handwritten statement. "Penny and I found this on Lord Ravensbrook's stuffed and preserved body, in one of the Hall's secret rooms. It's a confession, written by Alexander Glenbury, head of the family when Ravensbrook came to call. And, the lord's illegitimate son. Alexander says he killed his father because he was paid to do it by agents of King James and because his father refused to acknowledge him."

Marion was starting to look like a fighter who'd taken too many hits to the head, but she was still ready to fight her corner.

"What has this solution to a centuries-old mystery got to do with what's happening now?" she said stubbornly.

"The past is always with you, in Glenbury Hall," I said. "The details in this confession make it clear why Lucas had to die. For purely personal reasons; nothing at all to do with the security aspects of his work. When Lucas arrived at reception, he found himself face to face with the Ravensbrook display, and he couldn't help boasting to Arthur about the important paper he was going to present to the Society. I'm pretty sure it was based on an early draft of Alexander's confession. The text in this letter is far too smooth, with no contradictions or crossed out lines. Which suggests there had to be an earlier version. This was to be Alexander's confession to history, so it was important he get it right.

"Lucas told Arthur what he was going to be saying, and the splash he was sure it would make when he revealed its contents to the Historical Society. And, later, to the world. He had no way of knowing this was something Arthur could never allow. Because once this knowledge became public, it would change how everybody looked at Glenbury Hall. No longer the scene of a famous mystery, and a place of ghosts and wonders . . . but merely the setting for a squalid little murder.

"Arthur had nothing left but the Hall, and his new business, so Arthur killed Lucas to silence him. The world had taken so much away from Arthur . . . he couldn't bear to lose what little he had left.

"Now, as Penny commented when we first arrived, old manor houses like this always turn out to be riddled with secret passageways. And this house had more reasons than most. At The Smugglers Retreat, the barman told us this whole area used to be smuggling country. And the Glenburys were famously determined to always have the best of everything at a time when the only way to be sure of that was to have your own supply. What better way to ensure that, than to fund the local smugglers and allow them to hide their nocturnal business behind the Glenburys' evil reputation? No one would come anywhere near the Hall, because the locals believed the Glenburys were monsters. The smugglers would be allowed to hide their illegal goods in the Hall's increasing number of secret rooms until they could be moved out and distributed across the country, as long as the Glenburys got their cut.

"And yet Arthur went out of his way to insist that there weren't any hidden rooms in the Hall; that he'd spent his whole childhood searching for them, without success. He even invited us to tap on the walls, and listen for ourselves. But Penny and I have since discovered that the hidden rooms were specially constructed so no one would hear anything. On top of that, I'm convinced there are any number of secret passageways, connecting most of the rooms in the Hall. Arthur has been using them to move around the Hall unseen, manufacturing all kinds of ghostly manifestations to distract us from the truth.

"He was the figure I saw crawling on all fours. As long as he kept his head down, and stuck to the shadows, no one was going to recognise him. But he gave himself away when he used a secret passage to emerge from the bathroom, because he didn't flush the toilet before he came out. Which he would have needed to do if that was why he'd gone in there."

Catherine turned her head to fix Arthur with an accusing stare.

"Is this true, Arthur? Did you kill Lucas, and my friend Wendy?"

Arthur met her gaze briefly, but still wouldn't say anything.

"Yes," I said. "Why did Wendy come to Glenbury Hall, if it wasn't to support Arthur in his hour of need? I believe she was the one who discovered that a first draft of Alexander's letter still existed. She told Lucas, and he used his resources to track it down. And of course he would have brought it with him, as evidence to back up the paper he was going to present to the Society. Wendy came here to look for that first draft, to make sure the truth about Lord Ravensbrook's murder would still come out.

"Arthur decided he had to kill Wendy, because she kept saying that she knew what was really going on and that she was determined to get to the truth of what was happening, whatever it took. He couldn't risk that. And he was beginning to realise that not everyone was buying into the supernatural atmosphere he'd worked so hard to create. He must have believed a second mysterious disappearance would help to convert any doubters.

"He was at the reception desk when Wendy came hurrying through the lobby, following Catherine. Arthur saw his chance, and intercepted her. He probably told her he had happened across Alexander's first draft of the letter, but he needed to check it against the historical texts and documents Wendy had in her suitcase.

"She had no reason to see him as a threat, so it never occurred to her that it might not be a good idea to turn her back on him. But the moment they were inside her room, he broke her neck with the same rabbit punch he'd used on Lucas.

"He dumped her body in the corridor, and left her door key in her room, lying in plain sight. He then locked the door with his pass key, and hid Wendy's body in the same secret room as Lord Ravensbrook. He could always drop her in the well later. Penny and I found her there, and when I saw her neck had been broken, I knew what must have happened to her and Lucas Carr."

I stopped, to stare steadily at Arthur. "After the gargoyle failed to kill us, we went back into reception. Where you were breathing hard, and covered in sweat. You tried to make us think that came from moving boxes around, but they didn't look nearly heavy enough to justify that much exertion. It really came from all the running about you'd had to do: up to the roof to dislodge the gargoyle, then back down to reception where you intercepted Wendy, then up to her room to kill her and dispose of her body, and finally back down to reception again. No wonder you were sweating."

Catherine looked at Arthur as though he was a stranger. "I should never have let your parents send me away. What did Paul and Mary do to you, that you could end up like this?"

"You really didn't know about the cage," said Penny.

"What cage?" said Catherine.

Penny told her, and Catherine buried her face in her hands. Marion looked shocked, and then furious. Ellen looked sick. Marion put a comforting arm across Arthur's shoulders, but he just shrugged it off. Marion flinched back, shocked and hurt. Catherine raised her head, and stared at Arthur with tears in her eyes.

"If I had known what they were doing to you, I swear I would have taken you with me when I left, and to hell with the consequences." She turned suddenly, to glare at me. "None of what's happened is Arthur's fault. It's all down to what Paul and Mary did to him."

"Your friends," I said.

"I only saw the side of them they wanted me to see," said Catherine. She looked at Arthur. "No wonder you wanted to leave the Hall empty. To let it rot along with all the horrors that still haunted you."

"But what about the ghosts?" said Ellen. "All the things people have been seeing and hearing? Weren't any of them real?"

"I don't believe so," I said. "There were no ghostly phenomena before Lucas' arrival. Marion kept saying she hadn't seen anything supernatural, in all the time she'd been here. And neither did you, Ellen. Arthur only started encouraging Catherine in her ghost stories after Lucas disappeared, so the Hall would seem a weird and dangerous place, where Lucas' vanishing would be just part of the strange happenings."

"But what about when Lucas' spirit appeared to me in my room?" said Catherine.

"I'm afraid that was just Arthur again," I said. "Coming and going through his hidden doors. Because he appeared in the dark, and never spoke, he could be pretty sure you wouldn't recognise him."

Catherine stared at Arthur. "How could you? I was frightened out of my wits!"

Arthur stared back at her, but still wouldn't say anything. I was starting to find my big speech a bit hard going. I'd expected Arthur to crack by now, and admit everything. Since most of it really was just guesswork, I'd have a hard time proving any of it. I needed him to break. While I was thinking that, Penny took a step forward.

"Can I just ask Arthur how he was able to appear outside our window, when we were on the top floor?"

"Yes," I said. "I'm still having trouble explaining that."

Arthur smiled suddenly. "That one was nothing to do with me."

Penny sniffed. "Didn't you just know he was going to say that?"

"It doesn't matter," I said easily, though inside I was

rejoicing. By saying he wasn't responsible for *that one*, Arthur was implying he was responsible for the rest. "Put it this way," I said. "Arthur had put a lot of effort into creating his weird atmosphere, establishing a communal belief in the supernatural that had everyone believing the Hall was lousy with ghosts and weird incidents. It's possible that the sheer pressure of so much shared belief was enough to affect us too. For a while."

"I don't believe any of this," Marion said flatly. "I've known Arthur for over twenty years! He isn't the kind to plot and scheme and sneak around in the background, let alone kill people!"

"Of course," I said. "You've always had to be the strong one in your marriage. You had to make all the hard decisions, like leaving London and returning to the Hall. No matter how much he tried to argue against it. You won that one, because you had reason on your side and he only had emotions. He couldn't explain why he shouldn't go home again, because he never wanted you to know what had been done to him here. You forced him to return to Glenbury Hall, to a place he knew would bring out the worst in him. And he did it, to protect his family. Because he didn't want to be anything like his father.

"There is a curse on the house of Glenbury, but it comes from the line of descent. All those generations of inherited evil and madness. But Arthur could be strong, when he had to. Like when he tried to frame you for Wendy's disappearance."

Marion looked from me to Arthur, and then back again.

"What are you talking about? I was nowhere near her room when it happened."

"But Arthur tried to make it look as though you were," I said. "To point me away from him." I produced the cigarette butt and everyone stared at it, fascinated. "I found this on the floor of Wendy's room. Lying in plain sight, almost as though it had been deliberately left there for me to find. And of course the only person I'd seen smoking in the Hall was you, Marion. Arthur was there when I saw you doing it. I don't think he actually intended to incriminate you; he just wanted to muddy the waters. But his plan didn't work, because I knew Ellen also smoked cigarettes."

Ellen looked quickly at her mother, but Marion just smiled tiredly.

"I knew, dear. I could smell the smoke in your room sometimes. I never said anything, because I was in no position to preach." She glowered at me. "Arthur couldn't have left the cigarette butt in Wendy's room, because he would never have done anything to endanger his daughter."

"But he didn't know Ellen smoked," I said.

Marion put a hand to her mouth. "Of course. I never told him because I thought he had enough to worry about."

"I wasn't fooled anyway," I said. "Because when I examined the cigarette butt, there were no traces of lipstick. Which there would have been, if you or Ellen had smoked it. So it had to have been Arthur."

"I get it now!" said Penny. "The evidence that was important, because of what wasn't there!"

I put the cigarette butt away. Marion glared at Arthur.

"You stupid man! If there was a problem, why didn't you come to me so I could deal with it?"

He looked at her steadily. "Because this was my home, and my problem. But mostly . . . because I didn't want any of my family's evil to rub off on you."

"You're not evil!" said Marion.

He looked at her sadly. "Do you know why I was first attracted to you, Marion? Because you were strong and stern, just like my parents."

Marion shrank back in her chair. Arthur smiled sadly at her.

"Just once, I wanted to be the strong one. I did all of this because my family mattered more to me than anything else. I'd already failed you once. I couldn't let that happen again."

Marion reached out a hand to him, and he took it. She tried to say something, but couldn't. She reached out to him and took him in her arms, and Arthur clung to her. Tears ran down Marion's face, but Arthur didn't cry. And I remembered him saying how the cage had taught him there was no point in crying. Ellen's mouth trembled, but when she did finally speak her voice was perfectly steady.

"You did it all for us, Dad. I couldn't be more proud of you."

Marion nodded quickly, and pushed Arthur away from her. "You have to run. Get away from here. Ellen and I will buy you some time. Do it!"

She launched herself from her seat and wrapped her arms around me, pinning my arms to my sides. Ellen jumped up onto the table, ran down it and launched herself at Penny with such force that both of them fell sprawling to the floor. Arthur ran down the length of the dining hall, and was out the door and gone by the time I'd broken Marion's grip on me. I pushed her gently but firmly back into her chair, and raced down the room after Arthur. Catherine wouldn't even look at me. Penny had already wrestled Ellen into submission and pinned her to the floor. She patted Ellen on the shoulder, jumped up, and hurried after me as I ran out the door.

There was no sign of Arthur in the corridor, but I could hear his running feet ahead of us.

"He's heading for the front door," I said.

"He must have a car hidden away somewhere," said Penny.

"I don't think so," I said.

"But he must know he can't outrun us," said Penny. "So where's he going?"

"I have a horrible feeling I know," I said. "We have to catch him, before it's too late."

When Penny and I finally burst out the front door and into the grounds, Arthur hadn't gone far. He was standing by the wishing well, leaning over the side and staring down into its depths. I called out to him.

"Stay where you are, Arthur! Don't move!"

He turned his head, and nodded to me and Penny.

"Don't come any closer. I'll jump."

I put a staying hand on Penny's arm, and we slowed to a walk.

"Come back inside, Arthur," said Penny. "We'll sort something out."

"My only choices would appear to be prison or the asylum," said Arthur, quite calmly. "Neither of which appeals. And anyway, I have my family to think of. I think one last act of penance is needed, to make it clear I take all the blame. The authorities should leave my family alone then." He looked down into the well. "It's calling me. I've been hearing its voice ever since I came home." He slung one leg over the side of the well. "Move over, Lucas. Here I come . . ."

I sprinted forward, but it was already too late. By the time I got to the well, he'd disappeared into the darkness. Penny arrived to join me and we stood together, looking down into the depths, seeing nothing. We waited, but didn't hear a splash or an impact.

"Do you think Glenbury Hall was ever really haunted?" Penny said finally.

"It is now," I said.

Penny turned away from the well, to look at me steadily. "What did you wish for, when we first got here?"

"A case worth solving," I said.

Penny nodded. "Never trust a wishing well."